Skyline

Skyline

J.K. Pennerman

urlink
PRINT & MEDIA

Skyline

1603 Capitol Ave., Suite 310 Cheyenne, Wyoming USA 82001
1-888-980-6523 | admin@urlinkpublishing.com

URLink Print and Media is committed to excellence in the publishing industry.

Published in the United States of America

Library of Congress Control Number: 2022906276
ISBN 978-1-68486-157-6 (Paperback)
ISBN 978-1-68486-158-3 (Digital)

17.02.23

CONTENTS

Chapter 1
"An Uninvited Journey"

It is a bleak, mid-spring evening, when the crashing of wooden, window shutters echoes about the wattle-daubed walls of the cozy household, as its winds beat along with the heavy torrents of rainwater amongst the sleepy village of Nordeskye. All remains silent, as a gust of cool wind, sends a shiver over her tanned skin, as its breeze dances smoothly through her coilly hairs, which lays softly upon her cheek. All is silent, besides the entrancing night's downpour, and the subtle rolling of thunders, just outside the cozy rooms. Suddenly, it is disturbed, as a loud banging is heard along the heavy, wooden front door, its loud thuds sounding through the household.

"Arthur, Sir Arthur!!" exclaims a male voice, knocking along the front door.

"Sir Arthur, it's the lycans! We need your aid!!" yells the voice from the outside.

Frightened, the girl pitches up from her bed, a shallow canvas stuffed with straw and wool, decked with leather coverings. She listens carefully as footsteps are heard sounding down the hallway as the voice continues to call from the outside!

"Father?!" she mutters nervously, carefully placing her feet to the floor, moving silently to avoid any sudden creaks, as the cold boards shift beneath her feet. Silently awaiting an answer, she hesitantly reaches to open the room's door.

"Father?!" she calls out again, peeking her head down the bleak hallway, she glimpses a sword laying at the front door, aside a pair of leather boots.

"Father?!" she calls out once more, when finally, she sees the glimmer of a candle, casting a shadow upon the wall of the living room, suddenly, the shadow disappears, as a huge burst of light appears from the room. She quickly scurries down the hallway, entering the front room, looking by the wooden chairs, she sees her father cloaked in a dark robe, hovered over the fireplace. He appears to be getting dressed. He proceeds to the front door, opening it quickly, immediately, a male villager rushes inside, his cloak drenched of rain, and seeming out of breath. Panting in exhaustion and fright, he turns to her father.

"What is it, Lucian?" her father asks the male.

"It's the lycans, Arthur, one of the watchmen have spotted them along the eastern side of the wall!" he details severely, "The men are scared, we need your help!" utters Lucian panicked in telling. Meanwhile, Anna watches silently from the hallway. From the door, Lucian glimpses the listening Anna, and swiftly points her out to her father.

"Anna?" her father calls turning to her, his black, coilly hair dangling in his sweat, as his tanned skin glows in the fiery light, "I thought you were asleep," he mentions.

"I heard the noise, it woke me up," Anna replies standing unsurely near the hallway, "What is it father?" she asks curiously.

"I must help the men, it's the lycans… they're on the move," he replies gravely, placing the cloak's red hood over his head, as he buttons the shoulders of the garment.

"We must hurry, Sire," tells Lucian hastily, "I heard one of the men has been bitten," he flails wildly in panic, pointing Arthur to the outside. Arthur turns to him immediately, his expression of grief, as he looks towards the floor.

"May the fates, have mercy on his soul," murmurs Arthur solemnly, picking up his sword and sheathing it within his belt, hidden beneath the cloak. A pair of black leather gloves lay draped over the wooden chair, he takes them, fastening them over his hands. Donned with protective garments, ranging from his flowing black cloak to leather gloves and boots. Beneath his cloak, a black tunic, decked with silver buttons and embroidery, Anna admires the brave and noble fit. Meanwhile, another male enters the room, appearing out of the rain, capturing the attention of Anna, his head covered beneath his hood, yet wearing the same attire as her father. His gray beard hangs near his chest, being the only visible part of his face.

"Brother," answers her father, as he and the male grip forearms in greeting, "I didn't think you'd show?!" he tells reluctantly.

"This is a sin we must both correct, let us finish this, there has been enough bloodshed," tells the mysterious male forwardly. Confused, Anna looks to her father, who lowers his head, nodding in agreement. Lucian also stands by quietly in the room, seeming also to not understand the meaning of their discussion, and like Anna, equally concerned, and confused.

"Where are you going father?" voices Anna concerningly, standing among the three men, suddenly, the strange male turns to her.

"Arthur is this her?" asks the male, turning to Arthur in question.

"Yes, this is Anna my only child," he tells proudly in reply, placing his hand warmly on her shoulder.

"She's a lot bigger than I remember," answers the male reluctantly, as his face finally comes into light of the fireplace. His face is rough, and gritty, adding to his stern demeanor. He appears aged, with long grayish-black hair. Finally, Arthur turns to them, leaving Anna near the fireplace.

"Maurdis will pay for his slaughters," vows Arthur solemnly, tightening his fist about his sword's handle. With that, he leads the pair outside the door and into the torrent of rain. Speechless, as her mind races to fathom her father's sudden leaving, Anna darts behind him, pulling at his arm, as she is immediately soaked head to toe from the midnight's squall.

"F-Father w-what is this, where are you going?!?" she asks worriedly, seeing him leave without explanation. Arthur sees the look of fear in her eyes and stops. Placing his hand on her shoulder, he kisses her forehead.

"I will return Anna, I must protect the village, I must protect you, the lycans… Maurdis… they will never stop, this is the time where if we strike now, we may also have the upper hand, I have to go," explains her father gravely, "I love you, dear one," he smiles, kissing her forehead once more, before turning away to join the men, as he does, he drags something into her palm. It is a blue-ribbon bowtie, with a silver button at its center. As she looks up, the strange bearded male walks up to her.

"Your father will return safely, I will make sure of it," he assures stoutly, turning away, as the three disappear into the night. Anna nods silently, as she turns away to rush back inside, securing the heavy locks on the front doors, panting in anxiety she stares blankly at the front door. Where is her father going? When will he return? Anna's thoughts raced about this Maurdis of whom they spoke gravely of, could he be as sinister as told? Is it him that is the cause for the disappearances and slaughter discoveries of Skye? These questions would exhaust her mind, until she walks over to the fireplace, and sits in the wooden chair, patiently awaiting her father's 'promise of return.'

Meanwhile, Arthur watches as Anna has safely secured herself inside, his friend Lucian, seeing this, places his hand gently upon Arthur's shoulder.

"She will be alright Arthur, she is safe within the village, tonight we ensure Maurdis will never set foot here!" tells Lucian solemnly in promise.

"We must brother," replies Arthur, "She is all I have left," he tells, as they turn away, disappearing into the night.

The next day approaches quickly, as sunlight finds its way through the hairlines of the window shutters, its rays waking Anna, who fell asleep seated in the wooden chair, at the foot of the fireplace. Its flames have burned out, as the sounds of villager's voices and animals ring going about their day just beyond the walls of their stead, the house is unusually quiet, as Anna then pitches up from the chair, standing to her feet.

"Father?!!" she calls from the front room into the empty hallway. She continues to wait a few moments for an answer until, "Father?!!" she calls out once more, proceeding down the hallway and abruptly opening his room's door. She sees nothing but an unkempt bed, still messy from his sudden departure. A cloud of worry slightly casts over her, as she rushes on her wool tunic, lacing up her leather boots and darts out the front door in search of her father. Just outside their home is the busy village path, a dusty stony pathway along where travelers and villages buy and sell. It is bustling with people riding by on their horses, with bags of goods in tow, also many of those on foot with heavy bags draped over their shoulders stopping for trinkets, and trades for silver, the crowd stampede through the mud moving from store to store, as carriages pull along logs of wood. Anna pushes against the moving crowd, looking for signs of her father.

"Father where are you?" she mutters anxiously to herself. As she dodges an oncoming pair of travelers carelessly pulling their horses and supplies along, she overhears a pair of older male villagers talking.

"Were there any sightings?" the first goes on to ask.

"There was news of an attack yesterday, under the cover of night, these lycans... they're growing bolder, this one was just outside the village," the other mentions gravely.

"Nordskye has managed for years to fend them off by keeping the men on guard at night, but I fear these walls no longer offer our small village protection, soon there won't be a traveller to come anywhere near here for trade, the only thing keeping our city fed is our wood," the first male replies, "The forest has recently been deemed unsafe, our children are starving, and attacks have also began at the other cities and villages, Skye is at a never-ending unrest," he details further. Anna silently listens in on the conversation, to her, this adds even more concern of her father's wellbeing, as she hastily leads off into the village.

She traverses near the edge of town, past the noise of tradesmen, and simple travelers, entering its homestead. It is notably quiet along its stony paths, yet, it remains alive with hordes of familiar vagrants and beggars lining each of the building's walls. Anna follows her father's daily route through the 'sleepy town.' As she passes the brick laid houses, she is mindful the village continuously appears to be dwindling, much smaller than she remembers. It seemed like just yesterday, the streets appeared a bit more alive. Suddenly, a gust of wind blows by, hurling dust of the village's path towards her, she quickly shields her face from the wind, coughing, she dusts the dirt from her tattered, wool-woven tunic, continuing down the trail. Anna arrives at the village's well, normally a spot encompassed by neighbouring paupers, seeking out means for food, however, today it is empty. This strikes her as odd, meanwhile, something catches her attention. It is the sleepy, old bakery, sitting directly across from the well. Anna then wonders if her father may be lingering inside and quickly proceeds over to the bakery. As she pushes open the wooden door, she is greeted by and elderly male.

"Well, good day Miss, with it being so quiet in the city today I didn't think anyone would've stopped by," tells the baker jokingly in greeting, turning to her as she enters. He fixes a loaf of bread among the wooden shelves and walks near the counter to serve.

"How can I help you, young lady?" he asks with a warm smile. Anna steps further into the bakery, immediately, she is distracted by the loaves of bread and pastries, as her stomach grumbles at the sight of it all. It has been nearly two days, having since she's ate a filling meal. However, she quickly refocuses on the task at hand.

"Thank you, I was wondering, did an 'Arthur Valor' enter through here earlier this morning?" Anna asks humbly and standoffish in question.

"Why no, you would be the first customer in three days," he laughs jolly in reply, "However, did you say Arthur Valor? the forgemaster? the blacksmith? Are you, his family?" he goes on to ask intriguingly.

"He is my father sir," answers Anna humbly. The baker then pitches upright with a smile.

"Your father is a good man; kindhearted man, he visits often, although, I haven't seen him in three days, is everything alright?" questions the baker concerningly, noting Anna's disappointed expression.

"I-I um... He left last night, and I haven't seen him since, and I've searched everywhere," details Anna distressfully.

"Mhmmm," the baker mutters with a nod, "Well... I'm sure he will turn up soon, until then, here..." he tells tossing her a loaf of barley from the shelf, "Bread makes everything better," he jokes with a smile, as Anna leans into catching the loaf, inwardly leaping for joy of finally having something to eat.

"Thank you kindly," she replies gratefully, with pleasant grin running ear to ear, as she motions near the door to leave, waiving to the baker in farewell. Again, she steps out into the street, walking by the droves of lifeless vagrants lining the walls of the village's houses. Her heart grieves the look of hunger, and grief written on the faces of every person she passes by, knowing she has nothing to offer. Moments later, she approaches an alleyway, where the voices of quarrelling children can be heard. In the distance, three young boys can be seen shoving and pulling at what appears to be a young girl. Anna immediately stops, watching for a few moments, and is drawn to investigate.

"What's the matter?" she asks calmly, quickly capturing the four's attention, as she walks over, instinctively kneeling to protect the little girl. The three boys swiftly step aside, as the terrified, little girl immediately speaks up.

"Th-hey w-were trying to take my l-loaf of bread," she sniffles tearfully, looking to Anna, her clothes torn, tattered, and dirty, seeming patched with an array of cloths binding each tear. Anna turns to the petrified, and ashamed group of boys.

"I-I...we're sorry," apologizes one of the three nervously, looking towards the ground, their faces starved, malnourished, and spotted with dirt.

"We haven't no food to eat," the other mutters shamefully, as they each look away in shame. Anna pauses, breathing in, setting aside her judgement, she looks down at the barley loaf, and again at their faces.

"Here," she replies, reaching out her hand, as she extends her loaf of bread to the young boys. The faces of the three boys immediately light up with gratitude.

"Thank you!" the three utter harmoniously, as they immediately share the loaf amongst themselves.

"You're welcome," Anna replies generously, "But remember, it's better to ask than to take," she lightly scolds pointing in their faces. The young boys quietly nod in thanks, gratefully running off into the village. With that, Anna turns to the little girl, gently patting her shoulder.

"You be safe now! And head back to your parents!" Anna imparts caringly with a smile. The little girl silently looks towards the ground.

"W-What's the matter?" she goes on to ask, seeing her sad expression.

"I-I live with my aunt," the young girl replies lowly.

"And what of your parents?" asks Anna curiously in reply. The little girl pauses, as she quietly shakes her head. Anna is instantly touched by this and hugs the young girl.

"You head back to your aunt now, I'm sure she's waiting on you," she tells her with a warm smile. The little girl nods with a smile and turns away to depart, returning down the sleepy alley way. Meanwhile, Anna silently watches on, as the young girl departs, when, in the distance, she glimpses a woman approaching the little girl. The woman kneels down to hug her, as if she had been lost, shortly after, they are seen hand in hand, continuing until beyond sight.

Contented of the girl's safety, in the arms of the 'familiar' woman, Anna stands from her knees and continues down the path. Along the way back home, a sudden commotion seems to to have garnered the attention of many of the villagers, as everyone appears to be running in the direction ahead of her. Suddenly, Anna is bumped aside, she turns quickly to see who rudely knocked her from behind.

"S-Sorry I didn't see you there," a younger male voice, dusting himself from the ground, "I just washed this, this morning," he mutters patting off his brown tunic and trousers. Finally, he looks up, immediately, both faces light up at the sight of one another.

"Siff!" exclaims Anna ceremoniously, as she embraces him, rubbing her hands gently through his ash-blonde hair, his youthful, dusty face looks up at her with a smile.

"Where are you going in such a hurry?" she chuckles in asking her young friend.

"It's the village, the men have returned from the hunt of the lycans, they've gathered in the village square, that's all I know, I overheard some people talking about an announcement," details Siff vaguely, as they look amongst the moving crowd.

"Come on, they said its important, I don't want to miss this!" he exclaims pulling at her right arm.

"Were there any news of my father?!" Anna voices in question, speaking over the rolling of carriages, and murmurings of the nearby villagers. Siff, however, doesn't quite hear her questions among the commotion, and continues to pull her in the direction of the crowd.

"Come on we're almost there!" he urges on. The pair enter an open square, where sits in the midst, an array of pitched tenting, where lies marketers and tradesmen alike, weighing silver pieces, and carrying out small trades. About the square, lies the village's taller structures, its inns, and bars formed of stone and firm wood. To the right lie the empty gallows, petrified of having not been used, and to the forefront where many of the crowd appears to gather is a low, wooden decking, where a male's voice is heard addressing the people.

"Why are they calling us?" mutters Anna curiously.

"Stop being so paranoid," teases Siff, as he squeezes his way through the curious crowd, meanwhile, Anna being slightly older has a harder time keeping up behind him.

"Siff, wait up!" she exclaims nudging by the shoulders of a few older males.

"Anna, come on!" calls Siff quickly, crawling beneath the crowd up ahead. Anna then loses full sight of her friend.

As she soon nears the forefront, the commotion slowly grows to whispers and murmurs about the crowd, as the cries of women and children are heard, sounding just up ahead. This pulls at the nerves of Anna, who grows wary in concern, as she picks up the pace, and quickly squeezes her way through.

"Siff! Siff! Where are you? I'm here, Siff!" she calls, finally emerging from the crowd and at the forefront, there Siff stands, turning to her, his face is blank, and expression is of disbelief. Anna also glimpses Lucian, who visited her father's house last night, standing motionless up ahead. Lucian glimpses Anna, and quietly stands aside, as Anna slowly continues to walk forward.

"What's wrong?" Anna turns to Siff in question, he stiffens up, as his voice trembles shakily, not being able to answer. Suddenly, Lucian walks over to her, in his hand a silver blade. Anna recognizes it immediately; it is her father's sword. Her heart paces quickly, as her breaths grow heavy, and her palms begin to sweat.

Anna silently steps by Lucian, who quietly bows his head, as he steps aside. She glimpses her father's black leather boots and robe, lying aside a group of corpses, along the wooden, bloodstained deck, his clothes still appear damp from last night's squall, as his face is an unspeakable lifeless pale. Immediately, Anna covers her mouth speechless as a cold, shiver travels down her spine. Anna drops to her knees in the dust, aside her father's corpse, falling her head to his chest in sobbing.

"F-F-Father..." her voice trembles, as she whimpers uncontrollably, her tears filling her father's robe. The crowd silently looks on. Relatives and friends gather around, approaching the bodies of their lost loved ones, as a dark sorrow holds upon the village of Nordeskye. Meanwhile, Lucian slowly creeps up from behind, kneeling beside Anna, presenting her father's blade.

"Your father was cut off from the group, he pursued after Maurdis alone, we tried to keep up, but the lycans they were overwhelming, we got separated, picked off one by one, and we couldn't get to him in time," details Lucian sorrowfully in telling, as he wipes his eyes with his sleeve. "When I finally found him, he wasn't moving, the men told me we had to leave, or surely, we would all perish that night, and that we had to make it to the village to warn you all of how powerful the lycans had become, so I snatched up his sword and we ran. But it wasn't long before they found us, and once more, they tore through the group, and only few of us managed to escape. I hid myself within the brushes and mud of the forest, to lose my scent, and it kept me safe until the dawn. Only then, I got up and returned to Nordskye, to gather a search for the missing bodies, I kept Arthur's sword, to give to you," tells Lucian humbly, meanwhile, Anna's head remains rested on her father's chest in sobbing. Suddenly, she slowly lifts her head, her face reddened by her tears, as she turns to face him.

"Y-Y-You t-told me, y-you promised m-me, he would return safe, you promised me! AND NOW HE'S DEAD!! MY FATHER IS DEAD!! screams Anna tearfully in reply. Lucian is silenced with guilt, as Anna returns to sobbing on her father's chest, he then notices Siff, who quietly looks on at his friend, not having the slightest idea of what to do. Lucian then gets to his feet and walks near to Siff.

"Take this," he says handing the young boy the silver sword, "Ensure that she gets it," he informs before disappearing into the crowd behind them.

"B-BUT…" whimpers Siff, as he quickly brushes by, he then looks to Anna, who doesn't budge from her father's body. Suddenly, a male voice sounds, garnering the attention of the village.

"My dear city!" addresses a male elder to the crowd, standing above of the pile of corpses, "These are fearsome times, our men fear the creatures of the night, many our wives widowed, even our children, left fatherless, the land of Skye has never more been divided by fear! I urge you, ALL OF YOU, DO NOT take this warning lightly," he voices earnestly.

"He is coming!" he says vaguely. The people gathered in the town's square listen intently, as an aura of fear consumes their hearts. "We have allowed them to grow more powerful, all the while the people of Skye have grown ignorant, the order that once protected is no more, Skye is the more divided, meanwhile, starvation plagues our village, we are on the verge of collapse!" he rants wildly in telling.

The people slowly begin murmuring fretfully amongst themselves and for a moment, there is an eerie silence.

"He will take you…ALL OF YOU, there is no safety here!" states the elder dramatically, "How many more men? how many widows… starving children?" he details gravely, as he looks about the speechless, mourning crowd, "These walls won't last forever, the land of Skye must unite to quell this evil!!" he roars in protest, "Only when all of Skye chooses to make a stand against our enemies, will we finally be free!" adds the male further, looking among the listening eyes.

Finally, the crowd slowly disperses, the spoken words and deaths marked as another day, as the people of Nordskye now face further famine of trade, meaning even less food, supplies and harvest of much need wood. Siff kneels by Anna, placing his arm about her shoulder in comfort, as she sobs uncontrollably.

"He was all I had…" sniffles Anna tearfully, looking into his pale, stiff face. Her fist tightens, as her face runs, suddenly, a few of the village's men approach from behind. Siff turns, hearing their footsteps, as one of the men step forth.

"I plead your forgiveness, young one, my name is Erik Listor" the male greets humbly to Anna, who stops mourning for a moment, lifting her head to listen. "Your father was a great man, he served the village diligently, we think it only right to give him proper service," he tells further, "He was the greatest forgemaster Skye has ever known," tells Erik grandly, Anna remains quiet for a few moments, silently nodding her head in agreement. Seeing this, Erik signals the men in waiting, who approach with a wooden carriage. The four lift Arthur's corpse onto the carriage as Anna sits beside her father, gently caressing her hands through his hair. Anna looks over his robe, seeing something peculiar. A slit opening is seen through his robe, she lifts the cape of his robe revealing the hole piercing through the chest of his tunic, his clothes still damp of last night's rain. She continues to investigate, reaching underneath his corpse, placing her hands on his torso. Anna feels the tear of his robe also underneath. As she lifts her hands to her face, to her realization, it is soaked in blood. She could not be mistaken, her father's death had to have been handed down by the end of a blade. Her mind immediately races with possibility of deceit. Could her father have been betrayed? Left to die by the very village he swore to protect? Her mind is shrouded by the mystery, overshadowed by the surreal reality of his death. Her fingers run along the tears and bite marks of his robe and tunic, as the carriage approaches her home.

Anna quickly gets to her feet, turning to the men.

"Enough," she voices lowly, "I will take him from here," she tells stepping down from the carriage, with Siff following behind. This strikes the men as odd, as Erik steps forth from the group.

"Daughter of Sir Arthur?" he addresses to Anna.

"My name is Anna," she corrects bluntly, putting him at unease.

"My apologies, Anna, we think it only right that he receives proper burial," Erik goes on to suggest.

"He will," tells Anna stoutly in reply, "You can rest his body here," she instructs pointing to a wooden table around the home's side, "I would like to mourn peacefully," she adds. With head held down, Erik gestures the men to retrieve the body. They gently lay Arthur's body atop the table and soon depart, leaving Anna to mourn. Siff watches on as the men leave, and turns to Anna, who is leant over her father's body, as her tears drip from her cheeks to his face.

"Anna…?" mutters Siff tenderly, as her sniffles grow louder, his heart sinks for his friend, knowing there is nothing he can do.

"Please…go! I don't want you to see me this way!" she begs tearfully, her back turned towards him. Silently, Siff turns away, following her request and leaves her alone to grieve.

Moments later, Anna wipes her face with her sleeve, as she finally catches her breath. There she stands, as the day's cool breeze blows by. Finally, she leaves the table and enters the house, returning outside with an empty bale. Dropping it into a barrel of water, she takes a knife and cuts at her tunic's sleeve. Pulling out the filled bale, and placing the cutout rag in its water, she loosens her father's robe and tunic. Tears well in her eyes, as the bites, cuts, and sword wound appear, as she carefully wipes each wound.

Once more she steps inside the house, bringing out a large sheet, and covers her father's body. Anna glimpses to her left a mound of chopped firewood, it had been collected by her father the night before. Anna gathers the wood, laying them together and forming a flat rise. At this time, the sun has lowered to the horizon, as she pushes his body carefully onto the wooden surface. Anna's eyes begin to fill, as she places a piece of silver on each eyelid. After a few more moments of mourning, she then walks indoors. Darkness has finally fell, when suddenly, she hears a knocking at the front door. Anna proceeds to the door, as the knocking continues. As she opens the door, a cloaked male appears, with a familiar gray beard dangling near his chest, as it cleaves from his hooded face.

"Anna, daughter of Sir Arthur," he opens, with a commanding deep voice, "I am…" he goes on to say, when he is abruptly cut off.

"I know who you are," retorts Anna, "You're one of them, you came with Mr. Lucian, you took my father to his death," she condemns fiercely in reply. The male remains silent. "I do not wish to see any of you," she tells bluntly, slowly shutting the door.

"I knew your father well," he answers, putting Anna at a pause, "I know he loved the people of Skye greatly, and I can tell he loved you very much," he tells further.

"What did you come here for?" voices Anna impatiently, shunning away his words.

"To warn you, to stay away from the forest! Seek not revenge! I know the thoughts of his death within you be fresh, and that you may desire blood for blood, but the enemy you look for is far more powerful than you know… remain here in Nordskye, rebuild the forge and continue his legacy!" warns the male stoutly, as he departs the door, disappearing off into the night. Meanwhile, Anna is left standing at the doorway, her gaze peculiar, seeing as the older male disappears into the night. Quickly, she slams shut the door. Looking near the fireplace, she glimpses her father's robe and sword draped along the wooden rocking chair.

Anna draws a piece of wood from the fireplace, tying a piece of cloth about its top. She then dips the cloth into a barrel of oil, and proceeds to the outside. Lighting her steps to her father's shrouded corpse, she pulls away the sheet, revealing her father's body. Anna stands there, silently looking to her father's face, as precious memories race to thought. Her eyes shut tightly, as her tears squeezes through. She then pours the makeshift rise soaked with oil. As she stands near him, placing her hand on his head.

"Whatever it takes… whether it be my life… this I swear you; I WILL AVENGE YOU, FATHER," she whispers solemnly in prayer. With that, Anna sets ablaze the wooden flat, and watches on as the flames engulf the body. Meanwhile, she mourns, remaining unaware of the stranger watching from the shadows. On the other hand, small footsteps can be heard approaching, as an empty bale is accidently kicked over, causing Anna to turn about. It is her younger friend, Siff, returning to check upon her.

"You shouldn't be here," tells Anna, keeping her back turned, wiping her face with her soiled hands. Her face is covered in dirt, mixing along with her tears and sweat, as her hair is messy with stress.

"Anna, please... suffer not yourself alone, let me stay with you," he begs walking nearer. Anna takes a quick glance at him and continues to sob. Seeing this, Siff instinctively leans near, holding her in his arms, as there he sits with her, until they both slowly fall asleep.

It is the middle of the night, when the horn blares, followed by the shouts and voices of men, this commotion abruptly wakes Anna from her sleep. As she pitches up from the ground, she sees the row of torches lighting the path, as they walk by her home. Anna sits in wonder for a few moments, and looks down at Siff, still asleep beside her. Her fists clenched in thought, she scampers indoors, near the fireplace, and quickly covers herself in her father's robe. Approaching the front room's table, where sits, the gleaming silver sword. Anna runs her fingertips along her father's silver blade, and quickly sheathes the sword within her waist.

As she steps out the door, she is met by Siff, who stands center of the doorway. "Where are you going?" he asks curiously, noting her cloaked in black appearance. He takes a step back in disbelief, "Anna NO! You can't be serious?!" voices Siff, shaking his head in reproof.

"Do you even know what's out there?!! Neither of us have ever been outside the town's walls! Is it because of him? your father?" questions Siff forwardly, "Anna, I can't let you do this, you don't know what's out there! You might die! Every night someone disappears, the last person your father would want that happen to is you," he tells further.

Anna ignorantly shakes her head, "I must avenge him, they have taken everything from me, this Maurdis, the lycan's leader, whoever he is, he killed my father, his debt... must be paid," utters Anna solemnly, as she brushes by her young friend, leading out into the street.

"ANNA! WAIT!" calls Siff running up from behind, "I'm coming with you," he answers.

"Absolutely not, Siff, I will not bring you into this, this is my curse, my fight, I cannot escape my vengeance," mutters Anna, tightening her grip about her sword's handle. Siff steps closer looking up to her face.

"This is not your curse, but this is our fight," tells Siff boldly in reply, "You have no choice, I'm coming with you," he adds, pulling his tattered hood over his head. Anna realizes she can no longer argue with him and turns to glimpse the line of torches in the distance, as they exit through the large, wooden-crafted, front gates of the town's wall.

"Okay, you can come!" tells Anna seeing her window of shadowing the village's group dwindling, "But you must stay out of sight!" she scolds in telling. With that, the pair proceed up the path, encountering yet, another reality, having to escape past the village's guards. Surely, they wouldn't let a pair of kids leave the city alone, and certainly not during nightfall. The pair peer about the corner using the wall of a nearby home for cover, Anna cunningly sizes up the guards.

"Anna, are you sure about this?" asks Siff unsurely having second thoughts. Meanwhile, Anna sees the faint lights of the torches continuing in the distance, through the thin openings of the village's front gates. Across from them, she notices a stable, with what looks like a loose rope hanging near its door and comes up with an idea.

"Hey," she taps at Siff's side, "I have an idea, follow me," she tells vaguely, using the cover of shadows to creep across the way. Quickly, Siff follows after her. The pair arrive, unnoticed by the guards, as they enter the dark, open stable. Anna seizes the nearby rope hanging from the stable's door and quickly ties the rope to a post, low to the ground, near the stable's entrance. "Throw this to get his attention," mentions Anna, handing over a small stone to Siff, "When he chases you, lead him here," she instructs firmly.

"Anna? Are your sure about this?" stammers Siff questionably in reply.

"Yes, trust me!" utters Anna calmly, "Now go!"

Siff nods his head, and proceeds to the outside. His heart pounding out of chest, he uses the cover of a tall heap of hay, he jumps out from behind it, hurling the stone towards the guard's back.

"Hey!" he yells, as the stone strikes the guard, whose attention fixates on Siff who flees the haystack.

"Thief!" yells the guard furiously as he chases behind him. Siff leads the guard to the stable, as Anna waits hidden in the door's side. As Siff enters, the guard bounds after him through the doors and with a great tug, Anna pulls at the rope, holding taut, as the guard violently trips to the ground. Immediately, the pair abandon the shelter, shutting close the doors behind them, as they quickly squeeze through the front gates.

The pair have successfully escaped the safety of the village walls, entering into the mysteriously, vast forest that is Skye.

"Quickly, we must catch up!" hastens Anna as the pair trudge uphill, meanwhile, the torches can still be seen through the thickets of forest in the distance. Anna looks up towards the moon, floating amongst the clouds as a ghostly galleon.

"Siff, look up," she tells gesturing towards its light. "Beautiful, isn't it?" she goes on to say, directing his attention towards the iridescent moon.

"It is, however, it's what follows that concerns me," mutters Siff worriedly, looking ahead, as they feel their way through the bushes. The lights of the torches, appear to dimmer, a sign to them that they are falling too far behind.

"Siff, we must hurry before we lose sight of them!" mentions Anna hurriedly, as she picks up the pace, when suddenly, there is a loud crack followed by a thud. It is Siff, who trips blindly falling to the ground.

"What is that?!!" exclaims a male voice indistinctly, as the line of torches can be seen coming to an abrupt halt. Suddenly, one of them separates from the group, walking closer to where Anna and Siff lie crouched and out of sight.

"Do you see anything, Ellis?!" questions one of the men, holding ahead his torch.

"No, nothing's there, could've been a deer or some animal," he mutters turning away and rejoining the group.

"Pray the fates it is," replies the other reluctantly, as they continue through the forest.

"Come on, Siff!" whispers Anna, carefully getting to her feet. Siff follows and the two carefully keep a small distance between themselves and the group, while also remaining out of sight, as the party travels further and further away from the village. Hours pass and Siff slowly starts to tire.

"Anna, we should turn back, it's been hours and not a single lycan has been seen, we should head back to the village where it's safe," he tells pulling at her sleeve.

"We're almost there, I can feel it," she encourages still pressing forward, as the breeze about them slowly begins to pick up and the night's draft can be felt passing by.

Finally, fed up with Anna's ignorance, he pulls greater at her sleeve, stopping her along the low-lying brush.

"Anna I've had enough of this! This is not what he would've wanted, you're consumed by anger, avenge him, yes, but not like this, we are vulnerable, these men are searching for death itself, neither of us has ever left the village, the fates are not on our side this time!" Siff whispers in reasoning, "Please let's return before it's too late," he adds.

"I CAN'T TURN BACK!!" exclaims Anna lowly, riling towards him with tearful eyes, "He was all I had..." she sniffles, clenching her fists tightly, as Siff who being startled remains silent. "I can't turn back, his blood is on my hands, and this Maurdis... his debt must be paid," she tells furiously. Meanwhile, Siff looks on at the anger-absorbed Anna before him, speechless as to how such a gentle soul has become so consumed.

"Anna..." he mutters in answering, when suddenly, a great, light beams among their faces, as the cower their faces from the light, it is the village men, they have been found!

"How did you get here?!" voices one of the men in question, looking down at their hooded faces. The men step aside, as a lone male walks through, his straggly gray beard hanging to his chest, Anna remembers him instantly.

"How come you into the forest?!" he demands sternly to her. Anna looks into his shrouded face, with Siff sheltered behind her.

"We followed you," she answers forwardly in reply. This seems to anger the elder male.

"Foolish child, you endanger you both, allowing your anger to fester, pulling you into something you are not prepared for in the least!" he roars furiously, as the men standby in watching.

"MY FATHER IS DEAD BECAUSE OF YOU!!" yells Anna angrily in reply, as a silence comes over the men, whose eyes turn to the elder male, who remains quiet. "ALL I HAD… nothing else, I must avenge him," she tells further. Suddenly, the elder steps closer, when instantly, a loud wolf howl is heard, startling the men, who quickly reach for their swords and weapons. Alerted by the sound, he looks about the shadowy forest surrounding them, then turns to Anna and Siff.

"May the fates have mercy on your soul, you have no idea what you've gotten yourself into," he mutters solemnly to her. Turning to the men, "Steady your hearts the lot of you! STAY TOGETHER!" he orders among them. Meanwhile, Anna and Siff fearfully join the group, unsheathing her father's sword, as she nervously looks around. There is an eerie silence, when in an instant a jet-black figure hurls towards one of the men.

"LYCAN!!" roars one of them indistinctly, as the man's screams pull away into the silence of the forest. Fear settles on each of their hearts, as they pant in anticipation of another surprise attack.

"How many are there?!" shouts another in question, going unanswered by the petrified group.

"We must return to the village! We are at a disadvantage!" flails another in answering.

"No!" the elder replies, "We would only be picked off, we must stay together!" orders Wraithe loudly to the men. Moments go by, neither man moves from their spot, as another petrifying howl is heard in the night. Immediately, the bushes erupt, as a black flurry of shadow bounds toward them. 'It' is met with a swift strike of the elder's blade. Slain at his feet, the men hold their torches down towards the creature, it is a large, dark wolf. Suddenly, its body begins to shift, as its limbs begin to move and breathing slows. The wolf's body transfigures into a middle-aged male. Taking his last breath, he passes.

"He was… a man?" murmurs one of the men in discovery.

"That's what a lycan is," states Wraithe bluntly wiping his blade, "Guard yourselves!" he tells further. Suddenly, from both sides, the trampling of twigs and brush can be heard, followed by malicious snarls. "Ready yourselves!!" roars the elder once more. When in an instant, two shadows appear leaping atop one of the men, and biting down on his arm, whilst the other charges for Anna, who thrashes her sword at the beast, keeping it at bay. Another howl is heard and is enough to scare the men.

"It was a mistake to come here, we've doomed us all!" yells one of them, "We must return to the village!" he voices. With that, the men panic and disperse; this immediately frustrates the elder.

"Nooo!" he calls; however, the men ignore, frantically fleeing to their own way. Petrified, Anna and Siff remain at his side.

"W-What do we do?!" fumbles Anna looking up to him in question, keeping Siff behind her.

"I told you to remain in the village! You are not ready for what you seek!" he tells stoutly in reply. "We have to move," instructs the elder, leading off into the brush. Anna and Siff swiftly follow behind, fanning away the bushes as they plow through the forest. The moon is at its peak, boldly illuminating the shadows, as they approach an opening in the forest.

"Don't move!" mutters the elder lowly to them, gesturing to a sudden halt. Puzzled, Anna and Siff look to him.

"Why, they're right behind us," she tells in reply, Wraithe places his finger to his lips, pointing their attention up ahead. A creature starkly resembling a human creeps ahead of them, seemingly unaware of their presence. The creature bears human limbs, with longer arms and legs with elongated heels. They take note of its hairless, pale skin, which seems to lightly luminate within the moonlight, bringing to life its many veins, that line throughout its skin's 'cold' surface. What strikes the young pair as odd, is the creature's curved spine, that gives the strange creature a more grounded feral appearance.

"Vampire..." whispers the elder lowly, "Your people call them nocturnals," he tells further, slowly stepping them back.

Anna quickly shoves Siff behind her. When suddenly, a four-legged shadow leaps from the bushes behind them. The three immediately turn around, seeing the yellow-piercing eyes of the lycan snarling towards them. Panicked, Anna and Siff's gaze pans left to right, until the lycan makes a sudden charge for them. As it leaps towards them in attack, it is struck midair, wrestling to the ground, and with a great yelping cry, it is put down, as the nocturnal sinks its fangs into its throat. The young pair stifled with fear, dare not move, when finally, the creature abandons its meal, darting towards them.

Suddenly...

"DOWN!" yells the elder's commanding voice. Immediately, the two friends duck to the ground, and with a swift swipe of his sword, followed by a deafening shriek, the elder slays the creature. Both hearts pounding out their chests, the pair look on, their attacker bears no eyes, ears, or actual nose, only three lined openings along the sides of a meagre structure having vague resemblance to a human's nose.

"Get up!" orders the elder quickly bidding them to flee, as another a shrieking sound is heard. It is followed by a choir of the similar noise. Quickly, he turns to them, "They're coming!" he hastens, slashing his way through the bushes.

"They have no eyes; how can they see us?!" pants Anna in disbelief.

"The warmth, your blood, fear... they smell you!" details the elder, "And once one gets it, they all follow... cut off one head, only to have a hundred more take its place," he mutters miserably continuing ahead.

Siff starts to fall behind, unable to keep up with the pair, meanwhile, Anna quickly looks behind, ensuring he stays beside them. Suddenly, her concern is quickly turned to horror.

"Siff! Siff!" she screams, when from above, a peculiar shadow is seen diving towards him,

"Get off of him!" screams Anna, charging towards the beast, as she rushes it off of Siff. Tussling with the creature along the ground, Anna struggles to keep its biting jaws at elbow's length. Finally, she kicks it away, only for it to return, lunging violently towards her. Attacking from behind, the elder plunges his sword into its torso. From beneath, Anna glimpses firsthand, the blade's edge piercing through the creature's chest and quickly shoves its body aside. Siff pulls her to her feet, and they continue off. Forcing their way through the sticky branches, the trampling of forest can be heard gaining closer. Little do they realize, they near a steep ledge where the rapid's strong currents, can be heard pulling below. Anna quickly grabs hold of Siff, who nearly loses his footing, near the steep's edge.

"Over there, down the side!" shouts the elder flailing ahead, "We can lose them in the river!" he adds. In haste, Anna pushes Siff ahead, as the three scamper down the rocky cliff-side. When suddenly, with a great force, Siff is swept off balance, as one of the creatures hurls him over the side.

"AGHHHH...HELP ME!" he screams in fright, as they tumble down the wayside.

"SIFF!" shrieks Anna in panic.

"Hold on, boy!" calls the elder rushing to his aid, until a loud splash is heard, as they plummet into the raging rapids below. In that instance, the horde is upon them. The man leaps into saving Siff. Meanwhile, Anna hesitates at the edge, and makes the mistake of looking behind her; seeing the horde erupt from the forest. Panicked, she jumps from the ledge, plunging into the river's current. Meanwhile, further along the river's rapids, Siff continues his struggle against the nocturnal, whilst frantically trying to keep his head above the rolling tides.

"Get it off me!" he wails, bobbing above the surface for air, suddenly, he glimpses sight of the elder, who thrashes along the currents in an attempt to get closer.

"Hold on boy!" he calls over to Siff, pushing upon the creature's back. Quickly, he wraps his arm around its neck, unsheathing his sword and driving it into the nocturnal's chest, killing it instantly.

Finally, the creature's hold loosens, releasing Siff astray into the currents.

"NOOO!" Siff cries out in panic, frantically attempting to reach for the elder's hand.

"Here, boy!", he shouts to Siff, extending his arm towards him, when they hurled under the water's surface, as the river's force pull them apart. Meanwhile, Anna, splashing from behind, also struggles to stay above water.

"Siff!" Anna calls desperately looking around for signs of him. All the while, the elder finally gets within an arm's distance to grab Siff.

"Take my hand!" he tells again reaching out to him. Siff wades along the currents, as the pair finally draw closer. "Almost there!" he grunts, making a final push. Again, the water pulls both underneath, for what seems like an eternity. Tumbling them about the murky depths of the river. Siff futilely attempts to propel himself to the surface. When suddenly, he is struck, as the river's current drives him into a large boulder. in that instant, for Siff, everything goes dark.

"Siff!" breathes Anna fearfully, catching a glimpse of what seems to be his floating body, disappearing beneath the surface in the nearby distance. For a while longer, Anna continues her struggle against the tides, until it finally releases its grip on the young lady, ultimately driving them all to a calm, as it floats them upon the shore. Exhausted, Anna collapses.

As the rays of sunlight pierces through the sheets, onto her pale face, Anna startles herself awake. Confused and suffering from a severe ache of her head, she looks about her surroundings. Gathering herself, she realizes that she's in a tent. In its corner, she spots her father's sword, tucked away in a pack of supplies. Anna quickly creeps over, grabbing the supplies, and moves towards the tent's exit. Carefully, she peeks her head outside, seeing no sign of anyone nearby, she then quickly slips out of the tent. Placing the sword in her waist, Anna searches the supplies within the bag. As she turns the corner, a young lady, of fair skin, and flowing dark hair, dressed in all black tunic, carrying pieces of wood, appears in her path. Startled, both young women pause. The girl finally glances down at the bag held within Anna's hand.

"Put that back!" she demands, dropping the wood and rushing towards Anna, who panics, reaching for her sword. The girl quickly tackles Anna off her feet, and the two tussle, tumbling across the ground.

"Where's my friend?" demands Anna, momentarily mounting atop her attacker. Placing her left arm over Anna's hands, that grips upon her throat. The girl deftly closes her arm down onto Anna's forearms, breaking her hold on her neck, following up with an elbow to Anna's face, stunning and shoving her off. The girl quickly kicks Anna to the ground and climbs atop her, fixing her right leg onto Anna's left arm, while holding the other arm captive. Rendered helpless, Anna struggles against the girl's fierce hold.

Suddenly, a commanding male voice calls out.

"Terra!" he orders bluntly. Immediately, the girl looks up, swiftly removing herself off of Anna. As she looks up from the ground, Anna sees the male's shadow towering over her and swiftly rises to her feet, drawing the sword from her waist.

"Where's Siff?!", she demands sternly, vaguely recognizing the elder male. Anna nervously begins taking small steps back. "I will not ask again. WHERE IS HE?!" she cries tearfully. Slowly, the male lifts both arms in the air, carefully stepping forward.

"Calm down child, your friend is alive, if it were not for us, you'd both be dead," he voices calmly, attempting to remove the blade from her hand.

"Stay back!" warns Anna nervously keeping her distance. Suddenly, she stumbles over a stone, falling to the ground and dropping her sword nearby. The girl rushes towards her, as Anna frantically crawls towards the sword. Leaping onto her back and into a roll, she locks her right arm about Anna's neck, pulling a damp cloth from her pocket and quickly places it over Anna's nose and mouth. For a moment, Anna struggles, but falls into a deep sleep. Finally, the pair carries her off.

Sometime later, Anna awakes, her hands tied as she leans up from her slumber. Rubbing her wrists together in attempt to loosen the ropes, she realizes they are tied too tight. Exhausted, she looks up at the tent's ceiling, as her mind races, where is Siff, is he alive?

"Still trying to fight, huh?" answers a female voice sardonically. Startled, Anna looks over her right shoulder, and about the tent. In the shadows, she sees a woman, dressed in an all-black leather tunic, sitting, wiping a sword. She rests the freshly sharpened blade down, dipping her hands into a bowl of clear fresh water, and reaches for a nearby cloth. Drying her hands, she turns to Anna, who realizes, it is the same girl she fought earlier.

"What did you do to my friend?" demands Anna forwardly in question.

"You can calm down," The woman chuckles while stepping into the light, kneeling but a few feet from Anna.

"Where is he?" Anna snaps, struggling violently to get out of her constraints. "Did you kill him?!" she asks worriedly.

"Kill him?!" replies the girl incredulously, "Please! You guys do a pretty damned good job of that yourselves," she scoffs in telling. "Besides, if we wanted you dead, you'd be already."

"Then where is he?!" grits Anna impatiently.

"Your friend suffered from hypothermia, and what seems like a mild concussion," answers the girl in reply, as she gathers to her feet, brushing off her sleeves. Anna is shocked and utterly overwhelmed with guilt.

"He's in the tent left of us," mentions the girl. "Don't worry, he's recovered fine," she adds in saying, noting Anna's distraught expression. "When Wraithe pulled him from the rapids, he was blue. We had to treat him immediately."

"Why help us?" mutters Anna sullenly in question.

"Well… couldn't just watch you die, besides, you're the daughter of his closest friend, Arthur Valor," she tells in reply. "Besides, you kids are far from home, who else was going to save you?" she ends. There is a brief silence, as Anna tries to digest everything she's just heard, battling the thought of having carelessly putting her friend's life at risk for revenge, and having encountered firsthand the very beings that have Skye gripped in fear.

"The name's Terra," the foreign girl offers, breaking the silence.

“What?” turns Anna bluntly to her in question.

“My name, It’s Terra,” she repeats, pulling a knife from her sleeve.

“Who’s the old guy?” asks Anna curiously.

“Who? Wraithe?”, chuckles Terra.

“He seems too old to be wandering around here alone,” humors Anna in reply.

“Trust me, he’s seen things that’d keep you up at night,” Terra retorts in chuckle, as she walks behind Anna, kneeling to cut loose the ropes. “Get some sleep, you hit your head pretty hard earlier,” she grunts, standing to her feet and walks out of the tent.

Anna sits there quietly, puzzled and in pain, yet, after a few moments, she finally nods off to sleep.

Darkness surrounds her. The forest lays quiet. Nothing stirs, and not a single sound is heard. Anna frantically pans around in a circle. Suddenly, a light tug is felt on her left arm. Immediately, she spins about. Yet, to her realization, nothing is there but the darkness itself. Meanwhile, in the distance, she glances a faint light. Viewing it as a way out, she runs towards it without hesitation. Suddenly, she is struck down by a swift brute force. The area around her is set ablaze, as the snarling and growling of wolves can be heard nearby. Their soulless-eyes and flesh-tearing teeth, peer through the flames. Instantly, Anna’s body goes numb in panic, as she quickly scampers to her feet. Running for her life, Anna’s only thought is to flee to a glimmering light in the distance. Meanwhile, the howling fire gains on her. She can hear their trampling steps behind her, as the thick darkness seems to smother her breath. Finally, Anna nears within an arm’s reach of the light, when suddenly, a wolf leaps from the fire behind her and upon her back, hurling her into the blinding light.

“Aghhhhh!” she screams out in terror, coiling her body into a tight ball. For a few moments, Anna’s body remains curled up, until she realizes, nothing is there. Getting to her feet, Anna looks about the familiar surroundings. She pushes open the wooden door, opening to a bedroom. Immediately, she notices a pair of boots, the ones similarly worn by her father, they lie next to a torn-up cloak draped across the bed, its quilts soaked red with blood. Her heart racing, she slowly closes the door.

Anna continues to explore the house and notices a light glaring down the hallway, glowing from the living space. Curious, Anna makes her way down the hall, towards the light. Entering the shadowy room, she sees the fire, stoked and blazing in the chimney.

"I've been waiting for you," echoes a male voice from within the room. Surprised, Anna looks about her. A man wearing a gray fur coat, and boots appears leant above the fireplace. Anna remains still, as she stares down the stranger.

"W-Who a-are you?" her voice trembles in saying.

"Who am I?" chuckles the male questionably in reply.

"You don't know me, but you will," he states, turning towards her. He appears tall, of medium build, and middle aged. His fierce blue eyes gaze into her soul, as his curly, gray and black hair frame his cold, pale face with groomed beard, contouring his sadistic grin. In the bat of an eye, he shifts from the fireplace, to standing in front of her. Anna is frozen by surprise. Suddenly, her eyes widen in terror, as she witnesses his transformation into a gray-coated wolf, in that instant, all goes dark.

"NOOOO!", screams Anna jolting awake.

After waking up to the four corners of the tent, she finally breathes to calm down, realizing it was all a nightmare. She sits up, resting her head between her knees. Unaware of a familiar presence, Siff, who having been also startled awake by her screams, moves in closer, leaning forward to place his hand on her shoulder.

"Are you okay?" he asks comfortingly in concern. Anna, having not fully recognized the young voice, remains silent in thought, still quite shaken up from her dream. "Anna!" shouts Siff impatiently, shaking her for a response. "Anna!" he utters again, until finally, she lifts her head from her knees, looking into the smiling eyes of Siff.

"Siff?" she answers groggily in disbelief, gathering her thoughts. "Siff? Siff!" she erupts joyously, lunging into an embrace, squeezing him tightly in her arms.

"Anna. Anna! I can't breathe," he squeals, wheezing for air. Anna warmly releases her grip, finally allowing him to breathe. "I-I thought you were trying to kill me for a sec," he mutters jokingly in reply, catching his breath.

"Siff, I thought I lost you." cries Anna, clasping his face within her hands. "When you fell into the river, I-I-I only thought how I couldn't live with myself, if I lost you," she continues to sob, pulling his forehead to hers, with eyes filled of sparkling crystals. Seeing her well of emotions, Siff tilts up Anna's chin, revealing the overflow of tears from her eyes.

"I will never leave you," he whispers gently. "I'll always be by your side," he promises, leaning in to comfort her.

Meanwhile, the tent's front covers open, as Terra walks in. "I see you're up, finally," she quips upon entering, "I made you something," she tells, kneeling to hand Anna a platter of food. Anna looks down at the platter, as the aroma of the venison and eggs Terra prepared, taunts her appetite.

"I can't thank you enough," Anna replies gratefully, taking the meal and starting to eat.

"Sure you can!" Terra answers, "Just don't waste anything, it took some work to get that deer," she adds with a smirk, turning to leave the tent. After a few moments of enjoying their reunion, the pair finally leave the tent. Stepping outside, they hear a male voice.

"Where are they?" the voice demands. Hearing this, Anna peers around the tent, placing Siff behind her, realizing the voice belongs to that of her father's strange friend.

"It's him!" Anna turns to Siff in whisper. She then returns her attention ahead only to meet his tall stature standing in front of her.

"I warned you! And you did not listen!" he scolds firmly, "Your very lives could've been lost last night! I told you to leave blood for blood alone! You are a child; you are not ready for that what you seek!" he tells further.

"You were with him! You may have gotten to say goodbye, but all I have are his memories! He left me! All I had gone! This Maurdis has taken everything from me! His blood will be mine!" exclaims Anna sternly in reply.

"Then you will die an arrogant, foolish little girl! Maurdis is not to be trifled with, he has laid waste to many villages and cities within

Skye! Yours is nothing but another to his conquest, and you'd be wise to hide," adds Wraithe turning away in saying. Meanwhile, Anna runs up from behind.

"Why couldn't you save him?!" she begs in question, stopping him in his way. He remains silent, as her glassy eyes glare into his face.

"I tried…" he answers quietly. "The men got separated under attack and your father had pursued after Maurdis alone. By the time I had caught up, the fates had already decided their victor. In your father's final breath, he pleaded me to keep you safe from Maurdis, and bid that you do not seek revenge for his passing," tells Wraithe. "Maurdis shows mercy to no one! Challenge him, and your death shall be swift!"

"It matters not if I die, as long as Maurdis comes with me," Anna swears solemnly. Meanwhile, Wraithe turns away at this resolve.

"I cannot let you do that," he mutters in reply. "I will return you to Nordskye! There you will remain! You will not pursue this fate, that is the wish of your father!" tells Wraithe further, as he proceeds to leave.

"I am no coward!" roars Anna furiously in rebuttal. Finally, Wraithe pauses.

"I know, you have your father's spirit, that is why I cannot let you do it," he adds in saying. As he walks away, Anna clenches her fists in anger, and disappears back into the tent, followed by Siff. She sits in sobbing, in the comfort of her friend. When suddenly, the tent's covers are drawn back, it is Terra, slowly entering the tent. She kneels in sitting across from the pair.

"I heard stories of him, your father, from Wraithe, it sounded like he was a good man, and they had a fond relationship… I know this is hard for you, but try to understand his words, he may have a harsh way of coming across, but he understands what's at stake," tells Terra earnestly. "Live on, continue your father's legacy, forge a new life, don't let rage consume you," she adds in saying. "Return to Nordeskye, as he suggests… Please!" begs Terra caringly, as she turns away from Anna, whose face soaked with tears, and departs the tent.

"Anna, I feel your pain, but listen to them, we need to go back to Nordeskye," utters Siff in agreement, as he gently rests his hand on her shoulder. Anna silently nods, and with that, Siff draws her into a hug. An hour later, the two exit the tent, only to meet Wraithe and Terra packing supplies onto their horses.

"Gather your things, we must be on our way," instructs Wraithe forwardly, as the pair approaches. "Terra! The tent!" he orders bluntly. Quickly, Terra heads over and begins pulling out the supplies from within and breaking down the tent. Anna and Siff quickly assist her with putting everything away.

"Two days to put everything up, and just a couple hours to take down," she mutters reluctantly to herself, resting her hands at her waist. "Come on," she calls them, "Wraithe is waiting," she mentions, lifting the rolled tenting and tying it to her horse's side.

"Is everything ready?" asks Wraithe seated atop his horse, as Terra mounts her horse beside him.

"Yes," she answers bluntly in reply.

"Let's be on our way, although it be midday, the dusk sets upon us quickly," tells Wraithe further. "You two, behind us!" he orders, gesturing them to join atop the horses. Anna seats herself behind Terra, as does Siff behind Wraithe, and the four set off in return of Nordskye.

Chapter 2
"A Chilling Arrival"

As they follow along the trail, there is utter silence among them. Finally, Terra opens up in question. "Your father? Was he a man of trade?" she turns to Anna, seated behind her.

"He was a forgemaster, the best in Nordskye! People from all over Skye came to purchase his craftwork," she mentions in reply, as both women duck their heads beneath the hanging limbs.

"So, he was a blacksmith? Interesting," comments Terra.

"A blacksmith by day, and guard of the city by night. From I was born, Nordeskye has only known fear! Only the men are allowed to go out during sunset, and if they don't return before nightfall, they shut the front gates. After that, they usually don't return," tells Anna gravely in reply.

"Skye has lived in fear for ages, and before that, it only knew war, and that's all it'll ever know. Man may rule the day, but the lycans and nocturnals be the lords of the night. A delicate balance best not challenged," interrupts Wraithe stoutly in saying. Holding her head down in silence, Anna ventures lost in thought, as the chirping tweets of the forest echoes about them, and its breeze dances smoothly among the leaves. Looking up to the sea of blue and flurry whisps floating above the canopy, it is all a calming sight. A few hours pass, and they approach the edge of the forest, veering over a lush green hill. The atmosphere as they leave the forest is different, there is utter silence, as the air breathes thicker, and the clear blue sky is blanketed by a dark deep ash. It is within that moment, Anna and Siff are subject to horror. Their town, Nordeskye, is devastated. Smoke fills the air as the dying flames slowly burnout. The village's once sturdy wooden front gates, appear ran through, as cries and mourns sound from within the village walls.

As they enter Nordeskye, dust fills the air, and scattered corpses line along the main path. A pair of young children is seen, knelt in mourning over a woman's body, their faces gaunt, covered with the dirt and mud of their tears. Both Anna and Siff are speechless at the sight of it all, as they continue through the deserted alleys of the town. How did something so unspeakable happen in such a short span of time? Anna thought to herself in disbelief.

"This is the work of Maurdis, they followed the men after the attack, used it as an opening to enter the village, and destroyed everything," details Wraithe fully, as he leads down the barren path.

The four take a turn right into a quiet, gloomy alleyway, when Anna spots the body of a male in the distance.

"Look!" she points out further down the path, suddenly, coughing is heard. "He's still alive!" exclaims Anna hastily. The four cautiously move in closer. As they approach, the horrific sight comes into clearer view, as his clothes are torn up, and left arm severed, bleeding profusely. Suddenly, he lifts his head from the ground upon hearing their voices.

"Mr. Listor?!?" blurts Anna in disbelief, recognizing the injured male is none other than Erik Listor, who helped in the moving of her father's burial. Immediately, she bounds from the horse rushing over to him.

"Anna, WAIT!" yells Wraithe in cautioning, "Something's wrong!!" he calls out to her. Meanwhile, as she nears Erik's body, a gray lycan leaps from about the corner, biting down upon his head, and with a vicious twist, a loud snap is heard, shuddering Anna to a halt. Her eyes widen as it turns to her with its menacing snarl, slowly creeping toward her. Anna fearfully begins stepping back. Its gray fur recedes to human skin, as male draped in rags appears, his hair unkempt, untidy, and feet black as the dirt.

He gazes towards them, his face wearing a tired grin. "I know who you are!" he voices, pointing towards Wraithe and Terra, slowly limping forward. "You're him, and the lowly apprentice, you're the reven…" he barely utters, when he is struck by two blunt strikes of a sharp numbing pain, as Terra fires two arrows into his chest and shoulder. This enrages the male, who stumbles off-balance, suddenly transforming into a gray lycan. Crunching down upon the arrows, it spits them aside. Petrified, Anna stands motionless, as it turns its snarling gaze towards her.

"Anna, move!!" yells Siff from behind. Quickly, Anna dives to the ground, barely escaping the lycan's jaws, as it makes its charge. It then continues to Siff, as Terra quickly takes a knee, readying another arrow, and fires. Meanwhile, the beast ducks its head, as the arrow drives through the point of its ear, shearing along the fur of its back.

"Damn it," curses Terra having missed her shot. This only infuriates the lycan further, as it backs Siff into a corner, readying for its deadly strike. Suddenly, Wraithe lets out a loud war cry, pulling its attention, as he charges atop his horse. The lycan pounces, as the horse frightfully jolts rearing up, and tossing Wraithe from its back, allowing the lycan to deliver its deadly bite to its neck. The horse tumbles back, falling upon the legs of Wraithe.

"Aghhhh!" Wraithe cries out in agony, and quickly tries to push the heavy beast off his legs, when an human foot pushes down upon the animal's body, adding to the excruciating pain. Finally, Wraithe looks up, glaring into the male's face.

"Lucian?!" he mutters in astonishment, having recognized his former brother in arms, "Have you allowed yourself to fall into darkness," he goes on to ask, realizing his betrayal. Meanwhile, Lucian smiles quietly as his snout quickly retreats to a human mouth and nose, and his hairs once again to human skin.

"My Lord offers me something far greater than the sufferings of man, but immortality, we will have the lotus, and live forever," he details sinisterly. "I was never one of you, the council chose her father," mentions Lucian further, pointing over to confuddled Anna.

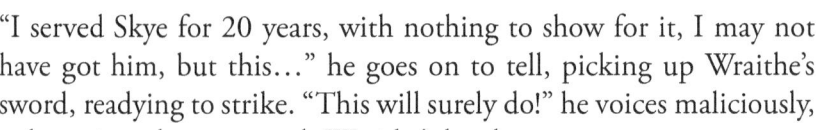

"I served Skye for 20 years, with nothing to show for it, I may not have got him, but this…" he goes on to tell, picking up Wraithe's sword, readying to strike. "This will surely do!" he voices maliciously, as he swings down towards Wraithe's head.

When suddenly,

"ARRGHH!" voices Anna in ferocious cry, followed by a swing of her blade, as flesh and sword meet, Lucian's blood spills to the ground. His hand severed, he falls to the ground in agony, holding his left forearm, as the blood pours profusely.

"I'LL KILL YOU!!" he whimpers in shuddering, getting to his feet. Shocked, Anna remains puzzled as to her next move, finding herself stiff. "I'LL KILL YOU!" utters Lucian maliciously. Meanwhile, Terra charges up from behind.

"Run!" yells Terra, pulling out her blade, when she is quickly met by a powerful backhand swipe, hurling her across the way, painfully landing to the ground in yelp. With not a second to waste, Anna dashes to Terra's aide. Lucian notices Anna approaching and turns to face her.

"You foolish girl, you've chosen death!" he roars furiously.

"You betrayed my father, led him to ambush, his blood is on your hands, and so will yours be on mine!" replies Anna stoutly, with her father's sword poised to strike. Lucian hunches to his knees, his mouth and nose grows outwards to a teeth-bearing snout, with ears sprouting upward into pointed tips, as his skin disappears beneath a sea of fur, with piercing yellow gaze fixated on Anna. It rushes towards her, as Anna then makes the grave mistake of striking early, and misses, the lycan bites down on her blade, hurling her across the way. Anna's sword is thrown from her hand; rendering her defenseless. Sitting up, she scampers backwards, seeing the fierce lycan gaining upon her. Seconds from attacking, a whisper of wind is heard, as the beast tumbles forward to her feet.

An arrow's tail is seen pointing from its left eye, as Anna looks across the way, seeing Terra exhale, dropping her bow in exhaustion. Quickly, Anna gets to her feet, as her and Siff rush over to assist with removing the horse's body from Wraithe's leg.

"Quickly! Come on Siff! On three… three, two, one!" commands Anna hastily, and with that the pair push, lifting its body just enough for the older male to weasel out. He slowly limps to his feet, as they turn to see Lucian's lifeless body lying in the middle of the alley.

"I knew Lucian for years, we fought side by side, yet, like Maurdis, he allowed jealousy to be his demise," mutters Wraithe in telling. Meanwhile, Terra joins them, securing her bow within her arrow bag strapped upon her back.

"He led them into an ambush, my father's death was planned," adds Anna, squeezing her fists. Siff quietly watches his friend fight back her tears. "He is nothing but scum," she shivers further in scorn.

"We are nothing but objects that stand in their way, there's no honor between wolves and men," states Wraithe bluntly in reply. Meanwhile, Anna continues standing over his body, when she hears the fiddling, and rustling of debris sounding from behind. Immediately, she turns around. It is Wraithe, sifting through the ruins of a collapsed, burnt-down home, as he picks through the ashen coats and silverware. Wraithe grabs anything he can salvage into a large sheet, which he then folds, swinging it upon his shoulder. Speechless, both Anna and Siff look on, as he returns beside them. Proceeding to Terra's horse, he begins packing the items within the saddlebags. Having seen enough, Anna finally speaks up.

"Do you not see the people here?" she questions outwardly to Wraithe. "You would take their belongings for yourself? You won't help them?" she flails in question.

"I cannot save Skye from what's inevitable, I can only survive it," answers Wraithe dutifully, stuffing the final pieces into the bags.

"But you would harvest their spoils?" voices Anna reluctantly in reply.

"A small, price of service, young one," he tells stoutly, "Skye has seen many of wars, and Maurdis has seen all of them, the Order was the only thing protecting us from his wrath, and the consumption of the nocturnals, but it is no more, Maurdis destroyed the Order, leaving behind only revenants, their spirits too broken to face him, he is too powerful," murmurs Wraithe in telling.

"Please!" pleads Anna, "Our village has seen enough loss!"

"So has all of Skye," answers Wraithe icily, "My advice is to find somewhere safe, hide, and survive," he goes on to suggest, mounting atop the horse, as Terra takes a seat behind him.

"So where are you going?!" races Anna after them in question, pulling Siff along.

"To do the same, Maurdis hasn't left Nordskye yet, he will come to finish them off, the lycans; the Order of the pact, they don't allow any survivors, when the dawn arrives, Nordskye will be no more," tells Wraithe gravely reply.

"Wait!" exclaims Anna running up from behind, "Please, take us with you!" begs Anna desperately. Wraithe pauses, looking about the village's smoke, and down to their fearful faces. "I will see your remaining council, inform them of what's to come, and then we are leaving," he answers straightly. With that, the four traverse through the village, feeling its gloomy emptiness about them, as the paths remain silent. The eerie cries of survivors ring throughout the village, as the bakery, markets, and homes be all devastated by the fires, as bodies line along the way, ravaged by the lycans.

Nothing hits deeper, than when Anna sees her home. Immediately, her body stiffens, as if seen a ghost. Her eyes look through the remaining structure. Meanwhile, Wraithe and the others stop in waiting, as Anna proceeds over to what remains of the front door. Stepping onto the wooden floor, Anna's foot collapses through the eroded boards, dropping her to her knees. There she sits in tears, sinking into the despair of having lost everything. Siff lingers nearby, cautioning in approach, and upon seeing her tears, withdraws.

"If Maurdis finds out she is the son of Arthur, he will surely torture and kill her, she must remove herself from this land immediately," mutters Wraithe lowly to Terra behind him.

"So where will she go?" replies Terra in question.

"We take her to Westskye, it's more developed; should Maurdis attack there, they are more protected, they would at least stand a chance. However, it's almost dusk, we must warn who we can!" stresses Wraithe urgently in telling. Terra quickly dismounts their horse, and slowly walks up behind Anna.

"Anna, we must leave, gather the survivors, prepare them for what's coming!" she urges earnestly at Anna's side. Anna wipes her face with her sleeve, pulling her foot from the collapsed floors, as she stands to her feet. She then looks to the sky, seeing the dusk's orange hue slowly settling in. Immediately, she sets aside her emotions, realizing the need to act quickly and returns to them.

"Although it only be the four of us, we must scour the edges of the village for any survivors, let them know that Maurdis will return, and bid them to seek out refuge for the night, for none will be spared upon his return!" informs Wraithe gravely to the three. "We meet back here once grounds have been covered!" he adds.

The three nod in agreement, and disperse, scampering through the village paths in search of survivors in spreading of Wraithe's warning. Meanwhile, Anna aids an elder woman, into the shelter of her home, one of the few unscathed by the fires having torn through the city. Moments later, the sudden blare of the village horn is heard and dusk is finally upon them, as every village door closes shut, remaining families cower within the deepest parts of their homes. Its heavy, wooden front gates pushed aside, offers considerable entry for an attack. Anna looks up to the sky, as the moon slowly creeps into view.

"Okay, time to head back," mutters Anna to herself, quickly pacing down the mainstreet. As she turns the corner, she notices Wraithe and Terra in the distance, standing in front of her homestead, however, there is no sign of Siff.

"Where is Siff?!" asks Anna stopping as she approaches, her sights panicked in looking about.

"No idea, we've been sitting here for five minutes," Terra shrugs obliviously in reply. Concerned, Anna looks along the dark pathways, seeing no signs of Siff.

Meanwhile, Wraithe steps forth, "We will tarry here a while longer, but the village's defenses are down, it won't take much for the lycans to make another devastating attack," he utters in telling. With that, the three take up shelter within the fallen home. Anna takes this time to walk about its ashes. She notices the formation for the chimney, the beams overhead caved in, reduced to coal. The house's floors breaking with every step, as she pushes open her father's room door, that breaks loose of its hinges falling to the floor. His bed, what's left of it, lay black as tar, its coverings eroded by the fires. Immediately, her heart sinks.

There she sits, leaned against the remains of a wall, as footsteps are heard approaching down the hallway and Terra walks in.

"This was your father's, right?" she opens to Anna in question.

"It was his bedroom. Funny, his footsteps, I would always hear before I go to sleep, he would join the men in taking shifts in guarding the village at night. When the dawn came, he would always work the forge; the bellows of his hammer upon heated irons would always wake me," whispers Anna sulkily in reply, looking to the moon through the house's fallen roof. As time passes, the moon has crept its way halfway to its peak. When suddenly, a great wolf howl is heard, pitching them up from their comfort. Immediately, Anna's thoughts race to Siff, who hasn't yet returned.

"It's the lycans," murmurs Wraithe, "Their here," he adds. Anna quickly creeps over to his side.

"I have to go find him," she whispers hastily, motioning to leave. Seeing this, Wraithe quickly pulls at her arm.

"Stay put child! This is no time to go off wandering," he mutters lowly in reply, keeping watchful eye about them. In seconds, a heavy thud is heard, sounding from near the front doors. A pair of large, gray paws, take the first steps into the home, where the three continue in hiding.

"It's inside!" trembles Anna in telling, leaned alongside Wraithe. Silently they listen, as its snout is heard sniffing along the floor; its paws can be heard slowly creeping through the petrified hallway towards them.

"What do we do?" whispers Anna nervously in question. Silently, Wraithe rolls across the room's doorway, as the lycan approaches the room. It lifts its snout, whiffing the air, seeming to catch a feint scent, as if knowing they're there. Meanwhile, Wraithe signals to Terra, from across the doorway. Terra then taps at the wooden wall behind them, as she and Anna lie leant tightly against the wall. Alerted, the lycan motions closer to the door, poking its head into the bedroom.

Suddenly, its harrowing yellow eyes turns to Anna, but is met with a silent swipe of Wraithe sword, as its human head tumbles to the floor, rolling along the ashes to the room's corner. Anna releases a deep, nerve-racking sigh. Checking if there may be anymore nearby, the three step over the body, and lead out into the night.

"Siff, we have to find Siff!" tells Anna anxiously, "He won't survive out there, he's too afraid!" she adds. Looking about, Wraithe quickly turns to her.

"Silence girl! You must be patient, it is nightfall, the enemies we face have us at a disadvantage, if he is afraid, then he is in hiding!" retorts Wraithe sternly. "Right now, we must seek shelter, lest it be us that won't survive!" he adds reluctantly. With that, he leads them further down the path. The night is silent, filled with the feint screams of horror, as the lycans sift through what's left of Nordskye. With every chilling noise, Anna's concern grows deeper for Siff, she must find him; he must live. They cautiously move by the marketplace, as baskets and supplies line its path. Its stalls, and vendors torn apart and destroyed; unrecognizable to what once was. They silently creep through, looking to every shadow, expecting at any moment something would leap out at them. Anna notices something shiny, and familiar, and quickly kneels to pick it up. She looks over the dust-covered knife, it is Siff's, he must be nearby!

"What is that?" asks Terra seeing her distracted.

"It's his, this is Siff's knife!" exclaims Anna in discovery, anxiously looking about for any other possible clues. A great howl is heard, alerting them, as a huge lycan emerges from about the corner, the three pause, completely exposed, yet unnoticed, as Wraithe lowly gestures them to quietly move to cover. Anna and Terra count their steps, moving as swiftly as they can behind the shelter of a couple of fallen tables, when suddenly, a shatter is heard, as a piece of glass is crushed beneath Terra's foot. Immediately, the lycan looks up, seeing the three straight ahead.

"Run!" orders Wraithe hastily. With that, the lycan releases a great howl, followed by a chorus of answering howls, and a chase begins. "Split! Quickly!" commands Wraithe, drawing the lycan's attention. Immediately, the three separates. Anna follows after Terra, bounding over tables, and scampering through the market's collapsed spaces. She struggles to keep up, when finally, they arrive to a fallen wall. Meanwhile, the lycan's snarls, and barks can be heard in pursuit, as Terra quickly strafes through. Fitting herself through the space, she accidentally bumps against one of the beams supporting the crevice, suddenly, there is a loud shift followed by a crash, as the space is closed shut by debris, separating the pair. Anna frantically searches for a way through, as the lycans can be heard gaining about the corner. Looking above a pile of barrels, Anna glimpses an opening of moonlight. Swiftly, she hurdles across the low-lying debris, and clambers up the barrels towards her escape. Not a minute later, the lycans arrive at the foot of the pile, and starts behind her. Fortunately, with a misplace of her footing, there is a shift, as the barrels come tumbling down upon the lycans. With a scarce leap, Anna then breaches to safety, atop the market's roof.

She continues to flee, leaping along the rooftops, as the vicious pack continues pursuit below, she makes a wide long leap onto a nearby roof, when suddenly, it caves in, dropping her to the floor. Anna painfully rolls over, as she slowly gets to her feet.

"Damn it," she grumbles painfully, as the thrashing and shaking of the front doors is heard, as the lycans struggle to get inside. Rising to her feet, Anna looks about, she glimpses shelves ladled with bread, bags of white powder, with pots and pans scattered across the floor, she then realizes, she is trapped within the bakery. Anna slowly limps her way to the back of the store, into a dark corner, when startlingly, from behind, she is touched by a person's hand. Panicked, she spins about, as Siff faces her, his fingers quickly perched to his lips, when in that instance, the front doors busts open.

Two males enter, tall and brawny in stature, and slowly begin exploring about the room.

"Come out! There's no use in hiding, we can smell you! WE KNOW YOU'RE THERE!" voices one of the men intently. Meanwhile, Siff pulls her to the kitchen, behind a stack of wheat.

"Your attempt at escaping only makes the hunt more enjoyable," murmurs the other, as they stalk through the room, entering the kitchen. One of the men approaches the pile of wheat, when Anna quickly unsheathes her sword.

"Arghhh!" she roars in war cry, running her blade through the unsuspecting male. He is impaled through, as Anna quickly draws her sword from his body, as he falls to his knees collapsing to the floor.

"A-Anna!" whimpers Siff pointing to her attention. Anna turns to glimpse the lycan racing towards them in attack. Shielding Siff behind her, Anna readies her sword. The lycan quickly pounces her to the floor, preparing to deliver its bite, when suddenly, Siff charges from the side, bludgeoning his knife into the lycan's neck. With a swift thrust of her sword, Anna plunges the blade into the underbelly of her attacker. The lycan yelps in whimper, toppling to its side. Anna then jumps to her feet, grabbing hold of Siff's hand, as they dart out the bakery's front doors. Along the pathway, they eventually bump into Wraithe and Terra, who being of equal surprise to see them.

"Come on!" notions Wraithe hastily to them, as he and Terra duck through a narrow alleyway. Immediately, Anna and Siff follow, until Terra notices something large.

"Over there!" Terra points out. Quickly, Anna and the others look left, noticing the village's canteen. The four race across the courtyard, arriving at the canteen's doors. Pulling at the wooden doors, they realize, it is locked. Wraithe repeatedly hammers at the door for a reply.

"Is anyone there!" he voices urgently, "Please, open your doors!" he calls out again, as the snarls and barking of the lycans can be heard approaching in the distance. Seeing his cries go unanswered, Anna quickly steps to the door.

"Please! Open up! We're children! Please open your doors!" she begs desperately. Suddenly, a pair of eyes appear from the peephole's slide. Anna quickly lunges herself to the peering eyes. "Please! Don't bid us to die!" she pleads once more. The peephole slides close, as the unlatching of heavy bolts and locks is heard being undone. The heavy door opens and the four quickly enter, as the male immediately begins locking the door behind them.

As they turn about, they realize the canteen is filled with villagers, crowded and sprawled across the floors, all pitching up as the four enter. Seconds after, the lycans are heard just outside the doors.

"They led them to us!" accuses an indistinct male voice. Wraithe looks about the poorly reinforced space.

"We need to enforce the doors and windows, give them no entry!" informs Wraithe urgently, as the village men all look to him in confusion.

"We have already used everything there is!" voices one of the men outwardly in reply. Meanwhile, Anna looks on at the people of Nordskye, seeing how they cower in fear, as the lycans lie in wait just outside the canteen's doors. Each villager arms themselves with a weapon, some even a blunt object, ranging from swords to soup ladles. An aura of silence fills the room, as every heart races in anticipation.

"So, what do we do?" mutters Terra to Wraithe in question. He looks about the room, for possible ways of entry, his attention stirs towards the windows, noting their wooden shutters locked close. He then glances over to the doors, pillared with sandbags and barrels. Finally, he turns to Terra.

"Mind the windows," he opens in telling, "The lycans may try to ambush from the sides, be ready," he adds further.

Suddenly.

"Are the monsters coming to get us?" asks a frightened middle-aged woman, when the heavy scampering of feet and snarls are heard sniffing just outside the walls of the canteen. Terrified, a fellow villager points out.

"W-what d-do you make of that?" stutters the male fearfully, trembling to his feet.

"Use your senses… it's them!" voices another lowly in reply. A loud thud is heard, as the front doors of the canteen shakes and creaks from the impact of outside. Startled by this, the male jumps to his feet, "To hell with this!" he exclaims flailing wildly, "I won't be trapped in here, when those things get in!" he voices further, stepping through the crowd, as he moves towards the windows.

Seeing this, Wraithe steps in, "Get away from the windows!" he roars in warning.

"They're trying to get in through the front doors, we can use the windows as an escape!" argues the male ignorantly, picking up a large mug from the floor. He takes aim at the glass window.

"You fool! You endanger us all!" roars Wraithe furiously, as he races to stop him. The male pitches the mug, shattering the windows glass, and quickly undoes the latch of the wooden shutters. In the split of a second, he is brutally snatched by a ferocious black beast. Securing a strong hold on his arm, it pulls violently at his shoulder, meanwhile, the other villagers look on, startled in fear.

"Terra!" yells Wraithe quickly. Immediately, she takes aim, when with a final pull, the lycan yucks the male from the window.

"AAAGHHHHH…PLEASE!! HELP ME!! PLEASE!!" cries the male, his pleas drowned by the eruption of panic of the villagers, as he is pulled away to the shadows. Terra lowers her bow, as it is too late. An eerie silence masks over the room. However, Wraithe quickly addresses the gathered.

"Everyone remain center of the room, there is to be no one near the windows… Have your weapons ready… if they want a fight, we'll give them one!" he voices courageously. Wraithe then looks over to Terra. "Be prepared!" he instructs firmly. Meanwhile, Terra in turn, looks to Anna beside her.

"Hey," calls Terra, "Be ready!" Anna quickly readies her sword, not a second late, when the front doors of the canteen busts open. Two men are seen entering the room, circling about the forefront. They look upon the crowd with malicious intent, until finally one opens up to speak.

"Behold, a message from our lord… Skye will be lycans!!" he flails wildly in protest, as they collapse to their knees, emerging as three large, snalring lycans. They immediately make charge for the crowd. Wraithe fearlessly charges them head on, with Terra at his side. The villagers retreat in fear, huddling near the rear of the canteen. Meanwhile, one of the lycans starts towards Wraithe, leaping at him with teeth bared. Diving below, Wraithe thrusts his sword into its underbelly, slaying the beast instantly. Meanwhile, across the way,

Terra engages the other, jabbing towards it with her blade. Suddenly, her sword is swiped from her hand, as the lycan rushes her to the ground. Terra shields its jaws at bay by use of her bow. The lycan then bites down upon the weapon, crunching it to bits, as it drags and tosses her aside.

"Lycan!!" panics a female villager. Her screams drawing the beast's attention from Terra. The lycan pounces upon the woman, throwing her to the floor, and with a ferocious ripping bite, spits her head across the canteen's floor. This immediately puts the villagers in a frenzy. Seizing its distraction, Anna swiftly rushes in, leaping onto the lycan's back. She plunges her sword into its neck, as it violently attempts to throw her off. Anna tightens her grip about the beast's neck, bludgeoning it repeatedly with her sword, until finally, it comes to a breathy halt, collapsing to the floor. Anna tiringly rolls from the creature's back, as it reforms into a human.

Wraithe swiftly rushes to reinforce the front doors, hurling over a few of the heavy nearby barrels against it. Suddenly, the windows begin to rumble, as the barks and snarls surround outside the canteen's walls. Grabbing a filled bottle of liquor, he then clogs it with a dry rag.

"Terra! Anna!" he calls bluntly to the pair. With a quick nod, Terra taps at Anna's shoulder, and the pair races towards the window, both girls readily hold at each shutter's side, awaiting his command.

"Now!" he exclaims lighting the bottle's rag from a nearby torch. Wraithe then hurls the bottle, shattering the window, as a pair of glowing, yellow eyes peers through. Its snout is met by the blunt strike of Wraithe's craft, as the bottle bursts into a large flame. The beast yelps and cries fleeing from the window. Suddenly, there is a silence, as the villagers slowly creep from their corner.

"Have they gone?" voices one of the women in question. Meanwhile, Wraithe and the others remain on guard.

"Quickly, fortify the windows, we must remain on guard, each person taking a shift," utters Wraithe in command. Anna and Terra nod, swiftly moving to collect tables and barrels to shove against the entry.

"I will take the first shift," Anna utters, lifting her hand in volunteer. "It's the least I can do," she adds humbly. With that, the canteen finally rests for the night, it is an escape from the nights of horror they've faced over the past couple days. Anna sits leaned upon the wall, keeping her eyes and ears open for any possible signs of entry, meanwhile, Terra slowly walks up to her side, taking a seat beside her.

"Hey," she calls, "I appreciate what you did earlier, you actually saved my ass," jokes Terra reluctantly in telling. "I'm sure 'he' would be proud," she adds in saying.

"Yeah…" mutters Anna lowly in reply, fidgeting her fingers.

"Hey, come on, it's my turn now, get some sleep!" tells Terra tapping at Anna's shoulder. Anna creeps to the side, as Terra takes her spot. Laying down to rest, her eyes remain wide open.

"Can't sleep, huh?" asks Terra seeing her discomfort.

"No," mutters Anna lowly in reply. "It's just… Wraithe? How did you come to meet him?" turns Anna to her in question.

"Who? Wraithe?" answers Terra, pausing for a moment. "My family were mainly travelers, we never stayed more than a week in anywhere we traveled," she adds. "Unfortunately, for travelers, sometimes it meant having to be out at night, more specifically, nocturnals! They took my family. First my father, as he stood to protect us. Then my mother, and lastly my sister. She took me and we ran, however, I was too slow, and so, they caught me. I would've been dead too, but she sacrificed herself… my own sister, torn apart before my very eyes," she recounts, sharpening her arrow's tip. "I wandered the forest for eight days. By then, I had seen and escaped many of things Skye itself had forgotten existed," she continues in saying. "It wasn't until I had fainted, did a man atop a dark horse stop to save me, his figure distorted by the blinding sunlight, it was Wraithe!"

"So, what happened then?" continues Anna in question, awaiting her response.

"So, he took me in," sighs Terra tiringly, "Taught me how to protect myself, and by the time it was for me to go on my own, I couldn't leave, he had become all I knew, he may not speak it but…

I know for him it was the same," she ends, stuffing the arrow within its bag. "Now enough with the questions, it's almost dawn, get some rest, you'll need it," she informs, laying back in guard. Anna quietly turns over and is fast asleep.

The next morning dawns slowly, as Anna awakes to a bumping at her leg. Spreading her arms wide, she awakes to Terra, standing over her, lightly kicking at her foot.

"Hey, wake up!" tells Terra, "It's morning!" she utters, collecting her arrow bag nearby. Tossing it over her shoulder, she proceeds to the front doors, and exits. Startled by this, Anna pitches up, fixing on her leather boots as she stumbles to the door. She is met by a great light, as villagers move about salvaging items and supplies. Anna glimpses Terra walking over to Wraithe, who appears to be in conversation with a couple men of Nordskye along the street. Curious as to their discussion, she heads over to join them. As she nears, their conversation grows clear.

"So, if you go down this path, you'll be able to settle accounts there," she overhears one of the male's voice indistinctly.

"How much do you think they would sell for?" utters Wraithe in question.

"Unfortunately, we don't know… few have travelled that far; Nordskye is pretty much a village on its own," adds the male in reply. Wraithe takes a moment, as Anna steps by.

"So how long?" interrupts Terra bluntly.

"Not sure, but the safest passages are here, and here!" tells the male, plotting the points out along the map, a petrified piece spread along the table.

"Both near the mountains, presumably nocturnal territory," shrugs Wraithe in observation.

"Nocturnals? I heard the stories, ruthless, bloodthirsty, they're like the ocean, a legion," adds another in mentioning.

"Anywhere is better than Nordskye, without protection, the people are doomed," tells the other hysterically. "The attack has left them defenceless," he adds fretfully. Meanwhile, Anna pans around at the desolation, the faces of despair of every passing villager, as they rummage through the ashes.

"These people are doomed either way," mentions Wraithe regrettably in reply. He then heads off to a white horse, hitched at a nearby post, and begins stuffing a few items into its saddlebags. "We must make haste," he urges, "The journey ahead will take about three days, we must leave now!" Anna quickly darts inside the canteen, finally, she glimpses Siff nodded off in the corner, and swiftly dives into waking him.

"Siff! Siff! Wake up, we have to go!" she exclaims, shaking him from his slumber.

He groggily awakes, wiping his eyes, as he leans forward, standing to his feet. Anna quickly drags him to the outside, where they meet Wraithe and Terra seated among their horses. Terra, however, seated atop a beautiful black steed.

"Let's go," voices Terra patting at her horse for the pair to join. This time Anna joins behind Terra, as does Siff behind Wraithe. With that, the four head off, passing by the rubbles and ash, that is now Nordskye. Again, they traverse by the remnants of Anna's homestead. Anna takes a final look at her home, the forge, and stake where once laid her father's body, as she turns hopefully towards the horizon, leaving behind all she has ever known.

As they depart through village's broken gates, a cool, unsuspecting breeze hampers by them, as they face the vast forest that is Skye.

Chapter 3
Equilibrius: The Lost Eden

A great howl is heard among the mountains, as the snarling and gnashing of teeth follows its bellowing call. A great, large black wolf makes its way up a rocky path, towards an empty, stone carved-out throne. The drapes of his cloak rests at its foot, as he sits comfortably within the throne. Finally, two wolves approach the path, heading towards the male donned in an all-black cloak, shrouded with a dark mane about his neck.

Within seconds, they transform, emerging as two normal men, with heads bowed as they stop near the throne.

"My lord," addresses the first, "Nordskye has been conquered, its resources reduced to ash! Still, no sign of it," he adds in mention. "There is word that he was there… the revenant, my lord," utters the other solemnly. Suddenly, there is a silence, as he stands from his throne.

"Brothers?!!" he addresses walking by the two, as a great rustling ensues about the forest surrounding them. Emerging from the forest as wolves, then standing to their feet as men, his subjects encircle about them. "Might I ask you, of our Order of the Pact?" he decrees in question.

"Upon failure… death or exile!!" their voices roar in sounding. Finally, he looks down to them in sinister grin.

"Upon failure… death or exile…" he repeats grimly. "These two before you are the last remaining of whom we've given the privilege of bringing us immortality, and restoring us to power; yet, there is no lotus, their hands empty of the privilege we've given them, we perish slowly from the weight of their failure!" he continues in rant. "So, I ask you! What be their fate… death? Or exile?" he roars in question.

"DEATH, DEATH, DEATH, DEATH….!!!" echoes the men repeatedly, jeering on their judgement. With a blunt gesture, he silences the men.

"The pact has spoken," he utters turning to the pair, "Your judgement… is death!" he condemns, "Sept! Tidas!" he calls distinctly from the group. Two young men, strapping in stature emerge from the sidelines, side by side.

"Which one of you will restore our honor?" he asks the two, looking moreover to Sept for response.

"I will! my lord, it will be my pleasure!" answers Tidas, who being slightly taller, and broader in stature than Sept, steps forth in challenge towards the 'condemned.'

"The honor is yours," the cloaked male replies, shooting a furious look of disgust towards Sept, who stands by, somewhat ashamed. Tidas arrogantly steps forth, as the two 'condemned,' prepare themselves, one anxiously charges towards him, and quickly transforms. Tidas grins, leaping over the beast, as it rushes in to attack. Quickly, he wraps his arms about its neck. Taken by surprise, the lycan loses its balance, toppling to the ground. The lycan returns to a man, reaching and struggling to free himself of Tidas' choke. Finally, with a feint twist of the head, Tidas snaps his neck, tossing the body aside, brushing himself off, as he gets to his feet. Meanwhile, the surrounding men chuckle in amusement. He is met by the other lycan, charging towards him, Tidas leaps to all fours, transforming into a lycan, and the two wolves clash, viciously biting and gnashing at one another. The battle is rather short, as with a crunching bite at its hind leg, the 'condemned' lets out a yelping cry, quickly silenced by a malicious bite to its neck. Tidas then steps forth as victor, kneeling before the cloaked male, as he approaches.

"Lord Maurdis, it is done," he tells, with head bowed in honor. Grinning as he approaches, he presses his hand to Tidas' shoulder.

"Rise, a worthy servant you've proven to be, you will serve greatly in our era of immortality!" tells Maurdis boastfully walking by. Meanwhile, Tidas shoots a taunting grin at Sept, who watches from the sidelines.

"My lord," addresses another of the men, "Of the deceased, a parting gift," he tells handing over a rent piece of cloth, two sided in color, black and red. Immediately, Maurdis recognizes its origin.

"So, the 'condemned' were right, the revenant lives, a little retribution to account for their failures," he scoffs pridefully. "Also, it seems he's been in hiding in Nordskye, he is the last remaining knight of the old Order, meaning he knows where it has been hidden, he must be found, tear it all apart and find him!" utters Maurdis in command, "FIND HIM!!" he roars furiously. With that, the lycans leave in search of Wraithe, and the unknown whereabouts of the white lotus.

Meanwhile…

Anna and Siff, having joined Wraithe and Terra, journey to WestSkye, a city tucked within a huge valley at the edge of the mysterious forest. It is a long journey, but one filled with anticipation and curiosity.

"I have something I must ask you?" utters Anna humbly in question. "This Maurdis… why does he seek to destroy all of Skye?" Seconds pass, and Anna's question seemingly goes ignored with the chirping of birds in the tall canopy's overhead.

"It is not simply Skye itself; it is the lotus he's after," answers Wraithe stoutly in reply. "With it, he can attain immortality, and then Skye would undoubtedly become his."

"The lotus?" repeats Anna in question, "Like the flower?" she asks further.

"It's the first bloom, the first flower to ever be created by the fates, its existence represents the preservation of life. Knights of the old Order sought to protect it from falling into the hands of the dark powers," tells Wraithe fully. "It was your father, Arthur, that helped unite the leaders of Skye under knighthood, thus giving way to the old Order." Immediately, Anna's eyes widen, as her face lights up in shock, her father never spoke of this to her, could this somehow be true?

"How did you come to know this?" questions Anna curiously.

"I met your father upon travelling to Nordskye. When word got out about a gifted forgemaster as himself, many would seek to trade with him, including myself. Shortly after, we became well acquainted, and years later, he would convince me to even join his cause. Seemed rather noble at the time, but the threats grew worse, far too worse until our numbers began to dwindle. We were losing knights faster than we could groom them. The fates were not on our side and pretty soon we became revenants," mentions Wraithe gravely in telling. "So, the Order split, its knights hunted down and slaughtered, and Skye was forced to hide from the darkness behind its walls," he continues in saying.

"Or they used to," mutters Anna lowly in despair, "So, why not restore it, why not return the old Order?" exclaims Anna anxiously in question.

"Because there are no more, all have been slain, and the people of Skye are subjected to fear. The knights who stood before are long gone," mutters Wraithe bluntly in reply. "It is soon sunset, we must find a place to rest," he tells, looking up to the reddening sky. Anna and the others also look up, realizing the day has quickly passed by. As they traverse along, each keep their eyes open for signs of a possible camp site.

"Over there!" points out Terra to a clearing near a seemingly empty cave. Seeing this, Wraithe tugs at his horse's reins, turning in the direction of Terra's finding. As they stop among the clearing, Wraithe dismounts, walking near the cave. He disappears into its hollow, yet, emerging after a few moments.

"We set up camp here!" instructs Wraithe bluntly, and with that, the four prepare for nightfall. A few hours later, the tents are pitched, as a small fire is stoked to blazing. The horses rest hitched near the cave's mouth, as they prepare for much needed rest. Meanwhile, Anna sits warming near the fire, soon to be joined by Terra.

"So, your friend, Siff, how long have you known each other," grunts Terra seating across from her.

"Seven years," answers Anna looking up from her dream, "I've known him since he was four, from playing about carelessly along the stony-brick streets of Nordeskye. He's an orphan, like myself now, I guess," sulks Anna in telling.

"He's without family?!" asks Terra surprised at this. "He's so young," she mentions in disbelief.

"He was much smaller when I knew him, father took him in when he saw us together. Whenever I ate, so did he. He's the only family I have now. He's lived across from me for years, so wherever I go, he's coming with me," swears Anna solemnly. Terra silently nods in listening.

"You would take him everywhere you go?" returns Terra in question.

"I would die to protect him," utters Anna boldly in reply.

"Mhmm, mind the journey you take, your intent albeit just, could untimely lead to his death, be careful," tells Terra earnestly in light retort, as she dusts herself of the dirt, and leaves to her tent. Meanwhile, Wraithe walks over.

"You and the boy sleep together, the tent is there, rest early, that we may end this journey quickly, we know not if Maurdis hunts our very steps," urges Wraithe thoughtfully, as he quickly departs closing his tent behind him. Siff then approaches, with arms filled of firewood, as both he and Anna linger on outside, lost in gazing at the stars.

"Everything is just so quiet," opens Siff in saying, as he turns to Anna.

"It is," she agrees softly, "It feels different experiencing it outside of Nordskye's walls," she goes on to tell. Siff gaze slowly falters to the ground, as he goes silent.

"What will happen to us when we arrive in Westskye?" asks Siff. "We have only little, how long do you think we'll be able to survive?"

he adds worriedly in concern. Anna remains silent, appearing to avoid an answer.

"Anna!" taps Siff at her arm. "Anna! Anna!" he calls pushing her arm.

"I don't know!" she mutters in reply. "I'm figuring things out, but we're no longer safe in Nordeskye, who knows if the lycans will return, we'd have no way to protect ourselves," she tells fully.

"Anna, it is our home," argues Siff stoutly.

"I never wanted to leave Nordeskye," voices Anna pitching up from the ground, "But there is nothing there for us, no family, no home, nothing, whatever was… there isn't anymore," she tells turning away sadly. Siff, caught speechless, sits quieted.

"Let's not stay up too late, we still have a long journey ahead of us," mutters Anna in telling.

"I know," he shrugs lowly.

"Get some rest," she tells, noting his glum expression. Anna then reaches over, lightly touching his forearm. "Hey, we're going to be fine, I promise," she utters solemnly, placing her hand on his shoulder. Siff silently nods, and the two lie, and are fast asleep beneath the speckled night sky. As the moon climbs to its peak, and the four are fast asleep, the forest comes alive. The leaves shuffle, as the flowers luminate in bloom, as a light cool breeze breathes throughout. Siff awakes in the middle of the night, getting to his feet, walking near the camp's edge to relief himself. As he loosens his trousers, he hears a feint snap.

Immediately, he is alerted; his eyes scouring about the nearby forest. Once more, there is a feint rustling, as Siff looks around to investigate. As he creeps through the nearby brush, the rustling continues. Spreading the branches aside, his face luminates, as an unusual glow lights nearby. He glimpses a tiny creature; its appearance resembling a human. Never has he seen something so peculiar. It appears to be stuck, struggling to remove a small branch off itself, even more interesting, as it moves, Siff notices something also very strange, it appears to have wings. Its ventral wings glow a vibrant, greenish yellow, as lush green shrubs, and flowers webbed about its body, as if woven by the forest itself. No larger than an average human hand, it wears an assortment of vinery atop its head, dangling above its pale, pearly-white skin, speckled with glistening, green dots at its cheeks

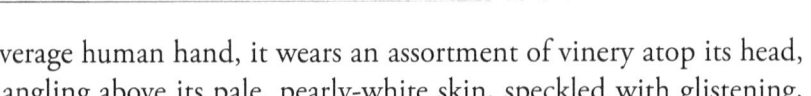

Siff is motionless with disbelief. Never had he seen such a beautiful, yet mysterious, creature.

"You're hurt!" exclaims Siff quickly kneeling to remove the branch. The creature gracefully lifts into the air, within arm's reach of Siff. Suddenly, the bushes rustle behind him, as Anna races into view.

"Hey, what's wrong?!" she exclaims in question, as she approaches. Siff silently points her sights to the creature. Immediately, Anna's face drops in amazement.

"Wha-What is it?" she asks, curiously stepping in closer, as the creature continues to hover about them. "How did you find it?!" she exclaims further.

"I left to go… I mean… Anyways, it was stuck, I moved the bushes aside and there it was! Glowing and everything!" exclaims Siff excitedly in telling. The pair continue to look on in curiosity.

"Do you know what it is?" looks Siff to Anna in question.

"Not in the least," she mutters lost in reply. Suddenly, their surroundings come alive as a strange breeze passes through. In an instant, the space rises with the similar floating glows, and shortly after, the pair are lost in a plethora of blissful lights, underneath a sailing full moon, and gloomy silent forest. The pair pan in every direction circled by the glows.

"This… is beautiful!" whispers Anna in amazement, as the creatures circle closer towards her. Within seconds, there is a shift, as the glows suddenly appears to depart.

"W-Wait where are they going?" utters Anna curiously.

"Anna, look!" exclaims Siff, pointing her sights ahead. It is the glows, they have formed a floating line, leading through the forest and beyond sight.

"It appears to lead back to camp?!" suggests Anna questionably. Siff quickly races after them, with Anna falling behind. The pair reenter the campsite; however, the glow's path leads straight through. To their amazement, the creatures follow through the seemingly empty cave. There is a moment of hesitation between the two friends, as neither knows what lies beyond the strange cave's mouth.

"Their leading us through!" utters Siff turning to Anna in excitement. However, Anna looks on questionably. She takes a hesitant glance back at their camp, it appears both Wraithe and Terra remain asleep, seeing their tents are undisturbed. Anna then returns her sights ahead at the path of the lights.

"We'll follow, but if they move us too far from camp, we'll be heading back," tells Anna sternly in warning. Siff nods in agreement, and the two are off, led blindly by the peculiar glows, entering through the mysterious cave's mouth. Making their way through, they realize the cave is much larger than it seems. As the pair venture around columns of tall rock, stepping over and across huge boulders, and ducking beneath the long points of overhead columns of stone. They continue, until something strange happens. The glows which led their way through, suddenly starts to dimmer, until there is nothing left but utter darkness. This immediately puts the pair into a sort of panic.

"Siff, where are you?!" exclaims Anna from behind, reaching blindly ahead of her.

"I'm right here!" he answers from slightly ahead.

"Follow my voice?!" he yells further.

"I know, just stay right there!" she tells, stumbling her way in the darkness. "I'm coming to you!" she adds, feeling her way along the rocks.

"I'm here!" he voices again, as Anna hearing this, quickly scampers closer to his sound.

"Okay good, almost there!" she exclaims, carefully placing her footing, as the stubble, sharp rocks play beneath her foot. Anna reaches out, grasping what feels the texture of leather, with the roundness of a shoulder.

"Siff?" she calls feeling once more

"Anna?! he answers, quickly collapsing into her arms. The pair have managed to find each other within the thick darkness. Looking over Siff's shoulder, Anna glimpses a glimmer of light in the distance.

"Hey, look!" she tells, pointing further ahead. Siff turns about, also glimpsing the feint light ahead. "You see it?" utters Anna in pointing.

"Yes," he nods.

"Come on, I think we might've found a way out of here," she tells pulling him along.

"Do you think it'll lead us back to camp," asks Siff, stepping carefully through the tricky rubble.

"I don't know, but at least once we're out of here, we can better find our way back to camp," grunts Anna in reply, hurdling over a large rock. They follow closer and closer towards the light, which grows greater with each step. Until finally, they step out into its blinding shine, shielding their faces from the shift of atmosphere. Finally, the pair fully open their eyes.

To their utter astonishment, they are both speechless as a beautiful, sunny oasis, reveals itself. It is alive with assortments of living creatures. Flocks of birds are seen soaring above, following along a great, glistening river that seams throughout the oasis as far as their eyes can see within the light. Looking down from their elevated ledge upon the lush valley, it is breathtaking. Butterflies can be seen hovering just above the canopy, as well as small herds of deer galloping carefree below.

"I must be dreaming," scoffs Anna reluctantly in disbelief, "Tell me I'm not dreaming!"

"I don't think you are," Siff replies, his mouth also gaped in awe. Both linger, mesmerized by the beauty of the wondrous landscape.

"Pinch me! This absolutely cannot be real," scoffs Anna in saying. Meanwhile, hearing her request, Siff turns, mischievously pinching at her left arm.

"Owww!" she yelps painfully, punching his right shoulder.

"Oww!" he laughs humorously.

"I was only doing what you asked," he laughs wittingly, holding at his arm.

"Yeah, but you know what I meant," she scolds playfully, as they quickly turn their attention back to the breathtaking view. They admire it for a few more moments, and quickly give in to the temptation to explore their newfound discovery. The pair descend the elevation, down its runoff, pacing their momentum along its lush grassy side, flowing seamlessly into its colorful forest. Beauty surrounds them, as flowers bloom, appearing significantly larger than ones found in Skye. As they continue to curiously explore below, the forest seems to come even more alive, with trees towering into the heavens, as nature's songs can be heard just overhead.

"Anna look!" exclaims Siff, excitedly pointing just up ahead. Her eyes widen, as a few deer gallop nearby, just a few steps ahead of them. Their appearance is different, with fur of pure white, decorated by patches of matted green moss, speckled along their backs. Vivid, colorful flowers bloom along their antlers, as the deers pause suddenly, also admiring the two strange young visitors. With a satisfied twist of their snout, they quickly return to their frolicking. Tortoises emerge from the brushes, with sprouts of mushrooms, and forest moss spread along their shells. Bluebirds are seen carrying wreathes of flowers, and small twigs within their beaks to their nests, as the forest appears to have trails of paths leading throughout. Running her hands along the nearby shrubs, Anna realizes, the forest's leaves are all moist of dew. Something seems to catch her eye, as she kneels, looking closely to a white butterfly speckled with greenery, as it quietly sips dew from a nearby flower. She somehow notices something unreal. The dew from the plant's leaves appears to be moving!

"Siff!" she exclaims calling him over, "Look at this!" she says pointing to his attention. The two witness the glistening dewdrops traveling up the stems of the leaves, lifting gracefully into the sky, as a great mist. Pairs of swift birds' rush into its mists, collecting its waters, while also creating light squalls of rainwater among the pair's heads. Anna then takes her finger, picking up a droplet of dew from a nearby leaf, watching as its droplet hangs from her finger, moving around to her fingernail and lifting into the air.

"That is unreal!" she exclaims in disbelief, turning to Siff, who looks on with enthused smile. "It actually flew from my hand!" she laughs gleefully. Distracted by their peculiar discovery, they are unaware, as a huge shadow casts over them. Siff turns, noticing the sudden change in light.

"A-A-Anna?!" he stammers shakily. Anna then turns to him, also looking up towards the overcasting figure, its sheer size blocking out the sunlight. The pair stand frozen, shaking in their boots, as the behemoth lifts a large club into the air.

"MOVE!" she yells, tackling him aside, seconds before the gigantic club smashes where they stood. The creature standing nearly twenty-feet tall, is clothed in forest moss with skin of ivory, rich with the dirt and greenery of the forest floor. A long locced beard drapes from its jawline, curtaining its heinous looking teeth, alive with insects and moss.

"EVAEL SITH TSEROF RO EID!!" the creature bellows, in a loud, and hostile voice. The two quickly scamper to their feet, fleeing for their lives.

"It can talk?!" pants Anna, as they dash into the nearby forest. Weaving and dodging along the tall trees, they evade the brute swings of its crushing club, that clears everything in its wake. It violently bowls over trees, and stomps through the brushes, as terrified smaller creatures swiftly flee for cover, as the behemoth continues its rampage.

"EVAEL SITH TSEROF RO EID!" It bellows again, in its harsh voice.

"What's it saying?!" pants Siff frantically from the chase.

"I don't know!" exclaims Anna, ducking below the oncoming tree limbs.

The behemoth continues its relentless pursuit, keeping behind the pair's every turn. Anna then glimpses a large, petrified log covered by moss, and quickly comes up with an idea.

"Over there!" she points to Siff. "The log! When I say go! Make towards it!" she pants in instruction.

"Okay!" exclaims Siff.

"GO!" she commands, as the two split, Siff darts towards the log, as Anna continues, distracting the creature. It swiftly gains upon her, preparing to swing, when Anna quickly dives into a slide along a slippery patch of moss. The creature's club passes just over her head, its breeze curdling through her hair. Anna with a quick change of direction, dashes towards the log, as the behemoth, being confused, slips into falling along the mat of moss. It quickly gets to its feet, continuing its pursuit. Meanwhile, Siff waits at the mouth of the log, anxiously calling to Anna, watching as the creature gains from behind. It lifts to make another crushing swing, when Anna dives into the log, seconds before it crushes the logs entrance.

As it removes its heavy wooden club, the pair cower further into the log, frightened of having narrowly escaped. However, they have now trapped themselves inside.

"What're we going to do?" panics Siff desperately.

"I don't know!" shudders Anna in reply, searching for means of escape. Suddenly, the log quakes, as a tremoring blow crushes through its roof. A pair of brownish-green eyes glares into the log. The behemoth glimpses the pair, and delivers another bellowing crush, exposing both Anna and Siff. She pulls Siff in tightly, as the creature raises once again.

"EID NIMREV!" it roars furiously, preparing to deliver the final blow.

"AGHHHHH!!" the two-scream huddled defenselessly. Suddenly, a fierce male war cry is heard, as he slashes the hind of the behemoth's leg, drawing away its attention. To the pair's astonishment, it is Wraithe. He has nobly arrived to their rescue.

"GO! SIFF! GO!!" tells Anna quickly pushing him out of the log, as they swiftly make their escape. Anna is felled, feeling a strong tug upon her right leg. Suddenly, she is quickly pulled by a violent breeze and tossed in the distance.

"Anna!" hollers Siff at the top of his lungs as she is thrown across the way. Her body hits the ground with a deafening thud. A blurring vision followed by a high-pitched hum; she wakes to from the fall.

"Anna! Anna!" cries Siff to her from the distance. Wraithe once again comes into view challenging the large creature. Siff then uses this opening to rush to her aid. Suddenly, he sees the swift movement of shadows, and freezes, as the heavy club smashes the ground, inches ahead of him. Realizing he was but a footstep away from being crushed, he stands petrified, looking up to the behemoth of a creature.

"EID RESSAPSERT!!" roars the creature fiercely. "EID!!" it bellows, hurling its club towards them. Terra appears, quickly rolling them out of the way. Meanwhile, Wraithe charges, leaping his blade into the creature's side.

"ARRGHHH!'" it roars painfully, finally dropping its club. With a blunt swing, Wraithe is struck to the ground. The behemoth drops to its knees, crawling towards him as it reaches for its club. Getting to its feet, as it prepares to finish Wraithe, an arrow pierces its right arm. Terra quickly prepares another arrow, aimed towards its leg. She swiftly releases, her arrow piercing through the muscles of its shin. The giant drops to its knees in pain.

"MOVE! NOW!!" she exclaims bluntly. Wraithe rushes towards the behemoth, as it attempts to fend him off, however, he weaves around to its rear, leaping atop the creature's back and plunges his sword into its shoulder. This infuriates the beast, as it roars to its feet, Wraithe swiftly bounds from its back into fleeing. It quickly grabs and hurls its club behind him, as he slides evading the spiraling tree just inches from his face,

"What is that thing?!" asks Siff to Terra from the sidelines.

"It's a troll," replies Terra, quickly prepping another arrow within her bow.

"Troll?" he pants catching his breath.

Meanwhile, Terra readies another arrow, and rushes in to battle. Firing her shot, she misses by a hairline, as the arrows winds strafe near the behemoth's face, drawing at its attention.

"Damn it!" curses Terra, as the troll corners Wraithe against a large tree. "Hey?!" she calls to Anna tossing her the bow and arrow bag. "Cover us!" she instructs firmly.

Meanwhile,

"LLA LLIW REFFUS OHW RETNE EHT TSEROF!!" roars the troll fiercely, surrounding Wraithe's escape. Suddenly, Terra slides underneath its leg, quickly jabbing her blade into the troll's inner thigh, again, infuriating the beast.

"EID NIMREV!!" yells the troll, violently smashing around at Terra, who rolls, twists and slides as much as she can to avoid its torrent of attacks.

"What's it saying?" mutters Anna to herself in wonderment. Finally, she has a thought. Anna remembers the dew, how it rose up from beneath. She remembers how the night, suddenly shifted to daylight, as they'd entered the oasis, a stark opposite of the outside world of Skye.

"What is it?" asks Siff, growing concerned, seeing her occupied with thought.

"I'll be back! Stay here!" she tells, rushing in towards them.

"Hey! Anna! What're you doing…?!" exclaims Siff reaching to stop her, as she pulls away.

"Stay here!" she tells vaguely, leaving behind the bow, and arrows.

Wraithe and Terra, take turns charging in, struggling to get closer, as the troll's attacks holds them at bay. Suddenly, Anna places herself between the three, with both arms flailing in the air.

"Tiaw! Tiaw!" she exclaims, drawing the troll's attention. "Ew naem uoy on mrah!" she voices, putting Wraithe and Terra at a puzzled standstill. However, the troll itself stops, appearing to understand her words.

"Ew dewollof eth swolg," she exclaims with her hands. "Esaelp!" she pleads, reaching into her waist's belt. Seeing this, the troll prepares its club, and Anna immediately throws up her hands. "Esaelp!" she begs once more. Again, the troll pauses, lowering its weapon. Anna carefully lowers her hand, reaching into her belt for her blade, as Wraithe and Terra look at each other uneasily. She reaches slowly, pulling out her blade, and tosses it aside. The troll stops in bewilderment, as Anna slowly lowers her hands to her sides.

"Ees ew naem uoy on mrah!" she voices further. Meanwhile, Wraithe, Terra, and Siff all look on in confusion. Suddenly, the troll lifts its weapon to strike. "Nooo!" cries Anna, shielding herself defencelessly. There is a silence, when moments later, Anna finally opens her eyes. She looks up, as the troll's attention has been distracted; turning to the others, Anna also notices them looking towards the sky. A human-like figure, descending towards them, eclipsing the sun, it is a female. From her bosoms to her thighs, are decorated, in the most colorful, and brilliant textures of flowers, and greenery. Her luminescent-blue ventral wings gracefully float her into their presence. Dropping to its knees, and placing its right hand to its breast, the troll bows its head in respect.

"Greetings, and welcome travellers," she greets gracefully. "And greetings to you as well! 'Siff Dillon' of Nordeskye!" she tells looking to her side. Terra slowly reaches for her hidden blade, tucked behind her torso.

"Peace, warrior," she tells calmly. "If I meant to harm you, I would've done so," the being goes on to tell. Appalled, Terra removes her hand from her weapon.

"Thank you, Gatekeeper," the being tells to the troll, which calmly gets to its feet. "You may depart!".

"Gatekeeper?!" whispers Anna puzzled in thought, as to their astonishment, the ferocious, giant troll obediently departs, as if nothing occurred.

"Yes, the Gatekeeper," answers the being in reply. "The devoted protector of the forest."

"Y-You… heard me??" stammers Anna shockingly.

"The forest sees, and hears all," tells the being, gesturing openly about them. "I am one with the forest, and my power extends as such." Meanwhile, Siff pushes his way between them, to take a closer look. Immediately, he is fascinated by her. Her skin ivory, with hints and glimmers of shimmering crystals. Her hair, which curls dark and thick, assorted with white and red flowers. Her eyes are an enigma, with colors of light blue, and accents of green. Her rosy, sultry lips, purse smoothly, as she speaks. She is beautiful.

"Who are you?" asks Siff, enthralled in all her beauty. The female smiles.

"I am Mitrefys," she replies kindly, "Keeper of the forest, and Mother of both its life, and death; I am Mother Nature," she proclaims, leading off towards the forest. "Follow me," she tells gracefully to the four. Approaching the forest's edge, something miraculous occurs. The nearby brush suddenly clears her path, creating a lush green rug, leading beyond sight. With her gentle step, withered limp plants, dead trees and shrubs vibrantly revive to life. The four marvel at her abilities, as forest animals emerge to greet her; foxes of pure white fur, hares of luminescent light-green, and other living creatures all with unique textures of the forest emerge from the bushes.

"This is not possible," whispers Terra in disbelief, meanwhile, Mitrefys turns, smiling in amusement.

"Oh, but it is, my dear," she chuckles in reply.

"I don't mean to be rude," opens Anna timidly, "But, where are we?!" she exclaims curiously.

"My dear, we are in Equilibrius… the Forest of Beginning… and Fount of balance between good and evil," she answers, gracefully turning to Anna. She leads them further along the path, running side by side to a small nearby stream. Although the run leads downstream, the water travels against its runoff, in a surreal reverse.

"Siff look!" exclaims Anna, pointing towards the stream. "The waters! They travel backwards! Just like the mist!" she tells excitedly. Wraithe and Terra also notice the strange phenomena.

"W-Wait, the water? Why does it travel backwards?!" turns Anna to her curiously in question.

"In Equilibrius its not considered backwards," corrects Mitrefys gently, "Its returning to the heart," she goes on to tell. This puzzles the group.

"The heart?" repeats Anna questionably in reply. Mitrefys then smiles in amusement.

"This way, I'll show you," she turns calling them along. The nearby animals also follow, running along the forest's path. The birds of the air fly above, moving further ahead, as if instinctively drawn to what lies ahead. A large opening seems to be further along, as they trek up a small hill, revealing a harboring inner oasis. Creatures are seen gathering near the waters circled about a tall tree, bearing flowers of pure white, falling into its clear waters below. The four look on in utter amazement of the surreal sight. Anna takes note of the small creatures seen circling about the canopy of the tree, they seem like an unusual flock of birds.

"What is that?" she questions curiously to Mitrefys.

"That young one is the divine tree," she answers proudly, looking forward to the oasis. Anna continues to admire the view, as her curiosity sparks about the circling 'birds' above.

"What are those flying things, and why do the circle about the divine tree?" points Anna towards the tree. Mitrefys smiles.

"Those are my subjects, an organic race I've created since the dawn of Equilibrius; the 'sprites;' caretakers of the forest, and forged from the very fabric of Equilibrius itself," tells Mitrefys fully, as Anna and the others look on. "Come, they are waiting," she urges, leading them down into the oasis. The creatures watch as the entity guides the strange beings near the waters of the tree, unsure of their unfamiliar scent and appearance. Suddenly, the trees flock makes swift change of direction, headed for the four. In a flurry of breeze and luminescent wings, they encircle about Anna, meanwhile, the others look on.

"What is this? What's going on?" asks Anna spinning nervously, as the 'sprites' make wind about her.

"As I suspected," answers Mitrefys vaguely.

"What is it? What do they want with me?" Anna continues, growing of concern.

"They haven't formed like this since a human found us twenty years ago," utters Mitrefys in discovery.

"W-Wait what? W-Who were they?" asks Anna further. Mitrefys smiles reluctantly.

"Arthur Valor… your father," answers Mitrefys bluntly in reply. Immediately, Anna's eyes widen, as this unspoken news is heard.

"W-Wait you knew my father?" stammers Anna in question. Again, Mitrefys smiles.

"He forged the Omni," replies Mitrefys, and with a wave of her hand, a silver runic staff whimsically appears, forming from the air itself. It is an aged staff, seemingly metallic with runic symbols and carvings decorated throughout. "My beacon of choice, and instrument of preservation," she details further, extending the staff towards her.

"My father forged this?" whispers Anna lowly in disbelief.

"From the minerals of Equilibrius itself! There is no other instrument like it, only commanded by the lotus," adds Mitrefys in telling, holding out her palms, in them, a gray symbol of a flower, with petals bloomed. "Without my lotus, the omni's power cannot be used; the 'beacon' is only encrypted to my command, with it, I can instantly forge any weapon desirable" she adds, wielding the staff into a shimmering two-edged sword.

"My father never spoke of this, this can't be true," mutters Anna in disbelief. Mitrefys disperses the sprites, stepping closer to Anna.

"It is true young one, that is why the sprites brought you here, your father's likeness and presence is buried within yourself. The sprites sensed it and brought you here to Equilibrius under the impression you were your father," tells Mitrefys fully. Anna then looks down in thought, her mind struggling to grasp this reality. Finally, Anna turns to her.

"H-How come he never spoke of this?!" she exclaims wildly in question. In that moment, Wraithe steps forth, preparing to speak.

"Because he was a knight," he interrupts in mentioning, catching Anna off guard. She is stunned.

"He was a what?" she begs to clarify.

"Your father served in the old Order, as a fellow knight at the roundtable, he was also one of its forefathers," Wraithe begins to tell. "He led us into many great battles, of which, we were victorious, he was the only knight to have fought a fate, lord Fenrifrys, alone, and survived. A courageous, noble man he was. Also, the finest blacksmith in all of Skye; it was he who crafted the very swords of the Order's knights," adds Wraithe.

"You knew this? And didn't say anything?!" mutters Anna in reply turning angrily to Wraithe.

"It mattered not until now, to be an offspring of the Order is a curse, Maurdis prides himself on our heads, need I say more of everything we've had to face, for what? To live a life of ruin?" he exclaims, "You would do yourself a favor in forgetting what was said today, should you choose to live," warns Maurdis sternly. Anna looks down in thought, and quickly turns to Mitrefys.

"You're the creator of Equilibrius?!" she exclaims in question.

"I am a 'fate;' Equilibrius is my garden, I am its caretaker, as does it thrive in my presence; its forest is my strength," she goes on to tell, as a soothing breeze passes over them.

"If you can control fate itself, how do you not save Skye from the creatures that harm us!" Anna questions forwardly. "For years, the people have lived in torment, too afraid to leave the gates at night, as this Maurdis destroys everything within his wake. These past couple days I've witnessed things from the very nightmares of men," mutters Anna gravely. "My village; our home, GONE! Nothing left!" she exclaims. "We travel in search of a new beginning, somewhere else safe, we do not know what awaits us at the end! But you, you have the power to free us, and restore peace to all of Skye! PLEASE, HELP US!" pleads Anna wildly, as the others standby in listening.

"I know all that occurs in Nordskye, young one," answers Mitrefys gently in reply. "But powers such as fate and choice are beyond my control. I only offer balance; the order of which can and will be. Maurdis follows the teachings of the 'fallen one,' and carries on the desires of capturing the very thing that remains under my protection," tells Mitrefys further.

"The white lotus," answers Wraithe stepping forward, looking towards the divine tree.

"Yes," agrees Mitrefys, also turning to the oasis. "He hunts the flower in search of immortality; if captured it would mean the destruction of both Skye and Equilibrius, nothing will be left standing under his rule," she tells the four. "I only offer protection within the preservation of the forest and the divine tree."

For Anna, this isn't enough, she then proceeds to stand before Mitrefys. "Maurdis will never stop until it is his, a lot of good people have died because of his ambition. Don't you see? Protecting this forest, the divine tree, is not enough," states Anna shakingly in reply.

"Good will always produce evil, as does the latter," Mitrefys answers blatantly. "One can only balance the powers of the two; thus, distort chaos," she adds. "There will always be those who challenge good, just as those who challenge evil. The balance of creation is simply designed that way, there are always those who fight for what they believe, those who choose to protect, and those who choose to destroy," she tells openly.

"And this is where your belief lies?!" exclaims Anna reluctantly in reply.

"I protect the nature and order of life, I have no definitive belief, I am neutral, surrendering all outcomes to fate, and destiny itself," utters Mitrefys straightly. Meanwhile, Wraithe tires of the back and forth, and interrupts lowly, before Anna begins to speak.

"You had something to show us?" asks Wraithe turning to Mitrefys, stepping between the pair. With a silent smile, Mitrefys leads off, following into the oasis. The roots of the divine tree sprawls from the rocks, floating it over the waters, as its immense overgrowth sprawls along its crystal-clear surface. As they arrive at the foot of the tree, Mitrefys looks to Anna in question.

"So, Anna Valor of Nordeskye..." she begins to say, when Anna suddenly interrupts.

"I carry the name of my mother, 'Nero,' it's one of the few things I know of her," tells Anna, pulling out a linked necklace with red circular charm hanging near her bosom, "This is one of the few things my father kept in remembrance of her," she goes on to tell, slipping it back into her tunic.

Wraithe's eyebrows raise, at the sight of the charm. Meanwhile, Siff's catches eye of Wraithe's peculiar gaze. "What's wrong?" he asks tugging at Wraithe's sleeve.

"It is nothing," he mutters shakenly in reply. Meanwhile, Anna returns to Mitrefys in question.

"If Maurdis gets the lotus, what will he go after?" she presses.

"He will replace me, as the balance of this oasis, and also the supreme lord of Skye, he will only grow more powerful," tells the entity gravely. "He will even be able to defeat the nocturnals, the balance of the world will be distorted, everything will perish, there will be only him..." Mitrefys concludes severely.

"Maurdis..." murmurs Anna inwardly. "From where did he come from?" she utters looking to Mitrefys in question.

"As did your father; Maurdis also was once a knight of the old Order," answers Wraithe, joining the discussion. "He was one of the most decorated and skilled of us all; also, the most harsh, quick to act and slow to reason, but he was willing to die for what he believed in, and anything he felt the need to protect. Your father and him received many 'disagreements' within their friendship," Wraithe goes on to add. "In short, the Order didn't take too kindly to his episodes of misconduct and brash actions, and further forbade him an official seat at the roundtable, where both commands and decisions were to be made by the wisest of Skye's knights."

"So, what happened to him?" speaks Siff curiously in question.

"He slowly began to resent the Order, feeling they were too incompetent enough to make decisions, seeing at how long they would take to come to final choices and attacks, it was this and a few other factors, that led to his abandonment of the old Order," adds Wraithe.

"Did any of it have to do with my father?" turns Anna to him in question.

"Your father questioned Maurdis' capabilities of becoming a knight at the roundtable, as did the other knights, who thought him brash and not a great fit for the overall decisions of the Order. Yet, Arthur chose to watch more closely over him; to aid Maurdis with his uncontrollable temper. And with their many noble battles, protecting Skye's people from both the lycans and nocturnals, they became close," tells Wraithe in reply.

"It was your father that introduced me to Maurdis, shortly before it was rumored, that he would be leaving the order," Wraithe continues in telling.

"My father left the Order?" asks Anna in disbelief, "But why?" she asks further.

"Your father had served Skye greatly and felt there was more to his life than noble servitude," details Wraithe in reply.

"It wasn't long after, when Maurdis had fallen in love with a woman named Sceptra, who loved him deeply, and for a while suppressed the tempers of Maurdis. But she felt the pull of his relentless pride, and ambition, eventually proving to much for her to bare. She then sought out advice and guidance from Arthur, and in turn found a growing love for your father, an unspoken love until now," mentions Wraithe fully. "The rift between your father and Maurdis had finally began," he utters. "Decisions were consistently met with furious bursts of insubordination, and blatant disregard of duty by Maurdis. He also went as far as to garnering some of the lesser experienced knights to rally behind him."

"The day finally came when your father simply left the order, and its knighthood, moving upwind, to what is now known as 'Nordeskye.' There, I got word that he had found a wife, and bore a child, a year after Maurdis' firstborn," he continues. "However, for Maurdis, this did nothing to slow his ambitions, he grew more impatient, and desired to be given a high seat at the roundtable, following the absence of your father. Yet again, the 'table' refused. They had sought out Arthur, your father in his absence, and when asked about his thoughts on Maurdis being a competent knight at the table, your father agreed with the fellow knights, a just decision, and revoked Maurdis' demands. he was simply, too unstable!"

"So, what happened next, did he rebel?" questions Siff, listening intently.

"There was a war, Fenrifrys, ruler of the lycans, one of the mighty 'fates,' had led the lycans against Skye and its knights, a battle that lasted for three full days; the 'Triad War.' It was hard fought and took all the might of Skye to fell his powerful army!" he recounts in saying. "On the third day, we had finally gotten the upper hand, Maurdis and his men had given us an opening and as lambs to the slaughter, we followed through with it," tells Wraithe gravely. "Fenrifrys, and the lycans had drew back into the mountains, I wish then, we knew it was an ambush, I barely escaped with my life, and Maurdis had been abandoned by his men, his ambitions proved too much, and soon he found himself alone against them," utters Wraithe despairingly. "There was little hope in him still being alive; your father spoke of his mistrust of Maurdis' decisions and predicted the battle's fate, yet, he aided Maurdis' ambition, which we thought ultimately led to his demise, the lycans proved far too powerful."

"Suddenly, there was rumor of a revenant of the Old Order, in SouthSkye, the description matched that of Maurdis, he was alive, your father and I quickly sought out to see him, to witness the impossible; his survival," Wraithe exclaims. "But when we arrived, he was barely alive; worst of all... he had been bitten!" Wraithe continues bleakly.

"Bitten? What do you mean?" asks Anna.

"A Blood Moon," speaks Terra bluntly in answer.

"Yes," agrees Wraithe with a nod. "under normal circumstances it would prove to be none other than a common wound, but a bite from a lycan, under control of a blood moon, would corrupt a man's soul!" exclaims Wraithe severely. "Under oath, a knight at the round table cannot raise their sword against another, the punishment would be severe. However, Maurdis was never appointed at the table, yet your father out of compassion chose not to finish him off, instead, seeing the dire state he was in, he simply surrendered Maurdis to fate, thinking he would wither away from his wounds, but somehow, he survived… When word got back to the 'roundtable' about his survival, the Order quickly sought to correct what your father had done and finish it, but by the time the remaining knights arrived, Maurdis had disappeared, sensing now the Order would be after him."

"And what became of him then?" questions Anna curiously.

"Maurdis felt betrayed by the Order, the very ones he swore to protect, now after his own life, so he abandoned it, surrendering himself to the 'Order of the pact;' the very teachings of Fenrifrys," states Wraithe gravely in reply. "It was there, he further fostered his hatred for the Order, and with the very same ambition seeking to protect, he now sought only to destroy, many knights fell victim to his wrath; dwindling the Order to nothing but revenants, dust to be scattered amongst the winds… that would not be the stop of his ambition. Maurdis would quickly take his place at the side of Fenrifrys, and would lead the lycans into their raids, it was during an attack, he learned of the birth of his child," adds Wraithe

"He sought out his lost family, but when his wife, Sceptra, found out about his ambitions, she took their child, and fled, into the arms of your father, the young child, about only a year old, she begged to leave it with him, for fear of Maurdis taking it," tells Wraithe dramatically. "Your father reluctantly accepted, reaching out to me for assistance in protecting the child, as Maurdis would indefinitely make him his successor; an heir to the lycan pact."

"Maurdis would relentlessly pursue her, until he found her stowed away, in a small village near Eastskye, the lycans would tear the village apart, and Maurdis, in a fit of rage, would slay the very one he loved, cementing his descent into darkness," he ends in telling, as the others look on speechlessly.

"He took the child, after leaving everything in ruin, and only the fates know where he has been hiding all these years," mutters Wraithe in saying, "Times have changed, this time, I fear he has gotten stronger,"

"So why? why is he attacking now? Skye suffers, no food, little supplies, and being unable to trade, we live in fear, never leaving outside the walls!" cries Anna desperately for an answer.

With a deep breath Wraithe continues, "Maurdis demanded the Order give him the white lotus, the key to immortality and if they were to refuse, the land of Skye was told it would run red with blood, starting with the Order, still, the roundtable refused, and Skye has been under attack ever since,"

"So, we have to help them!" exclaims Anna shaking her head vigorously, "We have to help them!" turning to Mitrefys, "With your help, we can finally put an end to them, and our people wouldn't have to live in fear!" Anna proposes vigorously. "We can save them!" she exclaims.

Mitrefys notions quietly. "What you speak of young one is beyond my power, I cannot aid you in this fight," she answers forwardly in reply. Anna is gaunt with disbelief.

"No, no, but you can, they would not stand a chance against you!" voices Anna desperately. meanwhile, Mitrefys remains still.

"I cannot disrupt the affairs beyond this forest," she tells bluntly.

"But why?! WHY DON'T YOU INTERVENE!!" bawls Anna inconceivably.

Finally, Mitrefys reveals herself.

"My powers do not extend to the outside world, my only duty is to the balance of nature, not of fate," Mitrefys replies, "As a 'fate' our duties are to care for what we were created."

"But can't you control the powers of both good, and evil?" argues Anna, unsatisfied with this response.

"It is not that simple young one," states Mitrefys calmly.

Finally, Anna's emotions boil over. "What do you mean!" she yells in disbelief.

"There are powers more potent than my own; fate and choice, I have no control of, I would be vulnerable to those powers, possibly disturbing the overall balance of nature itself," Mitrefys explains calmly.

"That is ridiculous," scoffs Terra wittingly hearing this.

"Anything can be considered foolish to those who simply can't comprehend," rebuts Mitrefys stoutly. "There is a deeper, more sinister power, much more potent than what is soon to befell you!" she adds cryptically.

Mitrefys turns to the Divine Tree. "I am connected to this lifeform," she tells, "It embodies the very fabric of immortality… If I perish, so does the tree and all that abide here, we are connected."

"So, what do we do?" asks Anna solemnly.

Mitrefys then looks to Anna in calm reply, "Get some rest, the journey ahead of you is a long one, you will need to restore the old Order, that Skye will once again be able to defend itself against treachery."

Chapter 4
"A Forbidden Treachery"

"Come, follow me! So, I can show you where you can find comfort in resting," tells Mitrefys, leading them along. She leads them around the divine tree, as the four admire its massive trunk, the tree of luminescent silver, and mossy green extends its branches housing the sprites. The four stare in awe, as white lotus flowers vibrantly bloom along its lively branches. Mitrefys then carries them up a path, again through the forest, until they ascend to a small plateau overlooking the whole of Equilibrius. The view is unsettling, as the clouds smoothly roll along the deep sky, as the sun and moon sit across each other, along the horizon, both sharing the light. Meanwhile, animals below can be seen returning to the forest, as whispers of cool breeze blows by the forest's canopy.

"Here is where you can rest," tells Mitrefys, pointing them to a comfortable bed of lush grass, facing the oasis.

"We haven't no time to rest," utters Wraithe mindfully, "With every second we waste, Maurdis gains, he will seek out Westskye, I'm sure of it, it's the last city that hasn't felt his wrath."

"Peace warrior," answers Mitrefys, "In Equilibrius, time itself, is at a standstill, a day in your world is an hour in mine," she tells comfortingly. Meanwhile, Anna and Siff sit near the cliff's edge, admiring the view, as Mitrefys suddenly stands alongside them.

"I see why you never leave here, it's beautiful," mutters Anna in saying, "This was once Skye before fear became our way of life," she adds in thought, Mitrefys then looks down to her in question.

"I must ask you Anna of Nordeskye, why must you save a world destined to ruin?" she asks. Anna quickly turns, looking into the entity's eyes and utters.

"Because so many have suffered and lost, many even more than I have, I long for a time when Skye can no longer live in fear, when its people can come together in unity and thrive, that's what my father believed in; you may believe in the 'order of balance,' but I believe in true peace."

Mitrefys is silent, looking ahead with bewildered smile, she turns to Anna in reply, "Those were the very words of your father, when he stood atop this rise, you are truly Arthur's child." Immediately, Anna looks up to her, seeing as Mitrefys turns to depart, she returns her gaze to the horizon as the sun slowly begins to dip behind the canopies. Wraithe waits in gazing across the way, distant from the others. Seeing this, Mitrefys heads towards him, approaching to his side.

"You are troubled warrior, an unspeakable guilt befalls you," she utters in saying. Wraithe looks to her in silence.

"It is the girl. Her father's spirit be strong in her; she believes in a united Skye, and victory over the enemy. She will only influence Skye to take up arms and do battle. Albeit noble, it is a fool's errand," mutters Wraithe troublingly in thought. Meanwhile, Mitrefys smirks inwardly.

"So, you believe in her?" she turns to him in question, as Wraithe then pauses.

"Her heart is pure... but mistaken," he utters doubtfully in reply.

Mitrefys then offers in saying, "There are no mistakes in choices, the mistake follows failure; yet, to inspire and unite the hearts of many would be a noble act worthy of acclaim," she adds, "However, it is not this that troubles you, isn't it? It is a choice made, one that you have to live with for the rest of your life?" adds Mitrefys knowingly. Suddenly, Wraithe turns to her.

"You know?!" utters Wraithe wide-eyed in saying. "I ask you, speak not of this!" pleads the revenant in reply. Meanwhile, Mitrefys nods silently and with that, turns to depart.

"Control over fate and choice I have not, interfering is not in my nature," she utters disappearing down the hillside. A whistling breeze blows by the four, when finally, the moon captures the sky. The forest is heard shifting, as nearby flowers and plants wither away; a peculiar sight to the once vibrant Equilibrius.

"Look at this!" utters Siff, pointing to a patch of dying plants. "They're dying immediately, how is this possible?!" Meanwhile, the others approach near to him.

"The forest blooms, and withers as the maiden sleeps," mentions Wraithe cryptically, as the others look to him in curiosity. "It's Mitrefys," he answers, "She is asleep. It means that we should all do the same, we cannot stay here; the other cities deserve to know of Maurdis' treachery." Anna smirks at Wraithe's seemingly newfound change of heart.

"Come on," she tells Siff pulling him along, "Let's get some rest." As everyone is fast asleep, Anna lingers awake, looking to the stars, she then witnesses something amazing. The sprites all rise from among the trees, luminating above the forest below, appearing as a sea of glows. Excited, Anna turns to wake Siff, shaking him from his slumber.

"W-What is it, Anna?" he mumbles sleepily. Anna continues to point, pulling at his arm.

"SIFF! Look! You have to see this!" she exclaims, dragging him along. Rubbing his eyes, Siff opens to see what Anna brings to his attention, still drowsy of his slumber.

"See what!? What is it?" he asks, reluctantly looking below. Anna then turns, her smile retreating to a look of disbelief, as behind her lies a quiet forest.

Embarrassed, she stammers, "It was the glows, uhh… sprites, they were flying, they lit up the forest just a few seconds ago! Believe me!" Tired, Siff shrugs walking off, finding a comfortable patch of soft grass, and returns to his slumber. Meanwhile, Anna is dumbfounded, puzzled as to the sprite's sudden disappearance. Suddenly, A pat on her shoulder startles her and she quickly spins about, however, it is Terra.

"What's wrong?" Terra asks to her.

Anna quickly glances back to the forest, seeing nothing but the forest's breeze through the trees. "It's nothing," mutters Anna in reply, looking to Terra in disappointed gaze.

"You're not a good liar, Anna," utters Terra reluctantly, as a cool gust of wind passes them by. "This forest, Equilibrius, it is the most peaceful place I've ever been," adds Terra, breathing in, as she gazes upon the stars. "If I could, I would stay forever." Anna then smiles in agreement.

"It is peaceful, after all my life, living around fear, it feels so surreal to me," agrees Anna in return. Terra then looks to her.

"The fate, Mitrefys, she seems to have taken interest in you," adds Terra in saying. "She watches you closely; but I must ask you; what would you do once you were to warn WestSkye?" she asks curiously. Anna pauses, taking a moment to reply.

"I would seek out Maurdis, avenge my father, and my village, and unite all of Skye, just as my father had hoped," tells Anna boldly in reply. Pouting her lips in hearing, Terra takes a moment of silence.

"A noble task, but what you speak of is impossible, all of Skye's finest knights have been slain, their cities live in fear, the lycans grow more powerful, there is nothing gaining for you to win; if those before you have fallen, what chance have you?!" scoffs Terra, doubtfully awaiting her answer.

"I'm not those before me, Skye CAN become one, it is all I believe in; and what greater power there is than hope itself?!" offers Anna in reply. Terra immediately looks down in thought, then towards the night sky.

"In all my travels alongside Wraithe, I've never admired the stars before this night, it would be my fears that would keep me on guard for any attack during our slumber. I have spent many of restless nights… it is truly not a life. I pray the fates grant me your hope!" tells Terra finally proceeding to leave. "Get some rest Valor, Westskye is still quite a journey ahead." she utters, strolling off, across the way. Meanwhile, Anna thinks on Terra's words a few moments longer, until tiredness settles in, finding her succumbed to a deep sleep.

Meanwhile.

On the devastated, ashen grounds of Nordeskye, the lycans have once again invaded the village. Rounding up the last remaining survivors, they are corralled by the ruthless circle of lycans. The snarls and gnashing of teeth are enough for the people to cower in fear, when suddenly, a tall, broad-statured male appears, donned in a dark-maned cloak.

"Maurdis..." trembles one of the men in saying, seeing him approach through the ravenous wolves.

"Seems like I no longer require introduction," chuckles Maurdis sinisterly, kneeling to ruffle the male's shirt. "My orders are simple..." he proclaims loudly to the frightful group. "I ask a question; you answer! If not..." he utters, when in a shearing of teeth, one of the lycans pounces upon a fellow villager, slaying them within seconds. Maurdis turns towards them, smiling devilishly. "A small truth; for a life. Truly not much of a bargain," he grins mockingly. "Now," mutters Maurdis, gripping the face of a nearby villager, "Where is the revenant?" he squeezes violently.

The frightened female villager begs tearfully, "Please! We know not of who you speak!"

With a bat of his right eye, a lycan breathes down a nearby villager's neck, whose tears instantly begins to pour, and in that instant, the lycan pounces upon him, slaying yet, another victim. Frightened, a young woman breaks way from the group, fleeing frantically down the path.

"GET HER!!" roars Maurdis fiercely. Immediately, two of the lycan start after her, they swiftly catch up, as one bounds upon her back, pinning her to the ground. Its teeth readily bared to her petrified face, awaiting the order of Maurdis.

"P-P-Please..." she squirms tearfully, her face red with tears.

"Bring her!" roars Maurdis in enjoyment. She is then pulled from the ground by two broad males, pulling both arms along. Maurdis then turns to his gripped hostage, squeezing her face tighter.

"You'd better speak, else we'll tear her apart, limb by limb!" he grins. Suddenly, a voice answers.

"WAIT!!" yells one of the male's indistinctly, pulling Maurdis' attention. Maurdis quickly gets to his feet, stepping near the frightened voice.

"Speak now or be torn apart!" orders Maurdis fiercely.

"T-They've headed west, to the large city, i-it was four of them, two maidens, a lad and t-the revenant of what you speak," stammers the male nervously in reply.

"Are you certain?" kneels Maurdis, snarling in question.

"Yes, o-on my life!" trembles the male.

"I like that," chuckles Maurdis reluctantly, suddenly, he snatches him from the ground, and with a swift, and powerful twist of his head, snaps the villager's neck, as his lifeless body drops to the ground. "Kill them all," utters Maurdis turning away coldly, as the vicious snarls and horrified screams sound behind him.

Meanwhile, beyond the walls of Nordskye, within the garden of Equilibrius. Anna abruptly awakes from her slumber. Mortified by a nightmare; she dreams of Nordeskye once again under attack, its people all slain and Maurdis in pursuit of them. After a few moments, her breathing finally slows, as she catches her breath. She rests her tiresome face within her hands, rubbing herself awake. She hears light rustling to her left and turns her head to see Wraithe tossing and turning in his sleep, along the soft patch of grass. She gets up and cautiously moves in closer to check on him, when suddenly, he abruptly awakes.

"ARTHUR!" he blurts out in saying, pitching up from his sleep. There, he meets Anna hunched over his face.

"I-I-I'm sorry, I-I only thought I'd check to see if you were alright," she stammers awkwardly in telling, "You were talking in your sleep." Wraithe looks on appearing distraught.

"You should find rest child, Westskye is not a short journey," he mutters miserably, turning back to his slumber, yet Anna lingers, taking a heavy breath, and curiously creeps nearer.

"My father, he rarely spoke of my mother… When he did it would be in short mentions, in that, she loved me and my stark resemblance of her, but he never spoke much further. So, I must ask you, have you seen her?" asks Anna desperately.

"Who?" replies Wraithe bluntly.

Clearing her throat, Anna repeats, "My mother… did you meet her?" she goes on to ask. Wraithe notions quietly, opening his eyes as he sits upright.

"Arthur spoke little of his family, for sake of the Order and what would be at risk for him, so from the fellow knights he hid you all, none have ever seen or truly heard of her," mentions Wraithe lowly in reply.

"Oh, okay," mutters Anna in disappointment, fiddling her thumbs. She steps away, moving to her pressed spot of grass, looking up to the stars. Closing her eyes, she returns to sleep.

Time stands still in Equilibrius, its forests blooms and withers as the 'maiden' sleeps. The stars remain planted in the sky, as the moon tarries in moving.

Meanwhile…

Just beyond the sleeping oasis, and the hollows of the dreary cave, a pair of piercing, yellow eyes lie in wait, spying along their campsite; watching as the smoke from the ashes of firewood ascend to the night sky. Suddenly, it silently disappears back into the forest.

"We've found them, my lord!" informs one of Maurdis' subjects, having returned from his scouting. Immediately, Maurdis gives orders to pursue; as he and his men swiftly close in on the campsite. The forest is quieted, as the lycans surrounds the tents beneath the cover of the forest.

"Take them!" orders Maurdis straightly. In an instant, the lycans erupt from the forest and begin tearing apart the campsite. The horses panic, breaking loose of their reins and flee the attack, leaving behind the empty campsite. The lycans then rip open each tent in search of them, but to their reluctant surprise, it is empty. Maurdis impatiently awaits word of their discovery and proceeds to enter the camping ground. As he does this, the returning subject approaches.

"My lord," he answers nervously, "T-The r-revenant is not here," he shudders in telling. Infuriated, Maurdis clutches at his throat, and tosses him aside.

"THEN FIND HIM!!" he roars loudly to the men. "FIND HIM!!!" It is in that moment, he turns away, glimpsing the cave's mouth, and calls over two nearby men.

"Search the cave!" he orders quickly, as the lycans then move to its mouth and begin scouring the inners of the cave. Their barks and snarls echo throughout, and it isn't long before they catch whiff of a strange scent. With a great howl, they then signal to Maurdis, who waits just outside the cave. Hearing the sound, he grins sinisterly upon entering into the hollow opening. The lycans hunt the scent throughout the cave, until finally, a glimmer of light is seen in the distance. The lycans emerge atop a hill, looking out over a beautiful sleepy oasis. Peering down at the night sky glimmering atop the flowing river's surface below. As Maurdis steps out onto the overlooking ledge he too is amazed.

"We found it!" he exclaims wildly. Puzzled, the men look to him.

"What is it?" asks one of them.

"Arthur spoke of a place, hidden within the forests of Skye, an oasis. It is home to the 'fate' that defeated and sealed our lord Fenrifrys; her power as vast as the oasis itself! In fact, it is where she draws her might. Our white lotus lives here!" Maurdis goes on in telling. "The fool has led us straight to it," he mutters lowly to himself.

Concerned, one of the men steps forth in question. "My lord, she has defeated Fenrifrys, mightier than all of us, can this 'fate' of what you speak even be beaten?"

Maurdis turns to them, answering viciously in reply, "We destroy it slowly, from the fount of its power; the forest itself, WE BURN IT!" Under the cover of night, as the forest sleeps and withers, they gather many branches and with the strikes of flint, spark the heap aflame. Lined with torches in their mouths, the lycans descend into the oasis, and begin setting the oasis aflame. The dry, withering forest quickly catches afire, spreading violently throughout. Meanwhile, all are sound asleep, unaware of the treacherous presence that gains upon them. The moon has descended giving rise to the gleaming sun. As its rays creep in shining upon Anna's tanned skin, a cool breeze brushes through her coilly hair, as her eyes slowly bat in waking. She feels a few taps, and the sudden shaking of her arm. Anna wakes to Siff, hovered over her pointing ahead. Shielding her eyes from the sun, Anna glimpses Mitrefys oddly standing near the cliff's edge, and quickly gets to her feet.

"M-Mitrefys??!" Anna calls slowly creeping towards her. Instantly, something feels off. The entity then turns to them, her face gaunt, as she reaches towards them. Both Anna and Siff witness the once lively luminescent skin of Mitrefys, slowly break away as floating ash in the still winds. Mitrefys weakly collapses to the ground, abruptly waking Terra and Wraithe, who both clamor to their feet and rush over.

"What happened?!!" voices Wraithe kneeling to help Mitrefys. Panicked and confused, Anna and Siff know not how to explain.

Anna stammers uncontrollably in reply, "I-I DON'T KNOW! SH-SHE just..."

Suddenly, a flock of frightened birds rise above the encampment, startling the four, when a familiar scent fills the air. Anna gets up, walking near the cliff's edge, and to her horror sees Equilibrius, the beautiful forest, smoking in flames. Mitrefys' eyes open weakly.

"H-HE I-IS HERE," she utters lowly, as bits of skin from her cheeks slowly breaks away, as floating ash. Looking below, something catches Anna's eye. As stepping out from the forest, in the clearing of the smoke, a tall male robed in a dark-maned cloak appears. And to her strange fright, he glares directly towards her. Meanwhile, Wraithe rushes up from behind to pull Anna from the cliff's edge, when as he grips her arm, he also glimpses down. In that instance, both Wraithe and the male make direct eye contact, as a haunting grin sheds upon the cloaked male's face. Anna notices this but is hastily pulled away by Wraithe.

"Who is that?!" she races in question.

"Maurdis," answers Wraithe panting in reply. "Grab your things, we must leave NOW!" he orders quickly. Terra obediently darts over, quickly gathering their supplies. Meanwhile, Anna struggles to lift Mitrefys.

"Give me your hands child," coughs Mitrefys weakly, pulling Anna to a stop.

"What?!" Anna replies strangely, looking into the eyes of Mitrefys'.

"We haven't much time, give me your hands," utters Mitrefys once more, sitting up from the ground. Anna looks to Siff, who glares back at her.

"JUST DO IT!" tells Siff hastily to Anna.

Anna obediently gives Mitrefys her hands. Suddenly, the entity clasps Anna's hands within her palms, and they luminate, lighting up Anna's amazed expression. Mitrefys then removes her hands. To Anna's astonishment, she glimpses a grey-hued imprint, resembling a flower, along the back of her hands. Anna turns to her palms, and sure enough, the imprint is also revealed in both palms. She nervously looks to Mitrefys.

"What is this?" Anna goes on to ask, when Wraithe and Terra swiftly runs over, and upon approaching, glimpses the unusual markings.

"I have encrypted to you my imprint, my gift; the white lotus, it is now a part of you," whispers Mitrefys in telling. Meanwhile, Anna's eyes begin to well.

"But, why me!?!" cries Anna doubtfully, "I can't do this!"

"You have your father's spirit; your heart is pure, and cause is just. I am contented in knowing I leave the lotus to you. Guard it! Protect it! DO NOT fall into darkness! With this very imprint, you summon the omni, forged by your father's hand, and encrypted with my gift. Any weapon can be forged at your will, take it!" tells Mitrefys straightly, handing Anna the silver runic staff. Mitrefys then turns to them. "You must all leave! Maurdis gains! Keep the lotus safe; I will grant you time!" Getting to her feet, Mitrefys stands firm. Suddenly, there is a shift within the atmosphere, as an eerie wind blows. The sounding thuds can be heard about them, as the birds of Equilibrius begin falling from the sky, withering away.

"What's happening to them?!!" voices Anna, as the winds begin to pick up through the forest's empty trees.

"The forest is dying," utters Mitrefys, leading them down the path to escape. "Quickly, there is a passage downriver, it will help you escape Equilibrius to return to the forest." Suddenly, Mitrefys collapses weakly upon a nearby tree, having to be helped back to her feet by Anna. Soon after, they arrive at the foot of the hill, facing the blazing forests, when an approaching shadow appears from within the smoke.

"He's here," voices Mitrefys, leant upon Anna's shoulder. Suddenly, a small flock of Sprites swiftly flutters by, called to, by the hand of Mitrefys. "They will lead you! There is an escape through the untouched part of the forest! My strength is quickly fading, and the forest can't uphold it for much longer."

"We're not leaving without you!" argues Anna stubbornly in reply.

"No!" grunts Mitrefys, "If they get your blood, all of Skye will be doomed! Don't you see? The lotus lives in you now!" Mitrefys then supports herself to her feet. "Get behind me, I will hold them off!" she orders the four.

As his bold footsteps sound emerging from the smoke, a dark-maned cloak vividly appears, draped over a firm, well-statured male. His hair is black with running streaks of gray, as does his short beard. His face of tan, with blazing scarlet-yellow eyes, and a demanding facial build. Black leather armor rests below his prestigious cloak, as he fully comes into view, wearing an arrogant grin.

"My, My, My…" he gloats gesturing about them. "After many winters, I've finally found it!" he chuckles hysterically. "Having also drawn out the one that damned our lord!" he utters looking to Mitrefys. "Even more so, as an added bonus; the one I once called 'brother!' For many years I've waited for this moment… and the fates heard my cry!"

"Maurdis!" roars Wraithe furiously in retort. "You insult the very fabric of this forest, laid waste to something you have yet to understand, you will find only destruction in your end!"

"Even in exile you preach to me, knight?! I shall not rest, until the very ground drinks your blood! Now where is my flower!" he roars in demand. Suddenly, a loud creak is heard behind them, Maurdis immediately looks up at the barren silver tree. Drawn towards it, he steps through the ankle high waters surrounding its trunk. Maurdis witnesses its bark breaking away into dust and ash before floating into the wind. Something catches his eye; it is a vibrant white flower breaking away from the tree. It descends towards the waters, until drifting into the very hands of Maurdis. Finally, his years of conquest would lead him to immortality, as his smug grin spreads across his face. When suddenly, the lotus' petals wrinkle, as a gray hue takes over its vibrant white, until nothing, but a darkened, withered flower remains. Suddenly, the breathing of Maurdis tenses; his heart skipping a beat, as his hands begin to tremble.

"No," he voices beneath his breath. When in sheer disbelief, Maurdis drops to his knees. Mitrefys then walks forth. Meanwhile, Maurdis watches as the soiled flower breaks away, into ash, sifting through his fingers, before being carried off into the wind.

"Your very arrogance, in pursuit of something you yourself are not worthy to have, has destroyed your very chance to attain it," voices Mitrefys stoutly in saying. When suddenly, she stumbles to her knees. "My power..." she utters, "It leaves quickly." Maurdis then darts through the waters, lunging at the neck of Mitrefys, lifting her from the ground.

"NO!!" roars Wraithe, ripping out his sword. Maurdis quickly tosses her aside, also drawing out his sword, as the two blades sound in a thundering clash.

"I have waited for this moment, for over 20 years!" snarls Maurdis pushing against Wraithe with his blade. "The fates have made me stronger! To kill you!" he utters, kicking Wraithe to the ground. "FRAIL!" he swings down towards Wraithe, who blocks late, causing himself to stumble backwards. "DEJECTED!" he roars, making another heavy swing, again blocked late by Wraithe. Finally, "WEAK!" he strikes again, this time knocking the blade from Wraithe's hand. He is now left defenseless, as Maurdis stands over him in gloating. Mitrefys, moves Anna aside.

"YOU WILL NOT HARM HIM MORTAL!! I SAID ENOUGH!" she storms, brushing her hand towards him, as a powerful current of wind blows by Maurdis, lifting and hurling him away. He then hits the ground with a sounding thud. Mitrefys stands guard over Wraithe. Meanwhile, the sky shrouds over; canvassed by thick smoke, as the forest screams to Mitrefys in agony.

"You are running out of time..." tells Mitrefys fearfully, when a commotion sounds from the forest. Instantly, the snarls and angry growls are heard emerging, as the lycans line behind their ruthless leader. Mitrefys' ivory luminescent skin fades darker into a dull gray, as her flowing vibrant hair ages, becoming brittle, and her once supple skin, ages with wrinkles.

"My time here has been distorted, my fate is certain; Equilibrius WILL die! But the lotus lives on in you," she murmurs looking to Anna. When moments later, a loud crashing is heard behind the curtain of blazing forest, as rows of burning trees collapse, hurling a torrent of ash and smoke towards them. The clouds engulf everything in its wake. Mitrefys takes one final look towards Anna, as if in farewell, as the smoke casts towards her. Mitrefys then steps forward, disappearing behind its rolling shroud.

"NOOO!" screams Anna desperately, seeing as she disappears.

Meanwhile, Wraithe quickly urges her, turning to flee, "Come child, we must hurry!!" immediately, there is a great shift beneath all their feet, as massive boulders and great trees come crashing down nearby, as the sun fully disappears behind the shroud of smoke.

"What's happening?!" exclaims Siff in panic.

"It's Equilibrius! Mitrefys is dying! So, the forest is tearing itself apart!" voices Wraithe over the sounding noise. The cries of dying creatures sound about them, their suffering unbearable from the relentless flames. Within the storm of smoke, Mitrefys searches for Maurdis. The entity then glimpses a glimmering silver object nearby and walks nearer. It is revealed to be the sword of Maurdis; she then quickly drops to the ground, picking up the blade. As she does this, the snarls and growls of the lycans encamp about her, hunting within the cover of smoke. Suddenly, one lunges towards her, appearing from nowhere, and is met with a swift strike of the sword, slaying it. Immediately, two more appear, and with a powerful wave of her hand, she hurls one with a powerful gust of wind, turning to the other, and thrusting the sword into its belly, not before it delivers its dying bite, injuring her shoulder. This causes Mitrefys to drop the sword. She then commands the roots of the ground to tie up two more that appear in attack; her roots restraining them about their necks and limbs and thrashing them into the engulfing flames.

Meanwhile, Wraithe and the others swiftly continue their escape, following into the taverns, under the guide of the sprites, whose glows begins to fade.

"Hurry! All of you!!" hastens Wraithe, turning quickly to them, his eyes widening, as he scampers back to Terra. "Where is she?!" he utters, looking behind them. Terra looks behind her, glimpsing Siff, being a step behind; however, there is no sign of Anna! "Damn child!!" curses Wraithe, "Keep going! I'll head after her!" he orders, leading back towards the forest.

Meanwhile, Anna trudges through the smoke, as her feet trembles with the quakes and shifts of the dying Equilibrius. In an instant, a huge tree collapses just ahead of her, nearly having crushed her, as its impacting winds slightly clears her view. Up ahead, she glimpses what appears to be Mitrefys, however, something else catches her eye, it is Maurdis. He stalks the distracted 'fate,' picking up his fallen sword along the way.

All the while, Mitrefys defends against the attacking lycans, she doesn't notice the creeping threat from behind. Anna quickly scampers over the large trunk, hurrying to get closer. Suddenly, there is another great quake, as trees and large rocks come crashing down from above, blocking her path. Anna glimpses as Maurdis closes in on Mitrefys, with sword in hand.

"Mitrefys! NOOOO!" cries out Anna in horror, seeing Maurdis drawing back his sword in attack. Anna's screams garner the attention of Mitrefys, who with a turning glance, is jousted through by a piercing blade. Mitrefys' eyes widen with a deafening gasp, followed by a sharp, numbing unspeakable pain.

"Ughhh!" she grunts, falling to her knees, as a great gust blows, clearing the smoke about them; followed by sheer and utter silence. Maurdis stands relishing in his impending victory, as he walks into Mitrefys view, quickly clutching her by the throat.

"NOO!" screams Anna helplessly, watching as Mitrefys struggles within Maurdis' grip.

"No more of your tricks! No more hiding! I know there is more! YOU WILL TELL ME WHERE IT IS!!" roars Maurdis furiously, tightening his grip about her throat. Meanwhile, Anna struggles over and through the blockage, in efforts to reach to her aid. From the corner of her eye, Mitrefys glimpses Anna attempting to come to her aid, and while choking for air, she extends her hand in Anna's direction. Suddenly, Anna comes to a pause, as thick roots shoot across, further blocking her path. Immediately, Anna realizes it is Mitrefys stopping her. Tears welling in her eyes, Anna watches as the very life is strangled from her.

"TELL MEEE!" roars Maurdis fiercely, as Mitrefys' eyes flutter losing consciousness.

"Y-You w-will n-never... g-get the lotus," chokes Mitrefys in saying, "T-That i-is certain," she squeals. Instantly, Maurdis feels a strong grip upon his legs, running up to his chest and torso. He looks down, seeing the thick vines of forest roots tying about his body, breaking his grip from Mitrefys' neck, allowing her to collapse to the ground. The roots tug tightly, dropping Maurdis to the ground, slowly dragging him towards the scorching forest's flames. It is Mitrefys, with arm extended, as she commands the roots to draw Maurdis into the flames. Meanwhile, Anna watches on, as Maurdis frantically fights and tussles to break free, as he is drawn closer and closer with every slow second.

"YES! GO! DO IT!" exclaims Anna encouragingly. When in the bat of an eye, Maurdis transforms into a large, fierce black lycan, and pulls with all his might against the dragging roots. It is now an act of wills between the two beings.

"No," grunts Mitrefys weakly, her strength continuing to fade, as her hand begins to tremble and lower. Maurdis continues to battle her pull, breaking free of a few of the roots.

"NO! NO! HURRY!" cries Anna desperately looking on, seeing the wavering battle shifting in favor of Maurdis. With the thrashing and gnashing of teeth, the lycan begins tearing and biting away at the roots. Mitrefys power is spent, and her hand drops, immediately, the pull of the roots is halted.

Anna is still, her mouth gaped, anxiously awaiting movement from Mitrefys. She glimpses the faint slow breathing of Mitrefys from the distance. With her slow, dying breaths, the roots constrained about Maurdis, and his men withers, drying hollow, and with a forceful push, he and his men break free. As Anna pants in desperation from looking on, Wraithe suddenly rushes up from behind snatching at her forearm.

"You'll damn us all, not just us four! But all of Skye! The lotus lives within you, if Maurdis finds that out, it will be you, he pursues after, and with your blood, attain immortality! Mitrefys bought us time! Don't let it be for nothing!" scolds Wraithe solemnly. Anna then hesitates, turning to Mitrefys, suffering just beyond her reach. With a great breath, Anna turns away, following after Wraithe. Quickly, the pair begin making their way back to the taverns. Meanwhile, on the tavern's other side. Terra and Siff anxiously await the arrival of Wraithe and Anna at their campsite. Both anxiously looking ahead into the dark, quivering cave.

"W-Where are they?!" mutters Siff worriedly in question. This only sparks a nervous shudder down Terra's spine.

She quickly turns to him encouragingly, "Don't worry… they're coming!"

All the while Maurdis is distracted, turning to Mitrefys, his eyes red with rage, as he kneels to pull her head from the ground. "Where have you hidden it!" he demands fiercely, her hair grasped within his hand. He glares furiously, as Mitrefys replies with her stubborn wheezing breaths. "Answer MEE!" he roars.

"Y-You are t-too late mortal, y-you will n-never find the flower," wheezes Mitrefys in whispering. Maurdis shudders with rage, as an evil grin sprawls along his face.

"It appears I might've underestimated you…" scoffs Maurdis in reply. "Tell me protector, look around you! Were their meaningless lives worth it?!" he chuckles evilly, as three of his men step forward from behind. "Kill them!" orders Maurdis bluntly. Immediately, the three transform to fearsome lycans, racing after Anna and Wraithe. Maurdis returns to Mitrefys. "Now! Where is it?!" he roars in demand.

Meanwhile, Anna and Wraithe arrive at the collapsing cave's opening. They look on as falling rocks and soil have begun closing its entrance. "Hurry!" exclaims Wraithe pushing her ahead, as they duck within the cave, diving through the curtain of falling debris. Moments later, the pursuing lycans gain upon them. When suddenly, they are halted by a great sounding crash, as the opening of the cave is collapsed shut by the thunderous landing of a huge boulder. Nearby trees and soil further cement the opening shut, putting the pair just beyond the lycan's reach. Wraithe then quickly pulls the fallen Anna to her feet.

"Keep moving, don't think a pile of dirt will be enough to sustain them!" he urges leading off into darkness. At this time, the sprites lead with a feint, flickering glow, guiding the pair along. Trapped on the outside, the lycans begin digging about the boulder and heap of debris. When suddenly, the nearby ground erupts with thick ropes of forest roots tying their way across the boulder and what's left of the entrance. Maurdis timely approaches, as the lycans step aside, now looking to their leader.

"Where did they go?!" he roars in question, looking to them in disgust. Finally, one of the men timidly speaks up.

"T-They've escaped my lord, the entrance swallowed up by the forest above," he begins to explain. "Though, if I may, there is little possibility of them surviving the tremors beneath the cave?" In a sudden burst of rage, Maurdis snatches him by the throat.

"You fool!!" yells Maurdis, choking the male. Gasping for air, the male transforms into a lycan, attempting to bite and free himself. Maurdis swiftly pulls him in, and with a quick twist of his head, snaps the lycan's neck. The men watch silently, as the male's lifeless body collapses to the ground. Looking up, Maurdis addresses them. "You fools! Do you not see who protects them! It is the fate! She has allowed them escape and trapped us within this perishing abyss! Remove what you must; I will finish it!" he orders, turning towards the path in return to Mitrefys. From the distance, Maurdis glimpses her, pulling herself along the ground.

"Even in dying you protect them?" scoffs Maurdis, approaching from behind. "But it is all too late for you, isn't it?" he grins. Mitrefys' face collapses to the ground, panting painfully. Her strength dwindling, as she withholds the taverns collapse upon Anna and Wraithe, who continue their treacherous escape. Maurdis kneels near her, pulling out his sword, preparing to strike.

Mitrefys pushes herself from the ground, sitting up to Maurdis in saying. "It doesn't matter what happens to me now; I gave them something special…Hope! Something you can never take away!" she whispers finally. Within seconds, her skin dries to a human pillar of silver dust, breaking away and flowing off into the wind before Maurdis' very eyes. The men approach from behind, also witnessing the spectacle, each knowing within themselves something has been lost. There, Maurdis sits silently, his men nervously awaiting his orders. Finally, after a few moments, he gets to his feet.

"MY BROTHERS!" he calls to them. "They have taken… NO, THEY HAVE STOLEN… THE VERY PURPOSE OF OUR EXISTENCE!" Quickly, the men gather about him. "THEY BELIEVE NATURE HAS PLACED THE BALANCE OF THIS WORLD IN THE HANDS OF MERE MAN! DOES IT NOT REALIZE WHO WE ARE?!!" rants Maurdis further. "WE ARE LYCANS! This is not our curse; but our privilege, PROOF THAT WE ARE GREATER; WE HAVE DEFEATED THE GREAT PROTECTOR! NOW MANKIND STANDS IN THE WAY OF OUR IMMORTALITY?" he voices fiercely. "So, I ask you today, WHAT IS YOUR DESIRE?!!"

"IMMORTALITY!!!" the men rave in reply, placing a proud sinister smirk upon Maurdis' face. "Sept!" calls Maurdis from the men. Seconds later, A young male appears, seeming timid, yet able bodied in stature. His skin tan, with dark coilly hair sitting atop his youthful face, and eyes of vibrant blue. The young male steps to Maurdis' side.

"You! Will hunt them down and bring us the lotus!" proclaims Maurdis placing his arm upon the young man's shoulder. "Skye will run red with blood; DO NOT fail me, my son!" Maurdis whispers fiercely into Sept's ears. With a disgruntled swallow, Sept quietly nods.

Maurdis looks once more to his men, calling forth another name. "Tidas!!"

Immediately, another young male appears, seeming the same age as Sept, with snowy white skin, his features strikingly handsome, with short brown hair. He also appears able bodied in stature, yet being slightly taller and broader than Sept. His scarlet, yellow eyes make direct contact with Sept, wearing a sly, mischievous grin. Tidas then proceeds at Maurdis' side, across from Sept.

"Tidas, you will make sure there are no failures in our mission!" informs Maurdis placing his arm upon the male's shoulder. Tidas silently nods, shooting a conniving look at Sept, who appears bothered at this choice. Pulling his son in closer, he whispers yet again. "Do not fail me!" Patting at his son's face, Maurdis then leaves. As he does this, Tidas glares slyly towards Sept, walking by him and bumping Sept's shoulder.

"Try to keep up… favored Son," he jeers wittingly.

Though irritated, Sept manages to hold his composure, proceeding to where the remaining men await further command.

"You Five!" singles out Tidas, pointing to them lined across the way. "You will accompany us! We all know our heading; we will take the lotus!" he utters grinning deviously towards Sept, "By any means necessary," he informs turning to them

"You've heard your orders," adds Sept stepping near, "We leave immediately!" Passing by one another, the two men both deliver an unsettling glare, as they ready themselves to pursue after Wraithe and the others.

"Fail us, and I will be the last face you see," tells Tidas, passing by Sept.

"The same goes for you!" resounds Sept, looking to him fiercely in reply. Tidas grins devilishly, finding enjoyment in the back and forth, and leaves, disappearing behind the cloud of smoke. Sept's breathing wells deeper, clenching his fists, he lingers a few moments, and continues behind Tidas into the smoke.

Chapter 5
"An Edgy Pursuit"

Having made their escape from the perishing Equilibrius, Anna and Wraithe miraculously join Siff and Terra back at the campsite. It has been completely torn apart, their belongings rummaged through.

"It was the lycans, they somehow followed us," comments Terra stepping through the debris.

"We must hurry, we know not how long the cave will hold them," utters Wraithe, quickly snagging remnants of their belongings. "The horses?!" he exclaims looking over to where they were last hitched.

"Does this mean we will have to flee on foot?!" mutters Siff in question. Meanwhile, Wraithe proceeds to the center of the campsite, delivering a loud, three-toned whistle. He sounds three pitches; each note higher than the last. Suddenly, a pair of whinnying is heard, followed by the thrashing of bushes, as two horses quickly emerge from the forest, trotting over to Wraithe and Terra. It is their horses, having returned upon recognizing Wraithe's call.

"Let's go, the tavern's collapse should take them awhile to escape, we can put distance between us and them, to warn WestSkye of what's coming!" urges Wraithe quickly mounting atop his horse.

"Why must we lead them there?!" voices Anna forwardly in reply. "For more people to die? We should flee; not guide them to another city!" Frustrated, Wraithe pulls his horse about, turning to Anna.

"It is not the city we put in jeopardy, but the whole of Skye if we don't prepare them; that city, is the only sanctuary to host the white lotus!" Wraithe answers stoutly in reasoning. Immediately, Anna's eyes widen.

"What??" whimpers Anna in disbelief. "So, they know about the lotus?" she goes on to ask.

"Not simple folk, but those with ties to the order; the city's council, within it's chambers lies a sanctuary; the only refuge of the white lotus other than the garden," he goes on to add.

"So, you knew about it?" murmurs Anna in saying, looking to him in disdain. Angered, Wraithe bounds from his horse, trudging up to her.

"Listen girl, I tire of your insolence, the fate of Skye hangs within your blood and the capture of that sanctuary, your meaningless discoveries mean nothing at this time, put aside this stubbornness of yours so we can actually do some good! The entity gave these to you, so damnit, PROTECT THEM!" scolds Wraithe hurriedly in reply. Meanwhile, Terra rolls her whistle reluctantly at this tongue-lashing. Wraithe turns away, mounting his horse once again, leaving behind a speechless Anna.

Terra then walks up from behind, placing her hand upon Anna's shoulder. "Hey, come on," she nods to her horse. "You!" she calls, looking to Siff, "Go with him!" Siff nervously glances over to Wraithe.

"B-But…" he whimpers speechlessly.

"It's okay, you'll be fine," tells Terra casually mounting and helping Anna upon her horse. Nervous, Siff proceeds over to Wraithe, joining atop his horse, and with that, the four head off, leaving behind the hidden garden and remnants of their campsite. As they lead through the forest, Anna nudges to Terra.

"How'd you survive with him?" she goes on to ask. Terra chuckles silently to her with a smirk.

Finally, she turns to her in saying. "He's pretty simple, follow his orders and you won't hear it much! You know, he's not nearly as bad as he seems. He taught me all I know! I was abandoned, no parents, no kin, just a little girl roaming the paths. Until one day, I was SO hungry, and there was this market in the middle of the village. One particular seller; a Mr. Carson, a rather miserable round fellow… would always have the finest fruits in all of the village," giggles Terra in telling.

"No, don't tell me you did what I think you did?!" laughs Anna in reply, capturing the attention of Siff, who looks back to them, shrugging at being left out.

"I had to, I was too hungry… so anyways, I ran up to his table as he was serving one of the villagers, and he saw me! Immediately, I panicked, grabbing a couple of the fruits and ran. It was then, I learned to never underestimate anyone. I got caught!" laughs Terra in saying. "Even worse, I had also dropped a few of the fruits along my escape. I was this close to getting the disciplining of my life," she winces in gesture. "But Wraithe saw me. long story short, he paid Carson for the food and watched over me while he was in the village. He said he helped me because he saw my 'determination to survive.' When it was time for him to leave, he couldn't get rid of me. So, he allowed me on his journey, and from there, taught me everything I know. How to survive, protect myself, right from wrong… and for that, I'm grateful," ends Terra in telling. Anna then ponders in thought. Seeing this, Terra continues. "I say this because the reason he's like that with you, is because he sees that you are special; you are the child of his closest fellow knight, and the living vessel of the white lotus! You must protect yourself!" adds Terra earnestly, refocusing her sights ahead.

The midday's heat wears upon the group, until Wraithe finally calls them to a halt. "We stop here for a few moments, relieve yourselves quickly! Allow the horses break; find brief shade; then we continue!" he tells, stepping from his horse. Terra taps at Anna, and the three quickly follow orders. Terra quickly tending to the horses, and Anna checking on Siff.

"Hey, you okay?" she asks Siff, as they seat along a fallen tree trunk.

Wiping some of the ash and dirt of his face, he answers lowly. "Yeah, I'm fine, it's just so much to take in right now." Meanwhile,

Anna comforts him, gently rubbing along his shoulders. "Anna, our village is destroyed; the lycans have destroyed the very balance of Skye and we are being hunted down by their leader himself! Anna, we are not ready for all this! I AM NOT READY FOR ALL THIS!" he sniffles worriedly. Unable to answer, Anna simply continues, rubbing at his shoulders. Suddenly, Wraithe who sits alone sharpening his sword, gets to his feet and walks off into the forest. Anna sees him wander off, and for a moment, she has a thought.

Suddenly, Siff taps twice at her lap. "Hey," he mutters, "I'm going for a walk, I need a breath." He then gets up and proceeds to walk off.

"Hey, try not to wander off too much, okay?" tells Anna softly in reply. Siff turns to her, with a silent nod and heads off into the forest. Anna then starts off in the direction of Wraithe. As she hurriedly makes her way through the trees, using them as cover. She glimpses him heading further up a small hill. There, Wraithe lingers along the hill's top, standing still among his thoughts. Creeping up from behind, Anna watches as he draws his sword. Wraithe silently looks about the blade; then lostly towards the sky. Something appears to consume his mind. There, he remains, lost in thought; however, Anna having seen enough turns away, leading off back to camp. Surprised, having witnessed seeing the hardened warrior, Wraithe, appearing distraught.

Meanwhile, Siff continues to explore the nearby forest. he hears the beautiful chirping and whistling of birds within the canopy above. Their delicate tune, slowly soothes away his anxiety. Looking up enjoying the sun's rays as he strolls along, he finds himself also beginning to whistle. As he moves further along, the birds' song changes. Siff's exact whistle suddenly resounds in the forest about him. Puzzled, he whistles again. Yet, as before, his exact tones are repeated among the chirping and whistling of the birds. Laughing in discovery, he continues, whistling a different tune, and quickly listening for the birds' response. Again, the birds repeat his exact tune. Siff continues on, hearing as their resounds ring nearby. He then decides to search for his 'songbirds.' He whistles lowly, as he clears the brush, as a flapping noise is heard landing behind a nearby thicket. Carefully attempting not to startle his 'friend,' he slowly clears away the bushes, and into view comes a small brown bird, sitting along a branch, a few feet above him.

It is a peculiar creature, with feathers appearing rough, with rigid bumps and buildups along its wings and body. Although small, it has sturdy stature, crowned with a helmet of hardened bone. Siff fascinates himself in the earthy fowl, and whistles once more, waiting to hear its beautiful sound. Yet again, the bird repeats the notes in gentle chirping.

"You're not so bad... are you?" mutters Siff staring into its hollow-dark eyes. Suddenly, it let's out a loud, hostile screech, followed by a chorus of the same screech, as Siff looks up towards the lively canopy. As he looks back towards the fowl, it dives towards him. Immediately, Siff ducks, as the bird hurls forcefully into the ground. However, it appears totally unharmed. Panting in surprise of almost being pummeled in the face. He quickly backs away, when another heavy landing sounds near his feet. It is followed by another, startling him once more, as he quickly traces backwards. Looking up, he witnesses a plague of birds, carrying along a loud, hostile screech, as they lift from the canopy up ahead, rising above the forest; their direction swiftly changing towards him.

"OHH SHII...!" he voices, quickly turning away in fleeing, as the thudding sounds of diving birds, sound behind his every step. Siff ducks and weaves along the trees, inches away from the hostile attacks of the flock, frantically fleeing in return to the others.

Meanwhile, back at where they are gathered, Terra has nearly fully packed all their belongings, as Anna looks around, realizing there is no sign of Siff. Finally, she looks over to Terra, who walks nearby to collect the last items.

"Hey, have you seen Siff, has he returned?"

Terra turns to her in reply. "No, I saw him last when you both were talking." Footsteps are heard approaching from behind, as Anna quickly turns, seeing Wraithe coming nearby. He walks by her towards his horse.

"We must return to the journey," he informs. Wraithe then pauses, stopping by the pair, as he turns to them in question. "Where is the boy?" he utters. Seconds later, a series of familiar screeches peaks his and Terra's ears, as the two immediately lock eyes.

"Listen…" utters Terra to Anna, who quickly lends her waiting ear. Anna then hears a familiar voice crying out, as it gains closer.

"Siff!" she murmurs in discovery. "He's coming?!"

Meanwhile, Terra quickly stuffs her handful into her bag, "Yeah, he is, and he's bringing 'friends' with him," scoffs Terra reluctantly.

"What?!" questions Anna, seeing Terra hurrying off to her horse.

"Screamers," answers Terra straightly, tying the bag to her saddle, "Some call them 'stonebirds;' highly territorial; they're one of the reasons this route is never taken… HURRY! Get to Wraithe, we must leave as soon as your friend arrives!" urges Terra hastily. Quickly, Anna darts over to Wraithe, as Terra also mounts her horse. With a whip of his reins, Wraithe starts off, meanwhile, Terra lingers for Siff's arrival. As his panicked screams are heard approaching, she glimpses the shadowy plague of fowls approaching above the canopy.

"Shit," she curses, "Come on!" Terra calls out to Siff hurriedly, when seconds later, Siff thrashes from the bush, immediately met by Terra, who rushes by lending her hand. Grabbing onto her quickly, she pulls him onto the horse, and the four race off, in escape of the 'screamers.' Zooming through the appearing trees, the rains of diving birds blanket their every move.

"How do we get rid of them?!" screams Anna in question, hugging tighter onto Wraithe.

"They're territorial! They think us a threat, they won't stop until we fully leave the area!" he yells in reply over the loud thudding sounds. As they flee, branches overhead come crashing down, as dirt hurls from the birds' diving impacts. The plague of fowls finally shadows over them.

"Don't these things feel anything?!" voices Siff to Terra, taking glance above them.

"I don't know, but I don't plan on getting struck by one!" she tells, drawing them away from an oncoming branch. The four continue to flee, when finally, the plague's violent attacks slowly begins to recede.

"I think they're stopping!" exclaims Siff, turning behind them, as he looks to the sky, seeing no sign of the pursuing flock.

"We may have left their territory," suggests Terra in reply. They continue a while longer, putting further distance between them and the 'screamers,' until Wraithe gestures them to cease, seeing no sign of threat. The four finally slow down, coming to a calm within the forest. "What part of not wandering off do you not understand?" turns Terra to Siff mildly in question.

"I didn't know they would've attacked?!" shrugs Siff innocently in saying.

"Nonsense boy! We not too long ago left a forest that was supposed to have not existed! Those fowls were mere deterrence's from its location; they were hostile obviously because we were too close to Equilibrius," scolds Wraithe in telling. "Nonetheless, we've escaped, we have to keep moving, no telling when the lycans will once again be on the move."

With that, Wraithe whips at his reins, resuming lead, as the four continue ahead, until finally, they reach the forest's edge, atop a small hill, overlooking a vast green prairie. Wraithe appears alert, and without notice, swiftly dismounts his horse. This immediately puts the others at concern. Quickly, they all do the same, watching as he kneels and begins to crawl through the waist high grass. Leading ahead, Wraithe signals the others to follow. The three stoops to their knees, and begin silently crawling up from behind, leaving the horses at the forest's edge.

Turning to them, Wraithe calls, "Anna," signalling her to his side.

"He's calling you, go," whispers Terra to her, crouched near her side.

Puzzled, Anna obediently starts creeping forward, worriedly arriving at the warrior's side.

"What is it?" asks Anna nervously keeping low. Wraithe however, remains silent, and slowly rises to his knees, then feet.

"Over there, near the hilltop, in the low grass," details Wraithe, pointing out across the valley. Meanwhile, Anna struggles to pinpoint his finding.

"Is it the lycans? Have they caught up to us?" she questions shakily in reply.

"No, a hare," answers Wraithe plainly. "Show me what you can do, by your bow, we will eat tonight."

"B-But, I don't see anything," complains Anna, looking out across the valley, seeing only the wind's waves dancing through the sea of tall grass.

"Look harder," urges Wraithe patiently. "Use your senses." Pulling in a calm breath, Anna concentrates fiercely, looking carefully across the valley. Suddenly, she glimpses movement, a fluffy white ball, bounces quietly in the distance, nibbling along the grass, it is a hare.

"I see it," she exclaims quietly.

"Good," answers Wraithe. "Use your bow."

"I have none," mutters Anna in reply. Wraithe silently gestures to her staff, given to her by Mitrefys. Anna looks down to the runic staff in discouragement. "I have never hunted before," She mutters discouragingly.

Hearing this, Wraithe quickly turns to her. "For fear of failing, you give up so easily, who will follow you?" Anna however, continues to hesitate. "If you do not shoot, we don't eat," adds Wraithe bluntly, "Now come… Show me!"

Closing her eyes, she wraps both hands about her staff, and gives a great shake, 'willing' her staff into a large, sturdy bow. As she opens her eyes, she sees the runic bow with arrow fixed against its string. Anna admires the mystic etchings detailed along its grip, Meanwhile, Wraithe also is taken by surprise, seeing the staff's swift transformation. Realizing she must strike before the hare escapes, Anna quickly positions, taking aim.

Knelt beside her, Wraithe whispers calmly into her ear, "Keep calm and breathe."

Anna then takes a deep breath, timing her heartbeat. When suddenly, a flock of birds sheltered within the tall grass takes off into the sky, startling the hare, causing it to flee.

"It's moving! It's getting away!" exclaims Anna discouragingly.

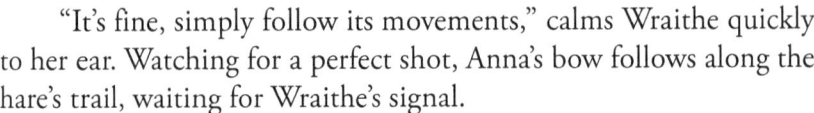

"It's fine, simply follow its movements," calms Wraithe quickly to her ear. Watching for a perfect shot, Anna's bow follows along the hare's trail, waiting for Wraithe's signal.

"It's getting away!" she exclaims, growing even more nervous.

"I know! Not yet!" he answers, with eyes following along. "HOOOLD... Now!" he confirms loudly.

In the space of a breath, Anna releases, their eyes follow the arrow as it strafes through the air; its thin shadow riding along the waves of grass. Suddenly, the hare is stopped. Anna's eyes widen and mouth gapes, as she leaps in excitement. "I got it!" she exclaims, quickly turning back to Siff, who being knelt beside Terra; jumps to his feet equally excited, as Terra also gives a smile of approval.

"Good," Wraithe replies remaining composed. "Retrieve it... it will serve us well." Anna hops in excitement, rushing through the tall grass to retrieve the kill. Moments later, she nabs the hare, scurrying her way back to the three.

"Lemme see! Lemme see!" urges Siff excitedly, as the four return to their horses. Anna quickly opens one of the saddlebags, pulling out a short-length rope, which she ties about the hare's body then to the saddle. Once finished, she joins atop Terra's horse.

"Keep moving," utters Wraithe, tapping his heels at his horse, with Siff straddled behind. They make their way across the prairie, traveling a few clicks up a steep hill, leading through the other side of the forest. This would lead them along for another hour and a half. As they near the peak of the hill, Wraithe suddenly dismounts, grabbing his horse's reins, and begins leading it uphill. Seeing this, Terra quickly does the same.

Puzzled, Anna asks openly, "What's wrong?"

"It's the horses," answers Terra in reply, "They're exhausted." Anna listens carefully, hearing its heavy breaths, and swiftly joins them on foot, followed by Siff. Another hour passes, as the four approach the hilltop. A calm, welcoming breeze, steadily flows by them, as they immerse themselves in the breathtaking view.

"Such beauty in a world full of discord," Wraithe tells in a moment of thought.

"I'm thirsty," mentions Anna, quickly searching her satchel for her water jug. She pulls out the ceramic jug, tossing it to her mouth. To her disappointment, there are but two drops, as she finds her jug empty. "We really should look for water," mutters Anna frustratingly.

"She's right," agrees Terra. "The horses haven't had a good drink in almost two days, pretty soon, we won't be able to get a budge out of them."

Wraithe then looks out over the valley and quickly turns to them. "Follow me," he utters, pulling his horse along. They proceed downhill, and into the valley, beneath the relentless heat. Suddenly, Anna feels a sensation, her staff, begins to pulsate. Holding her staff to her face, her eyes light up.

"Everyone, look!" she exclaims, showing the Omni's odd blue color change.

"How is it doing that?" fascinates Siff curiously.

"I-I don't know," tells Anna staring in wonderment.

Seeing this, Wraithe walks over, grabbing hold of her forearm. He then turns Anna to the right, to the direction of west, her staff then hues a slightly darker shade of blue. "Interesting," he murmurs. Wraithe then switches over, turning her to the left, in the direction of east. Suddenly, the staff returns to its runic silver. Wraithe again positions her facing west. When suddenly.

"Whoa!" blurts Siff, as he looks down. "Anna look!" he exclaims, pointing toward her hands. Concerned, Anna looks towards her hands, turning over to her palms, seeing as the lotus symbol, imprinted into her skin glows similar as the blue along the staff.

Wraithe swiftly turns to the horizon. "We must continue west!" he tells the three, starting towards his horse.

"W-wait what?!" asks Anna reluctantly as he darts by. "Weren't we always?"

"Yes, but for now, we will follow the Omni… It's showing us the way!" he further explains.

Confused, Anna turns to him in question, "The way? The way to where?"

"Water," answers Terra bluntly.

"That staff, your markings, they're like a compass," Wraithe goes on to add, as he leads off.

Amazed, Anna looks over the strange markings on her palms, measuring them up to her staff. They continue on, in the direction of west, when suddenly, Anna notices something strange, her imprints, as well as her staff have begun blinking.

"Wait!" she halts abruptly. "Look at this!" she quickly shows to them. Seeing her fixated towards her staff, the three halt immediately. To their astonishment, her bold, blue glow suddenly begins to flicker.

"I take it we must be getting close?" suggests Terra, turning to Wraithe.

"A plausible guess, I suppose. We must simply follow it!" Wraithe replies, looking about their surroundings. For a short while, they tarry through the forest, until finally, they approach a vast opening. Peering through the brush, they make their way across the stubble river rocks. A lift of relief dawns over them, as familiar ripples ring through their ears. Exhausted, and thirsty, they rush to the riverbank, its crystal waters reflecting the glimmering rays of the sun. Anna and Siff race towards the shallow waters; soon to be overtaken by the horses, galloping to the waters for a drink. Siff quickly slows, looking to Anna.

"Hey?!" he calls. "Do you actually think it's safe?" he asks, watching as the horses continue to drink.

"What do you mean?" mutters Anna in question.

"I mean the water… do you think it safe to drink?" mentions Siff, looking to her in concern. Anna pauses for a moment, turning her sights towards the pristine river. She hadn't considered if it might be unsafe to consume.

Terra then walks by the pair. "It's okay to drink the water, you actually can go right ahead. Horses only drink clean water… so it's fine!" Immediately, Anna and Siff turn, rushing towards the waters, and diving into the shallows. Both excitedly dip their heads beneath the waters for a drink. Wraithe casually joins them, reaching for an old wine bottle tucked within his satchel. He walks near the waters, kneeling to take a few much-needed mouthfuls. He then gets to his feet, wading further into the river, dipping his bottle beneath the surface and lifting it to pour onto his face.

Meanwhile, Terra cups her hands in the shallows, taking a drink as she sits along the shores. She removes her leather boots, and relieves her bag from the journey, tossing it along the riverbank. Finally, she places her hot, restless feet into the soothing, cool waters. She then steps further into the waters, diving below its surface, joining the others within the river. An hour passes, and the four linger near the river's bank.

"It's so peaceful," Siff utters to Anna, gleefully splashing water in her direction.

Anna laughs in enjoyment, until she looks ahead, glimpsing Wraithe leaving the river and walking onto shore. There he sits, tying his leather boots onto his feet. Anna sees him digging into his satchel, pulling out a smooth, black stone. He then picks up his blade and begins moving the stone up and down, along the blade's edge, sharpening it.

"Hey, I'll be right back," tells Anna quickly leaving the waters. She then proceeds over to Wraithe, who continues in sharpening his sword.

"Hey?" she waives, approaching near. Wraithe shrugs silently in reply. "Well… so much for a greeting," mutters Anna lowly in reluctance. Meanwhile, Wraithe continues, sharpening his blade, seeming oblivious to her presence. She moves closer, sitting across from him, waiting for his attention. Moments go by, and Wraithe doesn't utter a word. finally, Anna motions closer.

Clearing her throat, Anna opens in saying, "Hey, so… is there a more specific plan for what we're going to do when we arrive in Westskye?"

Without looking up from sharpening his sword, Wraithe answers bluntly. "We, but only a few hours ago, received instructions from a fate to protect you. Watching, as she gifted… YOU! The white lotus!" he points. "Don't you see?! The gift of immortality practically flows through your veins now. A target has now been set on your head! Who knows what will come after you, or what even to expect… And that child; no experience can prepare you for!" utters

Wraithe stoutly in saying. He then stands to his feet and begins to leave. Yet, Anna follows after him.

"Well, can you tell me of how Skye was once before?" she asks humbly. This stops Wraithe, who slowly turns to face her.

Wraithe mumbles indistinctly, as he quietly walks by her, taking a seat along a large stone. clearing his throat, he begins to tell. "The land of Skye was once unified and thriving. For a while, it maintained equilibrium, before dispersing into smaller, shared regions spanning across the landscape. Each would then colonize a corner: The north, south, east, and west. For ages the great region thrived, resources were plentiful, trade was high, and there was peace. The order spoke of the 'greater beings,' referring to them as the 'fates.' Their power trumping the strength of mortal men! They would be the powers that would soon subject the people of Skye. When news arrived of two powerful beings seeking to control the land, Skye grew worried, we had gotten complacent. We had entrusted our lives to these powerful forces that could overthrow us at any moment. Your father, Arthur, and a few others gathered the finest hunters, and wisest men in all of Skye, and proposed a knighthood, forging what would become the 'old Order.' They would be the defense that would save Skye, should those very fates seek harm upon mankind."

"Fenrifrys, the 'fate' of the lycans, a powerful race of halfbreeds, donning the likeness of man, whilst harboring the ability to transfigure into wolves. They were the first to turn on us! Fenrifrys sought out his fellow fates Mitrefys, and Noctrifys and demanded to see the white lotus, the flower from the tree of the beginning. One that hasn't withered since the beginning of time. Mitrefys knew this would lead him to take of it, he would be immortal, and possibly overthrow the others. So, the mother fate bid him nowhere near it. Fenrifrys knew he couldn't beat the two fates, so he departed, promising to return with an army of subjects to attain the flower's power. He then went out, garnering followers, and promising them 'a great redemption' and immortality. For the first time, Skye felt threatened; within itself… its very people, turning to the teachings of Fenrifrys. It wasn't long before he did as he said, forming an Order, three times the size of 'the Old,' their baptism into it, however, a blood pact."

"This sparked a fear in the olde Order, its men petrified of Fenrifrys. Many of the knights tried to flee. However, your father sought me out, upon meeting him briefly along one of the cities. Although, I was reluctant, I joined, I saw that running from it made it no better, they would only continue to be more powerful, and we would no longer stand a chance. Your father decided, he himself, would go and consult with the fates, a feat no mortal has ever done before. Many of the fellow knights thought him mad, I did too, all except Maurdis, his closest companion. Arthur left, promising to return. The knights would pray the fates guide him safely towards them, as this journey was unheard of, the garden of the beginning was never told to be discovered by man, but he found it!"

"Your father had been gone for about two weeks, many of the knights grew concerned if he would return at all, but there was a new reality we would have to then face, the treachery of Fenrifrys and his army. Arthur hadn't returned for some time, and the Order received news of an attack in Southskye, we would finally have to prepare for war! Maurdis stood with us, although the quickest to pursue brash action, he encouraged the Order to intervene before the lycans grew confident and siege the nearby city of Westskye, which was to be the main center of trade within the vast valley. Many were reluctant at first but Fenrifrys' lycan army proceeded north of Southskye devastating another settlement along their wake, it was clear the north and west would be next!"

The Order luckily intervened, they would make their stand against the lycans and Fenrifrys. Arthur finally returned, and when he did, he had an odd request, one that would test each of us. Arthur would propose a timed attack on the Blood Moon, a period where the lycans are most powerful, yet most vulnerable; however, a single bite would turn a man into the very thing he dreads! A lycan!"

"With this new, frightening reality, the knights would have to unite the leaders of Skye, the Order quickly rallied behind your father, who appealed to the leaders, convincing them that if they didn't ally together, Skye would fall. It wasn't long before, Fenrifrys and 'his pact' arrived. Arthur would lead them at the forefront, in a stand against the enemy. Maurdis and I, stood at his side and the battle would last three days; with the lycans maintaining the balance of power for most of the conflict. Fenrifrys would be separated from the pact, and cornered by the roundtable's knights, the leaders of the olde Order. in the end, each would fall, none proving a match for Fenrifrys. It wasn't until one of the fates, Mitrefrys, intervened, and with a final strike, their leader, Lord Fenrifrys fell, and Skye had finally won."

"Although we had won, the victory was insurmountable to the so many lives lost. The lycans went into remission, their numbers scattered across the land of Skye. Attacks were few, and in between, however, the knights of the now revenant Order, saw to it that any lycan captured were slain. For years after, they continued in protection of Skye and all its people and for a while, there was peace. The revenants had restored order. However, there was a treachery within the order. As told earlier, Maurdis was abandoned by the order, having been left to die, a mercy granted to him by your father, since he had been bitten during that final, dreadful night. Having survived, Maurdis abandoned the valiant knighthood, seeking out the teachings of the 'fallen fate.' In short, Fenrifrys granted the wishes of Maurdis, gave him power, acclaim and even made him his second in command. Maurdis would swear his allegiance to the Pact, restoring some of its lost power, and Skye has been at unrest ever since."

"That's really something… to have evaded one treachery, only to encounter another," mutters Anna lowly in thought.

"It never stops, young one," adds Wraithe in reply. "It was because of the Order, I lost many of privileges. My daughter… my wife," he continues with heavy sigh. "After the lycans defeat… I returned home; upon my arrival, I discovered everything had been destroyed! Even so, I had only worried for my family. It took me three days, through immense rain and storm, to find my wife torn apart, and my daughter laying mangled within her arms."

There is a silence among them, as Wraithe brushes his knees getting to his feet. Suddenly, "Get up!" he commands sternly to

Anna. Utterly taken by surprise, she is puzzled by this strange request; however, she reluctantly gets to her feet.

"Now, show me what you can do!" demands Wraithe, tossing Anna, her staff.

"Wait...What?" answers Anna puzzled in disbelief, "You want me to fight you?"

"Your staff," points Wraithe towards the omni, "HOLD IT UP!" Anna shakily holds up the staff, taking an unsure stance. "Now!" roars Wraithe, "DEFEND YOURSELF!" Wraithe charges towards her twirling his sword to strike. Meanwhile, Anna frighteningly makes a blind swing towards him and there is a loud clash as their blades meet. Opening her eyes, she holds a glimmering, two-edged sword. Anna glances shockingly at Wraithe, who remains undeterred from their battle.

"Fight back!" he commands, drawing back his sword to attack once more. His blunt strike immediately places her block off balance, as she clumsily stumbles backwards.

"W-Wait!" she exclaims, continuing to stumble back, as his strikes advance.

"In battle, victory is decided by one's will," he interjects continuing to joust and strike with his sword. Having had enough, Anna finally retaliates, hurling a few reckless swings towards him. Suddenly, she missteps forward, diving towards him with her blade, however, with a shift of his footing, he parries her attack, smoothly rolling her off with his shoulder, causing her to trip to the ground, losing her sword.

Wraithe then stands over her, his sword pointed towards her for submission. "Will you be defeated so easily?"

To her knees, with head bowed, as if, in defeat; she subtly looks for her sword. She then glimpses the blade near her left. Grabbing a handful of gravel and dust, she quickly hurls it towards his face. Wraithe guards, as Anna seizes her chance, rolling near her sword. Brushing the dust from his eyes, he darts after her. Getting hold of her weapon, Anna glimpses his reflection gleaming from the sword's silver blade.

"NOOOO!" she war cries, turning about, in an attempt to block his strike.

"Good guard…" mentions Wraithe, impressed at her awareness. "However, you are still beaten," he informs confidently.

"Not quite," Anna smirks in reply, glaring down towards his waist. As Wraithe looks down, he glimpses another blade, poised towards his loins. He is defeated, realizing Anna's upper hand; Wraithe yields with no resistance, removing his sword, he steps back, allowing her to her feet. Meanwhile, Terra smirks, as her and Siff look on from the sidelines.

"Clever," utters Wraithe, sheathing his sword. "We'll see, if your wit aids you in actual combat."

Terra then leaves the river, having been entertained by the sparring. She returns to readying the horses, when suddenly, she hears a feint rustling, and the snapping of twigs sounding nearby. Peeking round the horses, she hears the panting of encroaching snarls.

"GUYS!! MOVE!!" Terra yells out to the others, quickly drawing her sword from tucked within the saddlebag. Immediately, Anna and the other's heads turn, seeing Terra hurled over by a fierce lycan. They quickly rush over to aid her, when, with two plunges of her sword at its underbelly, the lycan yelps falling beside her, returning to a human's body. Wraithe and Anna quickly assist Terra to her feet when… "Oww!!" she cries out painfully, unable to place her right foot to the ground.

"What's wrong?!" exclaims Anna, diving to support her upright.

"I-It's my ankle! It's my ankle! I think it's sprained," grunts Terra painfully, biting at her lower lip. Meanwhile, Wraithe glances towards the lifeless body.

"It's an omega, sent to scout where we are, trust that more are on the way! We must leave at once, Maurdis hunts us!" informs Wraithe hastily. "Let the boy ready the other horse!" Quickly, Wraithe and Anna pull Terra over to Wraithe's horse. "Take the boy on the other!" he tells, hoisting Terra upon his horse.

"Here!" calls Terra to Siff, "Take this! Don't let any of them near us!" she tosses Siff her arrow bag and bow. As Siff catches them, he looks up unsurely.

"B-But I've never shot before!" fumbles Siff in saying. Suddenly, a commotion of rustling, followed by a chorus of angry growls sounding in the distance.

"No time!" exclaims Anna quickly, "They're here! Siff! You can do this! Exhale and release! We need you!" shakes Anna earnestly at his shoulders. Siff nods confidently, as they both rush upon the other horse, and immediately, the four take off.

"They're going to try to flank us! Keep your eyes on anything that moves! Do not hesitate!" instructs Wraithe firmly, leading off into the forest. They follow along the river, when finally, the lycans emerge from the forest, panting after them. "There they are! Fire!" he orders.

Siff draws back his arrow against the bowstring, taking aim, and fires. Piercing seamlessly through the breeze, it strikes one of the lycans in pursuit, toppling it to a halt. However, this does nothing to slow their pursuit.

"Great shot, Siff!" exclaims Anna, taking a quick glance back. "Keep them off us!"

Again, Siff takes another shot, this time falling short, strafing the fur off one of the lycan's shank. This appears to aggravate the lycans, who then increase their pursuit. Meanwhile, Wraithe notices a shallow pass through the river.

"Over there!" shouts Wraithe, "We can slow their pursuit through the river!" Immediately, he changes direction, and they race for the river's shallow. Their horses gallop through the waters, while the lycans struggle, having to swim after them. Once reaching upon the other side, the four head straight for the bushes. "Stay close! You must keep after us! This forest is called Nostalgia; it is not like the others! You see things, Hear things, from the past! Forgotten memories; all of it, they will tempt you, stay close!"

"Whatever you do, keep your thoughts clear, even the slightest feeling of nervousness or fear; the forest can draw you in!" grunts Terra in telling. "There'll be voices, but not random, they'll be of lost loved ones; a mother… a father… a sibling, or even a mate, for whatever relationship there is, whichever one is felt the most… that is the one that will follow you!"

"Allow nothing to cloud your conscience," adds Wraithe strongly. Siff tries to remain focus, as the lycans continue behind their every step. Moments later, the lycans catch up to them, flanking the four along their sides; using the cover of the forest to protect against Siff's aim.

"I can't get a good shot! It's the trees! They're getting in the way!" exclaims Siff frustratingly.

"KEEP TRYING!" tells Wraithe, cutting a sharp right turn, avoiding a sudden drop below. Anna then quickly pulls at their horse, turning swiftly, as one of the lycans leaps towards them, grazing by their horse and toppling down the falloff below. Immediately, the air around them pierces their skin with a sudden, sharp chill. Their breaths instantly become heavier, due to the air's humid, and thick aura. Racing further ahead, the lively forest trees change; appearing gloomier, with lesser cover, as large thorns and thistles web their way throughout their lifeless branches. The howling and snarling of the lycans breathes after them; when a cloudy, eerie fog, finally encompasses about the forest. It is so thick; Anna and Siff can scarcely see Wraithe's horse slightly ahead of them.

"Stay behind us!!" yells Wraithe, when suddenly, in a flurry of wind, Anna and Siff hurl over a runoff, toppling down its side into the muddy forest below. The forest is dark, as its eerie fog reaches also above the canopy, guarding away the sun's light. However, even more unusual, is the fog's luminescent glow.

Chapter 6
An Untimely Meeting

"Aghh… shit!" curses Anna, mustering to her knees from the mud. "Siff, are you okay?" she turns to ask. There is nothing about her but the silence of the forest. "Siff?! Siff?!" she blindly feels along the mud around her, as her fingers run along a straight, slender metal, it is her staff. Anna then gets to her feet and looks about at the fog, eerily lighting her way. However, there is no sign of Siff or their horse. Suddenly, she hears the distant snarls and howls of the lycans, searching behind the silhouette of fog. Anna carefully minds her steps, creeping along the forest, until she glimpses the lycan's shadows and quickly darts behind the cover of a tree trunk. "They won't let up," she mutters quietly to herself. She feels a sharp pain at her palm and holds it to her face. There is a nasty, open gash across her palm; however, her eyes widen as she witnesses something incredible. The blood from the wound recedes back into the cut, as her skin, within seconds, repairs! Her skin quickly seals away the wound, until there is absolutely no sign of injury.

"Wow…" she murmurs in amazement, looking over her palm. Suddenly, the panting of the lycans sounds closer. Peeping around the tree, Anna and one of the lycans lock eyesight. Immediately, it starts towards her. Quickly, she flees the tree, scampering further into the forest. Suddenly, a great howl is heard, as the lycan calls to its pursuit. Anna clumsily trips, stumbling into the mud; meanwhile, the lycan gains. As Anna turns, she glimpses the lycan bounding towards her, when in a quick second, a loud shriek is heard, as something rushes through the air, toppling the lycan aside. With a sudden yelp, the lycan is put down. Anna looks up from the ground, and sees a blind, hairless, pale-skin creature, staring her in the face.

"Shrieks!" she whimpers to herself in saying. However, the creature appears to have not fully sensed her presence, as it lingers, searching about the nearby area. Anna nervously looks for her staff; it lies over by a large tree. Losing interest, the shriek returns to the male's body. Anna then begins slowly crawling towards her staff. With a snap of a twig, she quickly stops, as this draws the creature's attention. Near the body, the shriek whiffs the air, attempting to sense a nearby presence. Meanwhile, Anna slowly continues to crawl towards her staff. She nears closer, when there is another loud snap, as a twig gives in, below her chest. Suddenly, the creature spins, charging towards her. Anna frantically gets to her feet, darting towards her staff. She dives for the weapon, spinning around, as the shriek leaps upon her, impaling itself upon the edge of her spear. It shrieks painfully, as it gnashes and thrashes to get at her. Anna then delivers a final thrust, and with that, shoves the creature off with her staff.

There is a choir of shrieks following as she gets to her feet, her mind immediately races with the thought of Siff. She flees through the forest, running blindly, in hopes of finding Siff and the others. Anna stops suddenly, as the feint yelp of one of the lycans, sounds nearby. A flurry of shrieks, head over to its cry, as Anna hears the disturbing screams of the male. Seizing her chance, she races on, until finally, she glimpses Siff's arrow bag; the one given to him by Terra. Surely, he must be nearby! Anna thinks to herself. She quickly tosses the bag over her shoulder and continues.

Meanwhile...

Siff trudges nervously through the forest, encountering a wall of bush, with a thin way through. He steps into the brush, inching his way through. "Ow!" he yelps painfully, picking at his left arm, and pulling out a large thorn. "I hate this place," he mutters to himself. Hearing the distant howls of the lycans in the forest about him, he swallows a sharp chill as he frightfully moves on. His sights nervously steer about the forest, as his anxiety builds, in hopes of him avoiding any sudden attack.

Seconds later, a cool breeze flows by, carrying along a familiar voice. "Siff?!" calls the voice to him in distress. Instantly, he spins about, alarmed by its call.

"W-who's there?" he whimpers in reply. The voice resounds once more. "SIFF…HELP ME!" Siff recognizes the familiar voice; there's no mistaking it; it is Anna! Quickly, he races after her.

"Anna! Anna! Hold on, I'm coming to you!" he exclaims following along her screams.

"Siff! Hurry!" Anna cries out desperately. Siff thrashes through the bushes, as hidden thorns tear at his skin, he hears the receding howls of the lycans in the distance yet continues to her aid.

"Hold on! I'm almost there!" he calls out in reply, creeping over a small rise. He glimpses a human shadow within the fog, rested upon a nearby tree.

"Anna?" calls Siff unsurely, as he approaches.

"S-Siff…I searched e-everywhere f-for you, p-please help me," Anna coughs faintly, lying lifeless at the large tree's roots. Without hesitation, Siff rushes over, seeing her clothes lacerated and clawed, her body covered with many bite marks, torn through her flesh.

"Nooooo!" he whimpers grievously, tearfully leant over her body. Wrapping her head in his arms, he caresses her head.

"S-SIFF," coughs Anna weakly, looking into his eyes. "I don't want to die." With eyes welling of tears, Siff remains silent, helplessly watching as his friend takes her final breath.

"ANNA!" his eyes pour, shaking to wake her. "Anna!" his voice trembles again. "Anna…." he chokes tearfully. "Please… don't leave me!" Softly, he rests his tear-soaked face upon her forehead.

All the while, Anna diligently searches for Siff, scouring through the forest, having not heard or seen any sign of the lycans, neither nocturnals. "Siff!" Anna calls out nearby. "Siff! It's me, where are you!"

A calm wind passes her by, carrying along a voice that stops her right in her steps, as her breaths shorten, and a nervous shiver carries down to her feet. "Why didn't you look for me…?" it whispers calmly into her ear. Anna stiffens, too disturbed to move, standing amidst the forest in disbelief.

"Father?!" whispers Anna to herself breathily. Instantly, a soft hand touches her shoulder, reaching along the passing breeze, as it draws her further into the mysterious fog. Anna swallows a sharp chill, slowly turning around. She is alone, watching as the luminescent clouds dance gracefully about the trees. Alarmed, she hears movement nearby, as another hand touches her shoulder from behind. Frightened, she spins around, squinting her sights ahead of her. Anna glimpses a male crouched to the ground. Immediately, her grip tightens about her staff. She slowly creeps towards him, until slowing to a stop. She listens carefully, hearing his heavy breaths, and sees him holding at his side.

"Hello?" Anna mutters unsurely. Immediately, the male stops, turning his head slightly to hear. "Hello?" she calls once more.

"A-Anna?" the male replies in question. "A-Anna is that really you?!" he adds in disbelief. Surely, Anna could not mistake this familiar voice and quickly moves in closer. She walks around him and into his view. Anna's breath escapes, nose flares, as her eyes widen with tears. It is her father, holding at his left side in agony. Looking into his dark brown eyes, her tears instantly give way.

"Anna?!" grunts her father in smiling. "I've missed you, young one." He reaches gently, wiping a tear from her cheek.

"W-What happened? W-What's wrong? I can help you!" she stammers tearfully, reaching for his wound. Her father's tunic and robe are torn up, soaked with blood.

"It was Maurdis, I fought him and lost," he grunts attempting to sit up. Quickly, Anna leans to help, fixing him leant upon the tree.

"W-What? W-Well I can help you, I'm with Wraithe, I can find him! He can help you!" exclaims Anna anxiously.

He looks into her concerned eyes, "It's okay," he whispers softly. "It'll be okay, we're safe now, the forest's fog, it shields us from the lycan's senses, I promise they won't find us here."

"B-But what of the 'shrieks'?" tells Anna, looking around them. Her father reaches for her face, gently holding her cheeks in his palms.

"It's okay, I promise, I'll keep you safe, young one," he whispers softly to her with a smile.

"But what about Wraithe, and the others?" Anna goes on to ask.

Her father expression changes, as he goes on to tell, "They've left us! The lycans pursued… they had little chance of escape; so, they had to flee, you and Siff; they've abandoned you both!" he utters, as Anna's face lights up in disbelief.

Finding this strange, Anna then stammers in reply, "B-But they couldn't have, w-we were supposed to warn Westskye, M-Maurdis, he will attack there next, we…"

"Anna, it won't work!" her father argues gravely, "Your warning, fighting back, none of it! The lycans are too powerful; the best decision is to stay here with me! There's nothing more you can do," he tells looking into her eyes. Anna is saddened by his words, as she nods quietly. "Hey," he whispers, tilting her chin up, "It'll be okay, now come on!" he grunts, fixing up against the tree. "Remove the blade from my side," he pulls aside his cloak, revealing a knife, stuck in his side." It is a ghastly sight; however, Anna quickly grips at its handle, preparing to tug.

"Okay," he grunts painfully. "We must hurry, your mother's waiting for us!" Anna suddenly stops, looking into his eyes. "It's fine young one, I'll be okay, you can pull it out," he goes on to mention. Meanwhile, Anna continues to stare peculiarly into his eyes. "W-What's wrong young one?" he goes on to ask. Anna then removes her hand from the blade, and uneasily sits back.

"Who are you?" Anna goes on to ask. Puzzled, her father laughs reluctantly.

"W-What?!" he stutters frivolously, reaching towards her hand.

"I said, who are you?" repeats Anna in demand, drawing her hand from his reach. Meanwhile, her father smiles, as Anna then feels a sharp pain at her wrist. She looks down and to her astonishment, she glimpses the wound at her wrist, bleeding profusely. In helping her father, has she wounded herself? Anna's heart races, as she slowly looks to her father, who wears a sinister grin. She then retreats, slowly getting to her feet, her eyes fixed to him in suspicion. "Who are you?! where are the others? What did you do to them?!!" she shudders horrifically.

"You always told me my mother died when I was younger... what's my mother's name?!" she imposes sternly, drawing back.

"But she escaped! We've found her, your mother's here! Within the forest!! Join us! Join us Anna!" his voice calls distortedly.

Frightened, Anna stumbles back over a stone, falling to the ground. Sitting up, she stares into his chilling grin. Watching as he gathers to his feet, his rent cloak is restored of its tears. The lacerations and wounds about his body instantly heals, as he slowly steps towards her.

"You're NOT MY FATHER! LEAVE ME ALONE!" screams Anna aloud. The male stands there opening wide his mouth, his jaw unnaturally dropping to his chest. Suddenly, there is a violent, powerful gust of wind. As Anna shields her face from the powerful winds, she witnesses her 'father' pulled backwards into the fog. Seconds later, the winds cease. Removing her hands from her face, she looks around at the empty forest. Anna then keels over to her hands in repeating. "It wasn't real, it wasn't real…" she utters. For a few moments, she remains still, breathing in. Until finally, she picks up her staff, as she gets to her feet and presses forward. "I must find Siff, I must find him!" she mutters. Clenching her eyes closed, Anna shuts out the eerie cries of the forest. "It's not real!" she murmurs inwardly. Opening her eyes, she quickly focuses, heading off in search of Siff.

Meanwhile.

Siff mourns over Anna's body, when he is faced with another problem. His attention is drawn to a loud shriek, sounding from within the canopy above. Trembling as he looks up, and around at the ghostly surroundings. Again, the shriek resounds. His eyes search the forest about him, as he looks to Anna's body straddled within his arms. Yet, to his astonishment, she has disappeared; his hands empty, as her absence leaves behind an unforeseen eerie wind. Siff is alone, seemingly surrounded by shrieks.

Suddenly, there is a rustling of the nearby bushes, as Siff hears movement along the trees ahead. His eyes widen in relief, as Anna rushes from the brush. "Siff?!" she exclaims. "Siff! It's me, I've been looking everywhere for you!" Although excited, Siff hesitates. Anna notices this and steps closer. "What's wrong? Siff? It's me! Anna," she goes on to tell.

"How do I know that?" he retorts. Pulling out his short blade in retreat. "I watched you! I watched you die in my arms!" he tells in reply, worriedly looking to the trees above.

"Siff look!" Anna steps closer, revealing her palms. He notices the lotus symbol within her hands. "No matter if the forest plays tricks; it can't mimic a person's abilities, and they certainly cannot mimic my mark," assures Anna in saying. Siff slowly lowers his blade, stepping in to embrace Anna, as the pair offer a breath of relief.

"We have to get out of here!" he hastens to her in telling. "Have you seen…" he barely finishes when suddenly, a shriek is heard from the canopy above. Quickly, Anna pulls them against the tree, as a heavy thud is heard landing along the side of the tree's trunk. Anna looks to Siff, silently placing her finger upon her lips. Siff nods nervously, as she pulls him along the tree, slowly circling away from the approaching shriek. Meanwhile, its loud breaths, draw in the nearby scents, through the three linings along the sides of its nose-like structure. It loudly whiffs closer and closer, following the pair along the tree's side. Siff then clenches tightly at Anna's hand, as its breaths can be heard creeping just around the corner. Anna's staff wields to a silver sword, quickly drawing Siff out of the way. Anna rushes forward, thrusting her blade into the shrieks head, as it peeks about the corner, not before bellowing a loud dying shriek and toppling to the ground. Suddenly, a chorus of similar shrieks follow just beyond the trees ahead, as if called by its cry. Anna nabs Siff's hand and immediately, the two flee.

As they cluelessly scamper through the brush, they both bump into a sturdy object. Looking up, they glimpse a large horse. Turning to them; to the pair's surprise, it is Wraithe and Terra. "Duck!!" orders Wraithe quickly. Lighting and arrow from a torch held within Terra's hand, he fires, as the pair cower to the ground. The arrow whistles, strafing just over their heads. It disappears into the fog and erupts into flames, decimating the nearby area. The crying shrieks of the nocturnals consumed by the flames resounds. Meanwhile, Anna and Siff look on in amazement.

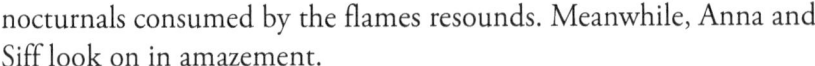

"W-What just happened?!" stammers Anna in disbelief.

"It's the fog, it's burnable, we found that out earlier," scoffs Wraithe reluctantly.

"And nearly killed ourselves in doing so," adds Terra in reply.

"Quickly, we must go!" urges Wraithe hastily, pulling at his horse. Anna and Siff look to each other.

"B-But we lost our horse, we won't be able to keep up!" turns Anna to them in saying. Wraithe then looks ahead to the forest, and quickly utters a loud three-toned whistle. Moments later, it is answered by a familiar whinnying. As the trampling of bushes can be heard approaching. Suddenly, their horse is seen, emerging from the fog. The horse trots near Anna and Siff, who's mouth sits opened.

"It recognized you?!" comments Anna in disbelief. "Over all the other voices?!"

"The forest mimics voices, but not distinct sounds, now hurry!" tells Wraithe whipping at the reins. Quickly, the pair bound upon the steed, starting after Wraithe and Terra.

"Well, why didn't we think of that?!" shrugs Siff reluctantly, fastening tightly to Anna. Suddenly, the thunderous thrashing of bushes sounds behind them, as a horde of shrieks hounds after them.

"Where the hell do these things come from?!" exclaims Anna glancing back at the stampeding creatures.

"They act as a hive! Alone, you may be able to survive one, but once it calls the others, there is no escape; it is like blood in the water," utters Wraithe in reply. "They come by the droves!"

"They appear somewhat human!" mentions Siff, as the pair catch up alongside Wraithe and Terra.

"Nonsense boy," rebuts Wraithe harshly. "You have seen one before, was there anything humane about it? No trace of human conscience lies within them, they are the offspring of Noctrifys herself; the cursed" he adds dramatically. A branch snaps, dropping ahead of them, drawing their attention to above, as they glimpse the shadows leaping within the canopy above.

"They're on top of us!!" hastens Terra, as they race in escape. Finally, Wraithe glimpses the forest's edge, a break in the fog.

"Ahead! I can see an opening! The fog! We'll use it to cut them off!" exclaims Wraithe, whipping at his horse, as they pick up pace. "Hurry!" he hastens to Anna and Siff, a gallop behind. Meanwhile, Terra ignites her arrow and readies her aim. She awaits a clearing for her shot.

"They're gaining on us!" tells Siff glancing back. The forest's edge clearly comes into view.

"Keep going!" orders Wraithe. Finally, they emerge into the vast plain. In that second, Terra releases her arrow into the fog, igniting a huge flame that engulfs the pursuing shrieks. Their ferocious sounds scream in torment, as the forest catches a huge fire spreading throughout. Ahead of them, reveals a clear, blue sky. Beneath it, a lush open valley, alive with butterflies, birds, and gorgeous greenery, with series of hills flowing effortlessly as a green sea, rendering a beautiful landscape, sitting beneath the falling sun.

"We made it out," breathes Anna turning to the forest behind them.

"From the forest we've escaped, however, Maurdis and his men still make pursuit, we must hurry. WestSkye is still another day's journey, do not allow yourselves to think a bit of smoke is enough to deter him," notions Wraithe in telling. "Come on!" With those words, the four continue, as the looming evening's sky harrows over them.

"The fires spread so quickly!" comments Siff in sheer amazement. "Do you think that got them? I mean… Not Maurdis, of course, but the shrieks?!"

"Not in the least," answers Terra bluntly. "The best thing we can do right now is to keep moving."

"You'd think they'd all got burned alive and we'd actually catch a freaking break!" shrugs Siff frustratingly in disbelief.

"You'd be a fool to think so boy," answers Wraithe harshly. "The fires merely bought us some time." Siff glances back at the blazing red night sky, shaking his head, as he holds fast to Anna. "My guess is within five days," Wraithe suddenly adds in telling.

"Five days?" the three react puzzlingly.

"For what?" looks Anna to him in question.

Keeping his sights ahead, Wraithe answers bluntly, "For us to prepare for what's to come."

"And what's that?" joins Siff curiously.

"It's the blood moon," adds Terra. "Happens twice a year, it's when the lycans are most formidable, and… even more dangerous."

Finally, Wraithe halts, yanking at the reins, "Meaning, if they don't kill you; if you are bitten, you will become one of them!" These words disturb the pair, Anna looking down in dread, and Siff petrified with fright. "Above everything," he adds, turning to them in warning. "DO NOT GET BITTEN!"

The two nod solemnly as their tedious voyage continues.

Hours pass, and dawn creeps upon them, meeting the sun peering over the smoking canopy, as its rays share across the grassy plains waves.

<u>"An untimely meeting"</u>

Meanwhile, a lone lycan lays motionless amongst an unscathed, patch of green grass, amidst the charred forest. The sun begins to creep over its motionless body, as it then transfigures into a young male. There he lays, unconscious, sprawled among the ashes of the forest.

"Ughhhhh!" he awakes abruptly to a numbing at his arm. He feels at his arm, gently touching along the foreign object. Looking to his side, he glimpses the penetrating arrow, lodged into his shoulder. "Dammit!" he grunts sitting upright, holding at his shoulder. He tenderly places his hand near the sensitive wound, gripping the arrow, and giving a great tug. "AAAGGGHHHHHH!!!" he roars out in intense pain, pulling it from his flesh, as his teeth clench in agony. He remains still for a few moments, coping with its pain. Dizzied, he staggers to his feet, looking about him, encircled by the ashes of the forest.

He peers up at the clear, morning sky, through what's left of the forest's trees, squinting towards the bright morning sun. Taking a breath, he slowly trudges forward, following the rising sun, in the path of east. Along his way, he collapses to the ground, holding at his right shoulder. Its pain too unbearable to journey a step farther, without tending to his wound. Quickly, he bites at his right sleeve, and with a tug of his teeth, rents a piece of cloth. Wrapping it about his wound, he tugs it tightly, smothering his cries of pain with one end clenched between his teeth. He takes a moment to gather himself, looking about the forest. As he remains still, there is rustling heard in the distance. immediately, he turns to the noise.

He waits as nothing appears, then getting to his feet, a faint, familiar voice echoes to him within the forest ahead. "Nooo!" it cries out to his listening ear. Alarmed by this, he is put at full alert.

"Hello?!" he answers openly to the mysterious forest. "Whoever you are, show yourself!" he demands fiercely. However, the forest remains silent, as its white ashes hurl and blow about him. "You have no idea with whom you're messing with, I am Sept, son of Maurdis! NOW SHOW YOURSELF!!" he roars, awaiting the presence's response. Instantly, the pain of his shoulder returns, forcing him to grip at the wound.

"NOOO!" repeats the strange voice again. Sept's eyes widen, looking for a sign of any other presence. The voice calling to him is that of a female, sounding in distress, could he be close to capturing the young woman that escaped them at Equilibrius? Sept thought to himself. Compelled, to finish his father's orders, Sept wanders further, this time in search of the strange voice.

"My son!" the voice exclaims, ringing nearby. Sept spins about, as it speaks from behind. His face enlightens with disbelief, as a sharp swallow travels down his throat, and stomach begins to flutter.

A beautiful woman, with cheeks of soft delicate rose stands in his wake. Her face hugged by the thick, black curly hair sprawling down her back complimenting her flawless tanned skin. Her arms rendered warmly to him in greeting. "My dear Sept!" she utters joyously, with an incandescent smile.

"My My… how've you grown," she exclaims glaring proudly, as she approaches.

"M-M-Mother??!" stammers Sept in utter disbelief. "I-Is it really you?!".

"It's me Sceptra; your mother, I'm sure I haven't aged that bad," she smiles shrewdly in reply. Awestruck, Sept drops to his knees, his eyes glistening with tears, running down the side of his face.

"I-I-I t-thought you were d-dead?" he shudders in saying. Sceptra smiles gently, reaching for her son's tear-soaked face as she kneels beside him.

"My dear child, your mother's very much alive," she answers softly. "I've survived right here, hiding within the forest," she whispers with a smile. Sept quickly wipes his face with his sleeve

"W-Why didn't you return home to us?" questions Sept peculiarly, gazing to her in frustration. Hearing this, Sceptra turns away, shamefully removing her hands from his face.

"I wanted to," she whispers softly in reply, her eyes looked away in shame, "But I can't, I am bound by the forest." Sept's heart drops, looking to the ground in silence.

"What do you mean?! Y-You can leave, I can take you, father can be happy once again!!" exclaims Sept convincingly. His mother looks to him, gently touching his face.

"It doesn't matter darling, what matters is that now I can always be with you, and love you, my son, all you need do is stay with me, here… within the forest," her words whisper smoothly into his ears. Sept's look drops into a blank expression.

"You know, father said you were dead," he mentions lowly, capturing her silence, "He said… it was them… the humans," Sept murmurs hatefully. His mother gravely looks away, keeping silent. "What's wrong?" he asks concerningly, seeing her distraught gaze.

"Your father," she replies, gazing into his starry eyes and taking a deep sigh, before continuing on. "Your father, was a good man, not the best, but he loved us." Meanwhile, Sept listens intently to her words. "He was VERY protective of us," she emphasizes with a smile, before pausing briefly, as her smile retreats to a grave expression. "But power, and conquest consumed him."

"He maintained a loyal group of men, standing in support of him and his cause; so loyal, they would follow him into the darkness he'd become. They would obey, no matter how vile or how sinister it may be, they would follow!" she tells, with tears escaping her eyes. With a heavy breath, she continues on.

"Under the teachings of Fenrifrys, the fate of the lycans, Maurdis grew plagued by dreams of immortality and power attainable only by the white lotus, hidden by the mother fate herself. In conquest of finding it, it would lead him to destroy everything in his wake; all in the name of his new order… the 'Order of the Pact.' Maurdis, your father, spared no one, he was a tyrant!" she adds severely. Sept listens motionless by her words. As another tear escapes her eye, running down her soft cheek.

"I first found out your father was a lycan, after you were born," details Sceptra looking into his eyes. "He, and his men had just left, however, I felt something wasn't right. I hadn't seen him wearing the clothing worn by the Order, and Arthur, closest friend of your father, had not visited in a long time. I knew they had a few quarrels during the times your father remained silent, but it seemed different. I would slowly begin to realize your father wasn't the man I knew, or fell in love with," she sobs, turning away in dismay.

Confused, Sept leans forward to comfort her. "Mother?!" he answers, "Please tell me… what do you mean?" pleads Sept in need of understanding. Sceptra turns to him, sensing his need for closure.

Taking a deep breath, she details further. "Over 120 years ago, history speaks of an ancient order," she opens in saying. "This order was meant to defend humanity from its 'curses,' and serve as a symbol of hope, protection, and balance. Your father, Maurdis, helped establish that order, him and four other men."

"The old order," mutters Sept softly in reply.

"Yes," his mother answers with a nod. "Your father was a protector, and soon the order became a brotherhood."

"The order would defend the land of Skye from many attacks, both lycans and nocturnals alike, even from treachery within. Restless rebels wanting to take from other cities and small villages, the order would be Skye's defense. However, it would not last. For one night, during a blood moon, the lycans attacked a nearby town!" she begins dramatically. "Arthur, leader of the order, and a knight of its roundtable, joined by your father, and their men, led the town's defense!"

"There was so much bloodshed!" tells Sceptra gravely. "During that dreadful night, the knights managed to escape the lycans… but your father…" she pauses suddenly. This grabs at Sept's attention.

"What happened?!" questions Sept wide-eyed in curiosity. His mother doesn't reply, glaring grievously into his eyes. "Mother! Please! Tell me!" he begs earnestly.

"He was attacked, badly injured, and bitten by Fenrifrys himself! The very thing he dreaded; he would be 'cursed' to become!" cries Sceptra in telling. "With aid of the mother fate herself, the order would finally win the battle against Fenrifrys, drawing all his followers to flee. When they had found Maurdis, your father, they saw that he had been 'cursed,' withering away before their very eyes. The knights murmured amongst themselves, how they were to deal with him, for it was a blood moon and the pact's curse was strong. Maurdis was to be ousted by the order and given death by sword! Although it be contrary to the order's laws, that no knight be able to raise his sword against another; many argued, that this, would be an exception!" Sept's gaze wanders to the ground in thought, at the words of his mother.

Sceptra breathes in, continuing in saying. "It wasn't until his 'brother in knighthood', a man by the name of 'Arthur Valor,' your father's once-beloved best friend, saw that Maurdis had been badly injured, and the chances of him succumbing to his injuries seemed more likely than him being cursed into the pact, so he argued that Maurdis' death be decided by fate; and by fate alone, ultimately sparing him from the order's wrath. Little did he know, this would prove to be crueler, more so, than the thrust of another man's sword, and so it was decided, seeing that Arthur was a beloved knight of the roundtable, the order would abandon Maurdis, and he be left to die, upholding the law of the old order, no knight shall raise his sword to smite another; A mistake the order would soon come to regret."

"The knights would come by, bearing your father's sword and cloak. They had taken it and given me it for mourning. They told me that Maurdis had died in the battle; that he died honorably, as were the words of Arthur. I mourned for four full days, to me, you were too young to understand, yet, I saw in your eyes, you knew," she weeps in telling. "However, Maurdis did die. As did the man I knew. That man, no longer existed, he was to become something sinister."

"Fenrifrys knew of your father's impending death, and sought him out, finding him along his dying breath, and thus revived Maurdis. Your father would then feel betrayed by the order and having been left to die by the very regime, he helped establish and devoted his life to. He lost those close to him, the brotherhood. He also garnered a hatred for his once beloved friend, Arthur, and Fenrifrys would use this to draw Maurdis into joining the pact. Maurdis would then join that which he swore to protect against," she continues looking into Sept's eyes.

"Fenrifrys knew humanity would hate your father, so he welcomed him, and slowly fostered Maurdis' hatred for the order. He promised your father that their cause would be greater, that immortality, could be attainable, and doesn't belong in the hands of mere man. With each teaching, Maurdis would fall further into darkness; growing stronger in the pact and powers that its curse offered up to him. It would corrupt him, and soon the lycans replaced the order within his heart. Maurdis would swear his life to a new regime," tells Sceptra dreadfully. "The Order of the Pact."

"Your father grew powerful and would follow his lord into battle. This time, against the revenant order, in conquest of the white lotus. Many of the remaining knights were slaughtered and for the lycans the battle had all but been won. But again, Mitrefys would appear, defending the 'great garden' and would seal away Fenrifrys, putting an end to the conflict. Maurdis would be defeated and the location of the garden would be hidden from the likes of man, and fates itself. The mother fate grew weary of the threat of distorting equilibrium and the stealing of the lotus, and thus hid herself and all she created within the secret oasis. However, this would only pull Maurdis deeper into his rage. He would swear on his life, to avenge the death of his Lord, obtain the white lotus and restore the pact to an even greater power! Maurdis would go mad!"

"No..." mutters Sept, shaking in disbelief; her words conflicting within him. "T-This is... B-But what happened to you?" Sceptra enters a gaunt stare. "What is it?" continues Sept. However, his mother refuses to speak, with tears welling in her eyes. Meanwhile, Sept's mind races rigorously, battling with the words of his mother. He begins shuddering in denial. "NO, NO, NO, NO, NO!" he mutters, pacing about his thoughts.

"Tell me!!" he murmurs beneath his breath. "TELL ME!!" bursts Sept in anger.

"All right!" retorts Sceptra tearfully. "Maurdis returned, knocking along our home's door. He wore a cloak, that hid his appearance. At first, I couldn't believe it, it was as seeing a spirit; so estranged. Maurdis held us close, and once again, I felt safe. I was overjoyed of his return, somehow, the fates allowed him to find his way back to us. He had barely arrived before he would propose something strange, but I guess I was blinded by the joy of his return," she mentions, sighing in regret. Maurdis would secretly pull us away from the city, to be isolated within the forest. He would never speak of the order, nor the means of his return. When asked, it would be avoided, or lead to a silence; it was like his soul had been left behind; so estranged. Maurdis would always leave out, just before the dusk, never uttering the means of his departing, and he would never return until the following dawn.. I would cry and scream for him to tell me, for him to stay with us; he wouldn't reply, as much as I told him I loved him, I would receive no answer," tells Sceptra in weeping. "Until one night, as he slept, I had just left putting you to bed, and entered our bedroom, I found your Father, fast asleep. However, the sleeves of his cloak revealed the bite marks upon his arm, and that's when I knew; it would all finally make sense," her voice trembles in sorrow.

"As I slept next to him that night, my mind wandered. Maurdis willingly served under the pact, and under Fenrifrys! My only thought was you!" she tells straightly, holding at Sept's hand. "I had to keep silent. Your father would leave out the next morning, this would be my only chance to protect you. I swept you up, rummaging together everything we would need before he was to return. We left as quickly as I could, but not long after, he would arrive. His sound resonated through the forest, a great howl, calling to his subjects. We had to flee, having been chased by his pack of lycans. I knew he would be furious with me, seeing it as a betrayal, but I feared the man I knew, no longer existed, and in a fit of rage could kill us both! We would escape the lycans, seeking refuge within Eastskye, a protected colony gathered among the mountains, it was there, I sought out Arthur, and told him of Maurdis. This news would bring about great grief upon the beloved knight, who once claimed Maurdis as his brother. Arthur promised us safety, taking us in. At first, I thought us finally safe, until three days later, the lycans would attack. Maurdis and his army would lay waste to Eastskye. The Order withheld their aid; the previous battle took too many of its knights, and the arrival to defend the distant colony, would prove suicidal! The lycans had the advantage. Higher numbers, element of surprise, a full moon! It was the perfect attack. Their raid was swift; ravaging through the colony, rendering Eastskye barren. The lycans would leave no survivors in their wake. Fortunately, we escaped once again, by aid of Arthur, he would lead us and a few others into Nordeskye, a village tucked within a valley, north of the eastern mountains. However, this would not be the stop of Maurdis' search. He would hunt us, following after us to Nordeskye. Arthur knew it would be Maurdis' next move, his prideful ambition drew him to it. Arthur would then warn Nordeskye of Maurdis' treachery. This time, the remaining knights gathered to stand with him. The lycans would not so easily claim victory! Maurdis would arrive, but Nordeskye would be ready. This time, the brothers in knighthood would meet in battle as enemies!" Sceptra exclaims. "In the end, Arthur would defeat Maurdis, plunging his sword through his chest, and claiming victory for all of Skye. I loved your father, but couldn't stomach the monster he'd become, so, I left him."

"We would remain in Nordeskye. There, I took care of you by myself," smiles Sceptra earnestly. "Until one winter night, I pitched from my slumber under the sound of your screams. I rushed into the room, and there stood a cloaked man, with you, straddled in his arms. As he pulled the hood from over his head, my heart stopped!

Before I could move, I found myself to my knees, wallowed in my own blood, it was Maurdis! He had somehow, once again, returned! He took you that night and left me to die!" she sobs weakly.

"Upon betrayal… death!" mutters Sceptra lowly. "Those were the last words he spoke to me, before I took my final breath." she utters, as silent tears flow along her cheeks. Sniffling away her sorrow, she places her hand beneath her chin, holding upon her unscathed neck.

"Maurdis, lost control," she utters despairingly, running her hand down her neck, to unveil a large, gruesome bite. In a heavy breath, Sept's head lowers, shuddering vigorously in rage and disbelief.

"It's not true... I-It can't be true!" he repeats in denial. Meanwhile, seeing his distress, his mother places her hand on his shoulder, lifting his gaze towards her.

With a soothing voice, she whispers calmly, "My son...I know what you're hearing does hurt, but I am telling you the absolute truth, I loved your father incandescently, but in the end, I was slain by your father's very hand… in a well of rage, and the nature of what he had once dreaded!" Septs sits silently, wallowing in his thoughts. Meanwhile, his mother gets to her feet, pulling him up and into a warm embrace. Surprised, he stands stiff within her arms, until finally, he embraces her, hugging tightly as his tears give way.

"My son," she answers warmly. "All is not lost," she smiles. "We can exist together...right here...in the forest; you can leave it all behind and stay here; with me; your mother!" she shows to the forest about them. Sept however, is made unsure.

"Here?" he repeats, delivering a bewildered gaze. Meanwhile, he inches slightly from their embrace.

"Yes, my dear... what's wrong, here is where we belong," she elates with a smile. He pulls away, putting space between them.

"I can't do that," answers Sept regrettably, as he turns away, "I must seek out my father, he must give answer for what you've told!" he refutes in saying.

"My son, why return to him in questioning, your father is ashamed of you! He always will be!!" cries Sceptra angrily. "You have not his unrelenting will; his demand for power, nor his ambition…

in his eyes you are nothing but weak!" ends his mother harshly in reply. Shocked at her words, Sept keeps distant.

"I said, I can't do it, should I tarry here in torment with these things?! Or must I demand of my father the truth of these words?!" he roars to her in question. Sceptra however, stands off, flabbergasted at his refusal.

"Things?!" she laughs reluctantly, "The 'shrieks' are the protectors, centuries ahead of you mere lycans; their service is to the whole!" smiles Sceptra sinisterly, looking into his eyes, "My dear boy, can't you see, your life is already our own!"

Suddenly, the area about him shadows in, as her laughing resonates followed by the shrieks of her subjects, "Who are you?" he demands in question, standing in retreat, "You're not her! You're not my mother!" Sept steps back

Her face pales, sprouting vivid dark veins, as the clear of her eyes hardens black, her mouth gapes bellowing a strong breeze, "You FOOL!" she roars distortedly, "You'll always be a disappointment to him!!" she continues in laughing.

"Whoever you are! Whatever you are! I am not afraid of you!" retorts Sept standing his ground.

"Foolish wolf! Your blood belongs to the hive now!" her voice encamps him, shrouded behind the shadows. Suddenly, a shriek is heard, as it leaps from the darkness, upon his back. Quickly, Sept hurls the creature from his back as he transforms, darting off into the forest. He is followed by a powerful gust of wind, carrying along the pursuing shrieks.

"You will fail! And be cast out!" the voice laughs in rant. Meanwhile, one of the creatures bounds towards him head on. Sept with teeth bared, thrashes the shriek within his jaws, casting it aside as he continues to flee. His instincts guide him along the eastern path of the sun, as his howls call out to his pact from the forest. He flees and flees, until the sounds of the shrieks' pursuit fades. Finally, the eerie forest follows into an unrecognizable calm, as Sept then returns to his human state. Collapsing to his knees in exhaustion.

"Could it all be true?" searches his mind inwardly. Suddenly, a forgotten pain returns, as he quickly grips at his shoulder. He must urgently make his return and see his father. Willing himself to his feet, Sept trudges onward in return to the pact, and to demand the truths of his father.

Meanwhile, beyond the forests of Nostalgia, a pair of horses carry on throughout the forest.

"How much farther, until we're there?" asks Anna tirelessly, brushing away the branches from her face. Seated behind her, Siff lifts a bottle to his face for a drink. Yet, to his frustration, a drip follows, placing a disgruntled frown upon his face.

"Well, we're now out of water," he scoffs in telling, stuffing the bottle into the saddlebags.

"Chin up...we're almost there," laughs Terra encouragingly, notioning up ahead. Siff pitches up anxiously at this gesture, his spirits lifting, as they finally approach the end of their tedious journey.

Chapter 7
A Change of Scene

"Be alert!" tells Wraithe moments later. As they veer over a small hill, revealing a large town settlement, tucked within a vast valley.

"Whoa!" elates Siff, excitedly tapping at Anna's shoulder, pointing her attention up ahead.

"Yes, Siff! I see it!" laughs Anna in reply, as the four descend into the valley towards the huge city, masked behind an enormous wooden wall. "FINALLY!" she voices in relief, as they approach its great structure. For the first time the two young friends, breathe in the sights of a new city. Anna and Siff excitedly take notice of the many travellers commuting back and forth, through the wall's tall iron gates. The pair follow anxiously approaching the main gate, heavily guarded by the city's soldiers, when a middle-aged male, donned in armored attire, approaches the four atop their horses at its entrance.

"State your order of business!" he demands, looking sternly to Wraithe.

"Trade," answers Wraithe, equally blunt, putting the guard at a pause. The guard switches his glance to Anna and the others and slowly walks by them, looking amongst their saddles and supplies. After a satisfied 'inspection,' he nods to the gatekeeper, who then tugs at the lever, allowing the four to enter.

"Thank you, my good man," nods Wraithe gratuitously, leading through the gates. Excited, Anna also nods in respect to the guard, who reluctantly acknowledges with a scoff. Turning ahead, she is awestruck at how developed the city is, having never been outside the walls of Nordeskye. This city looked entirely different. Its scale much larger than that of Nordskye, its buildings made mostly of brick and wood, as its paths lay patterned with brick, more less, than the dusty dirt paths of Nordskye. The four make their way through the bustling main path and receive constant stares from passing townspeople, particularly curious of their unfamiliar faces. However, Wraithe and Terra pay this no mind, continuing ahead. Meanwhile, Anna and Siff remain fascinated at the tall buildings, of stone brick and firm, heavy wood. The brick lain pathways sprawl with people in every direction. Each building appears different, with distinct colors on each wall. Many of the windows are decorated with rows of flowerpots and ceramics fixed about their frames. Kids can be seen playing overhead along the stone-bridge pathways. Looking to their left, the pair glimpse a bakery, with a line of customers leading outside its doors and along the path. At their right, a distant courtyard, where music can be heard sounding, as persons gather to dance and play. The happiness within Westskye feels all too surreal to Anna and Siff.

Suddenly.

"Everyone down!" orders Wraithe quickly drawing the pair's exploring gaze.

"Hey, you two...focus!" mentions Terra, snapping at their attention. "We are all to stay close, it's easy to get lost in here," she gives mild warning.

"Everyone down," orders Wraithe again, leaning from his horse. Quickly, the others follow, as he leads them over to a tent, where the bellowing of hammers, and clinking of iron sounds from within. Ducking through its open covers, he greets the blacksmith.

"Good day, good sir," utters Wraithe respectfully, as he approaches. "Might I ask that you may point me in the direction of your market exchange?"

"Why, not a problem!" the blacksmith replies hospitably, sweeping his sweat covered face with his soaked sleeve. "It is but a short trip up the main, following a right, can't miss it!" he points outwardly down the path.

"Ahh, thank you!" turns Wraithe to him in gratitude, quickly flicking two shillings into the smith's hands.

"Of course!" the smith nods, quickly shoving the pieces into his pockets. Wraithe returns to the three, walking by them, returning to his horse.

"This way," utters Wraithe to them. "We're headed down the path!" Quickly, the three follow, as they make their way further along the city's main path. They then follow the instructions of the blacksmith taking its right, and into view comes a huge commotion, as droves of people gather outside the pillars of a tall building. As they approach closer, persons are seen clamoring atop the horde. Items are heard shattering as ferocious arguing and shoving ensues, as many struggle to get inside. More are seen along the path with heavy bags tossed over their shoulders. Vases, irons and swords toted in wheelbarrows pass them by, hastily carried towards the crowd. Items dropped along the way are quickly toppled upon and picked up by nearby scavenging children.

"Look!" points Anna out to them, at their left, it is a docking for the horses.

"Quickly! Come on!" tells Wraithe, yanking at the reins. It is a long wooden post, beneath it, a narrow well, allowing the horses to drink. After securing the horses, Terra quickly snags two of the saddlebags, tossing them to Anna and Siff.

"Go quickly! We'll catch up!" utters Terra hastily.

"W-Wait… W-What are we to do with them?!" stammers Anna cluelessly, fumbling the heavy bag.

"Head to the market, we'll gather inside!" orders Terra, helping Wraithe with the next horse.

Casting the bag over her shoulder, Anna looks to Siff. "Let's go!" she nods up ahead, as they quickly make headway towards the commotion. As they arrive, Anna barely hears the instructions of the guards. They stand positioned at the tall, wooden doors, shrouded by the people. The guards investigate each and every item to be brought into the market's chambers. Feeling a pulling tug at her tunic, she turns to Siff. Anna leans in, lending her ear.

"Anna, how the hell are we to get in there, there's no way we'll get inside!" he voices in her ear over the commotion. Anna looks around for signs of a way inside. To her right, she glimpses a chariot of horses, behind them a tote full of hay just along the corner, near the market's alleyway. Anna creeps closer, away from the bustling crowd, meanwhile, Siff remains a foot behind her, as a soldier appears, docking the horses upon the nearby post. He is then seen conversing with another.

"I will retrieve the keys, mind the horses!" Anna overhears indistinctly, immediately, Anna turns to Siff, "I have an idea!" she exclaims, pulling at his arm. Anna reaches into her saddlebag, pulling out a silver cup. Using the cover of a tall pillar, she hurls the cup past the guard, as its heavy clink hits the nearby wall.

"Who goes by!" he roars, taken by surprise, as he walks around the side of the chariot. Carefully, she looks around. "Now!" she whispers, pulling Siff along, as they dash over to the pile of hay. "Get inside! Quickly" she notions clearing some of the hay aside. Hearing the nearby footsteps, the guard rushes around to check. Anna swiftly shrouds the hay over her and Siff, barely seconds before he arrives to their side. Puzzled, the guard notices the fallen hay from the large tote and pulls out his sword. He swipes away some of the hay, as he checks for movement. The blade's edge, grazes by Anna and Siff, as the pair remain silent. He prepares to make another sweeping graze, when to their relief, the first guard returns, his keys heard jingling in hand.

"What are you doing?!" the pair overhears him ask oddly to the second, as he approaches.

"W-Well, I-I thought I heard something!" stammers the second guard embarrassingly in reply. Looking under the tote of hay the first guard picks up the gleaming silver cup, tossed earlier by Anna, and holds it up to the sun.

"Ahh, this will trade very well!" he utters, stuffing it into his side. "Enough messing around, let's get the hay inside, it won't be long before the horses eat us instead of it!" he orders hastily. Anna and Siff sigh of relief, and with a whip of the reins they are off, as the second guard takes the keys, opening the tall, heavy wooden doors of the market, bidding them to enter.

The stench of animals are the first things to greet them upon entering, as the bleating of goats, clucking chickens, and snorting of pigs are some of the noises heard by the passing heap. Their eyes looking past the curtains of hay, they glimpse a huge open area, where hordes of tents are gathered. Smoke and incenses are smelt burning nearby, as persons are seen pulling along their cattle and supplies. Noisy bids are heard taking place, as crowds gather, flaunting their offers for the various trades. Suddenly, their tour comes to an abrupt halt, as they are taken on a detour, drawing them away from the markets. Doors are heard opening up ahead, as a shadow casts over them, and hung torches are glimpsed flashing by, along the brick walls.

"What's happening?!" whispers Siff nervously to Anna.

"I think we've entered a tunnel," she shushes quietly.

"Halt!" they hear an outside voice command, as footsteps approach near the heap. Suddenly, Anna eyes a guard, standing just beyond the curtain of hay. "Over there!" he commands pointing out, as they then continue ahead, finally coming to a stop.

"We're stopping," whispers Anna quietly. When a loud creak is heard, as the guard leaves the chariot. Carefully, Anna listens as his footsteps recede. She then taps at Siff. "Come on!"

Moving silently as possible, the two exit the other side of the haystack, quietly landing their feet to the floor. Keeping Siff behind her, Anna uses the tote as cover. "Stay behind me!" she utters, watching as the guard reapproaches. Anna glimpses a stable across the way, and quickly pulls at Siff's hand, as they scamper across the way. Suddenly, clinking is heard as a cup drops from Siff's bag.

"Who goes there!" yells the guard put at alert. Meanwhile, the pair scurry along the inner walls of the stable, as another guard rushes over to the first.

"What's wrong?!" approaches the other in question.

"I heard something!" exclaims the first guard in reply. Instantly, he looks to his right, noticing a silver mug and walks over to retrieve it. "Thieves!" he yells, drawing his sword, as they both turn towards the shadowy doors of the stable. Anna covers Siff's heavy breathing and backs further into the stable, as the guards enter. Suddenly, a loud snort is heard behind them, as Siff backs into a sturdy structure. Quickly, the pair turns about, as Siff erupts into a loud scream, as a startled bull, riles up, thrashing about the pen. The guards hear this and close in on the pair.

Seeing the incoming guards, Anna looks towards the pen's gate, "Siff!" she yells, "We'll draw it to the gate!" Anna then pulls at his arm, leading over to the pen's wooden gate.

"Stop thieves!" yells one of the guards, rushing over.

Suddenly, the bull charges towards Anna and Siff. "Jump!" exclaims Anna, as her and Siff quickly dive aside. The bull crashes into the wooden gate, hurling it open and swinging it into the arriving guards, as it thrashes around to its escape. Quickly, Anna pulls Siff to his feet. "Come on!" she hastens, darting by the guards writhing in pain. They push open the heavy front doors, opening them into the bustling market, and quickly slams shut the doors behind them. Anna looks to her right, at a tent, setup with assortments of fruits and vegetables, and pulls Siff beneath the tables.

Finally, the guards push open the doors, immediately searching for signs of the two. Meanwhile, Anna and Siff look on, crept beneath the tables.

"Useless!" shrugs one of them, "They're long gone by now! Who were they?!"

"Probably nothing more than common peasant thieves!" pants the other reply, holding painfully at his side, as they then lead off into the market. Meanwhile, beneath the table, the two friends sigh of relief.

After a few moments, the pair creep out from beneath the tables. Siff turns and instantly, his eyes reflect the sights of hundreds of fruits lining along the display. Tempted, he snatches up a few of the nearby apples, stuffing them quickly into his bag. "Come on, Siff!" calls Anna, walking ahead. As they round the corner, they reluctantly bump into Wraithe and Terra.

"Where were you two?!" exclaims Terra curiously in question, seeing the scruffled pair seeming out of breath.

"We snuck inside!" Anna rolls her shoulder in telling. "W-Wait how did you guys get inside so fast?!" questions Anna in disbelief.

Terra grins. "We tipped one of the guards," she utters bluntly.

"Oh," murmurs Anna, as her and Siff look to each other in bewilderment.

"Well, no time to waste, you're here, so you've made it inside, we'll make trade, and attempt to speak with the city's council," utters Wraithe, leading off into the fray of townspeople. For the next hour, they visit each stall along the market's main aisle, trading items and silvers for rations and other supplies suitable for a journey. Anna finally grows impatient, moving up to speak to Wraithe.

"Hey!" she calls to him from behind. "We're wasting time, Maurdis and the lycans could be headed here right this minute, we should say something!" stands Anna firmly.

"Oh, I know that all too well, young one, but this time, I'll be trading before the city bursts into flames!" scoffs Wraithe in reply, as he brushes by Anna. He and Terra then continue over to a nearby blacksmith's tent. Shaking her head in frustration, Anna turns away, however, something catches her attention. It is the loud chatter, heard just up ahead. Anna slowly begins moving towards the noise. Her wanderings catch the attention of Siff, who scurries concerningly after her.

"Anna, what are you doing! Wraithe said to stay close!" mutters Siff after her.

"No, he didn't! Besides, he's trading, I'm only trying to see what the fuss is about," she tells continuing further ahead. Meanwhile, a cloaked stranger watches as the pair wanders off, and begins to follow among the disguise of the crowd. On the other hand, Wraithe returns to where stood Anna and Siff. Frustratingly, he turns to Terra. "This girl will be the end of us!" he utters, seeing no signs of the pair. He and Terra quickly begin search for Anna and Siff. All the while, just beyond the tents of the market, Anna glimpses a stand, seating three chairs, where guards are seen bringing a male towards the three seated individuals. Voices can be heard chanting and clamoring in applause and slanders; it appears to be a ruling.

"Siff!" exclaims Anna, "I think this is the high council!" tells Anna excitedly, looking ahead. Suddenly, a tall soldier appears, standing in their way.

"Remember me, Thief!" jeers the guard with a grin. Immediately, two more guards appear at each of the children's sides, firmly grasping upon their arms. "You're coming with us, the council doesn't tread well with thieves!" he mocks harshly.

Meanwhile, Wraithe and Terra search the nearby area, when Terra finally glimpses sight of them being carried off. "Wait! There they are!" she exclaims pointing up ahead. Quickly, they squeeze their way towards them. To the pair's surprise, Wraithe arrives, tugging at the guard's arm.

"Good Sir, my apologies, what seems to be the problem with these two?!" voices Wraithe to the guard in question, shooting a peculiar gaze at Anna and Siff.

"They're taking us to the high council," answers Anna, shooting a sly grin towards Wraithe.

"As the young woman said, they're off to be tried for theft, I would suggest you remove yourself, for you become of the same!" scorns the guard rudely in reply. Wraithe looks to Anna, then back towards the guard, and swiftly headbutts into his nose, dropping him to his knees in pain. Holding at his soiled nose, the guard orders the others to sieze him. Immediately, the guards lunge at Wraithe, who does little resistance, and subdue him. Getting to his feet, the guard walks by him, and thrusts his fist into Wraithe's abdomen. "Take them!" he orders furiously, "Take them all away!" They also seize Terra, who stands nearby, shoving and pushing them before the three-seated council, amidst the center of the market's open floor.

"Who be this you bring before us guard?!" answers one of the three, from the chair, the voice appearing female. The four are then forced to their knees, meanwhile, Anna looks up towards the ceiling, admiring its tall stature and around at its inside. It is a huge open floor, with rows of audience seated on each side. the commotion quiets down, as the attention shifts to the three council seats.

"What be their order of business!" reiterates another of the three, the voice being that of a male.

"Theft and treason, my lord!" answers one of the guards humbly, pointing to the first who continues to hold at his soiled nose. "They've also brought harm to a few of the others!" Wraithe then shoots a serious look to Anna.

"You had better start talking," he mutters sternly to her. Anna looks to the council, unable to put together a description of the three seated individuals, as the sun distorts her sight.

Anna then notions to speak, "I implore you!" she exclaims, grasping the council's reluctant attention, "We do not wish to bring about mischief to WestSkye! However, we bring an urgent word of warning! Your city, your families; everyone here, under the sound of my voice… are all in imminent danger!" tells Anna openly to the council, looking around at the gathered citizens. Immediately, there is an uproar of murmurings, as the people begin to laugh and make humor.

"Order! I said ORDER!" roars one of the councilmen, striking his gavel. Quickly, the murmurings cease, as he looks to Anna in saying. "What folly is this?! You commit treason, and rant fear into the hearts of our city's people, have you no honor, thief?!" he scorns towards her.

"I'm no thief!!" Anna retorts boldly, "I am Anna Valor, daughter of Arthur Valor, the blacksmith that be the reason you all live here in peace! And my words be true! Maurdis, lord of the lycans, be on his way here as we speak!"

"SILENCE!" roars the councilman furiously, jumping to his feet. "We've tolerated your insolence quite enough!" he adds, finally turning to the nearby guards. "Lock them away!" he orders quickly. Once again, the guards grab onto their arms, drawing them away.

Rolling his eyes impatiently, Wraithe speaks forth. "I'm sorry, good people, but if we are done with politics, can you give ear our cause?!" he pleads satirically to the audience. The counsellors quickly look up at this request.

"I'm sorry, what?!" looks the female counsellor to him in confusion.

"Can I have a word?!" clarifies Wraithe upon repeating.

"Speak!" she orders bluntly in reply.

"Thank you," bows Wraithe cheekily, as he looks to the council. "In less than FIVE DAYS! An army, unlike anything you've ever experienced is on its way here! Rest assured they will tear right through you, sword, shield, and everything, unless you hear our words and prepare yourselves!" he proclaims solemnly. "The white lotus; the flower you have oh so very, kept well hidden… they know where it is, and they will find it, he was there when they hid it, and now he has returned; with that flower within his hands, Skye will run red with blood." The eerie warnings of Wraithe stir a questionable silence among the people, as the aura of fear builds along the room; its tension thick enough to be cut by a two-edged sword.

The councilmen straighten up, having been made uncomfortable by his words. Finally, the last of the three speaks. "How did you come to know this, straggler" he questions prejudicially towards Wraithe.

Wraithe looks to them boldly in proclamation. "Because I…am the last true and breathing revenant of the old Order!"

Immediately, the counsellor sits back, scoffing in disbelief. He then leans over, mumbling in the ears of the two others seated beside him. Finally, the second male counselor fixes to speak.

"My good sir," addresses the counselor with a chuckle. "If that were to be true… you would be 40 years older than myself," he adds in humor.

"Indeed, I am 100 years old," answers Wraithe straightly, unmoved with his words

"You sir… are mad!" points the female counselor from the chair, as the audience erupts into laughter.

"Why thank you!" nods Wraithe sarcastically in reply. Anna rolls her eyes in shrug. Looking down, she stomps at the guard's foot, causing him to release his grip. As she yanks away from the other guard, she then rushes towards the seats of the council.

"Hear me, please! Within the past week, I've seen many of slaughter; mothers stripped from their children; fathers pulled from their wives and families... bodies lining the very streets of

Nordeskye… our streets! You can lock us up if you see fit, but I beg you, don't let the same be told of you."

"Mhmm," nods Lady Elaine. "And what proof have you of why we should believe your preposterous tale?" she goes on to ask. As the counsellor speaks, the heavy clunking of boots, singles out from among the crowd, as a figure approaches, chuckling hysterically, as he steps into the council's light.

"You'd all be wise to heed the young lady's words," he chuckles in telling, swirling his bottle to his mouth. "She's right!" he utters, stumbling into view. His appearance raises the eyebrows of each of the counsellors. As they glare in bewilderment at the tattered clothing of the male. Overdressed in rags and other decrepit cloths, he carries a seemingly heavy bag upon his right shoulder. His moccasin boots reveal his unsightly toes and feet. Meanwhile, his hands lay wrapped within filthy rags. The male's hair is long and unkempt, resting along his shoulders, as his straggly, filthy beard, hangs above his chest.

"What did you say traveller?" questions lady Elaine looking down to him with repugnance.

"The girl…" points the 'straggler' towards Anna, rudely lifting his bottle to his face, as some of the drink escapes his mouth. "I said," he gulps. "She's right!" he wipes away with his sleeve.

Finally, Lord Asher stands, looking to him in disgust. "I understand you may not have visited us here before in Westskye, but there is no drinking in the council, and I might add who are you?!" The straggler rudely ignores the counsellor and fixates towards Anna.

"With respect, MY LORD!" mocks the straggler in bowing towards the council, placing a disgruntled look on their faces. "I am Hulkur… I travel from the east," he hiccups in introduction.

"Hulkur, you say?!" repeats Lord Asher intriguingly. "And you, straggler; You believe this young girl's rantings?" he continues to ask, nodding over to Anna.

"Yes," drinks Hulkur in reply. "I do!" he hiccups with a grin. "If Maurdis is headed to this city's walls… your city be already damned!" The council and the audience, sit silent in listening. "Maurdis be backed by an army, but not just any army…No No, they are much much more," he lingers in saying. "LYCANS!!" he whispers wildly.

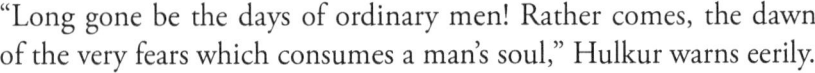

"Long gone be the days of ordinary men! Rather comes, the dawn of the very fears which consumes a man's soul," Hulkur warns eerily.

"I hail from a land, amongst the mountains of North," he begins in telling. "Our city decimated; we didn't stand a chance. I lost my brother…" he pauses silent with emotion. "I-I found his head thirty feet from his corpse," he utters, shaking his head in reflection. "Be you any concern for the survival of this city, or its people, you'd do what the lady says," he ushers boldly. The council adjusts uncomfortably within their seats, as his words weigh upon their judgement. Anna looks to Hulkur, his gritty appearance and heinous scars that run across his left cheek.

Suddenly, the council speaks; it is lady Elaine. "We heard your plea straggler, but we will not tolerate the foolish rantings of a drunkard within our city's council; You are dismissed! Guard! Withdraw this unsightly drunk!" she orders immediately. Quickly, the guards appear at his side.

"You do not believe me?" mutters Hulkur, taking a final drink, as they yank ahold his arms. "So be it!" he roars, shedding his decrepit attire, and emerging as a fearsome lycan. Immediately, the council and audience draw back in horror, as the crowd erupts and begins clamoring over one another to escape. A few nearby guards bravely make their charge towards it. Suddenly, it viciously turns at them, baring its teeth; Leaping upon the first guard, it rips at his throat. The other guards attack with swords drawn but are quickly hurled away by the thrashing kicks of the lycan's hind legs. It quickly bounds upon and mangles another. Meanwhile, Wraithe and the others remain constrained by the petrified guards.

"Free us, you fool!" yells Wraithe towards the guard. "He won't stop, else you want the council run red with blood!" The guard, however, remains too frightened to move; his trousers soiled of fear. Seeing the urgency to act, Wraithe quickly headbutts the frightened guard, freeing his chains from the guard's hold. The other guards scatter and flee, leaving behind the chained Anna, Siff, and Terra.

Wraithe darts across the council's floor, towards the lycan, as it readies to attack another. With a swift twirl of his chain's rope, Wraithe hurls the iron bands towards the beast, as the chains fasten quickly about its neck. The lycan then turns to Wraithe, who struggles to pull against it. Anna sees the body of the guard rendered unconscious by Wraithe, and scampers nearby to retrieve a group of keys tied upon his side. Fiddling them within her fingers, she tries them until finally, she frees herself of her chains.

"Anna, come on! Hurry!" hastens Terra. Anna swiftly dives to Siff, who is knelt at her side and begins trying the keys at his chains until freeing him as well. Quickly, Siff begins to flee. Meanwhile, Wraithe continues to dodge and constrain the lycan, using the iron chains as decoy and leverage. The lycan however, overpowers him. Seeing Siff scamper across the council floor, its instincts pursue, making chase after him, whilst dragging Wraithe behind it.

"KILL IT!" Wraithe yells to Anna desperately, while pulled across the floor.

"Anna, Quickly!" urges Terra desperately panning from Wraithe struggle, to her chains. Anna tries each key, as Terra's chains appear to not budge.

"I don't know! They won't open!" cries Anna in reply. She then looks over to her staff, lying nearby. Terra watches as Anna darts for the staff.

"Anna? Anna?! What are you doing?!" questions Terra nervously, as Anna returns.

"You trust me?" asks Anna vaguely, taking a deep breath. "Your hands, hold them steady!"

"Anna NO! Hell No!" squirms Terra in retort. "No way!"

"You're going to hate me!" mutters Anna, lifting her staff atop her head, wielding as a large silver axe, and with a thunderous swing, utter silence. Terra finally opens her eyes, as the chain bands are completely shattered, its pieces falling from her wrists.

"Shit," she whimpers in relief, looking to Anna. "You're one crazy b…."

"HEYY!! Now is not the time!" roars Wraithe for aid, as he continues to be dragged along the floors. "KILL IT!!"

Anna glimpses the lycan gaining upon her friend, her eyes widening in horror. "Siff!!" she exclaims, darting across the council. Bounding atop its tables, her staff transforms, into a runic, two-edged sword. Anna then leaps headfirst, thrusting her blade forward. Diving in attack, the sword pierces at the lycan's side. As she clashes into the lycan, toppling it aside, it cries out, followed by an utter silence, as they glide along the floor. The council's audience finally appear, from cowered behind the seats and pillars. Immediately, all eyes turn to Anna, who rises to her feet, standing above the lycan. Anna turns to Hulkur, who returns to his human state. Wheezing for air, Hulkur rolls to his back, as the rags covering his body saturate with blood. With blade in hand, Anna watches, as he wildly coughs up a few drops of blood.

"Finally," he breathes weakly. "I am free!" he wheezes, as his eyes blink in fading. "He's coming; T-This is a war y-you will n-never w-win… Maurdis WILL have his immortality," he coughs, resting his head to his final breath, his body sprawled beneath the council's seat.

Anna thrusts her sword into his corpse once more, quickly drawing it back from his lifeless body. She then looks towards the council and its audience. "Hear me, I beg all of you, if you think this be a fool's word, let this have opened your eyes otherwise. Trust when I tell you, Maurdis be on his very way! We must prepare ourselves for the lycan's arrival! Lest many of us face the fate that befell those here today! We must not allow Skye to fall under Maurdis' rule! This day we choose to FIGHT!!" she proclaims in saying, lifting her staff in uproar. Immediately, the audience clamor in applause, followed by the chanting praise of 'Anna.' The counsellors look on at the audience, seeing their spirits lifted behind the likes of a young peasant girl, and are appalled. Humbly stepping down from their seats, the three counsellors approach Anna and the others to speak.

"Your bravery here today was unmatched, and your words proven true! We will give ear to your cause!" utters Lord Asher, bowing respectfully to the young Anna. Meanwhile, Terra nudges at Wraithe's side with her elbow.

"Well, she did it, we got their attention," she whispers to him.

"Good," he answers bluntly. "Now the real work begins." utters Wraithe stepping forth to speak with the counsellors.

"If I may?!" mentions Wraithe as he approaches. "We haven't much time, we need you to take us to the ancient chamber," tells Wraithe to them. The three counsellors look on lostly, not understanding the location of which he speaks.

"Ancient chamber?" scoffs Lord Asher. "Ha! WestSkye has nothing of the sort, revenant!" he adds in laughter. Meanwhile, Wraithe quietly walks by them, looking down at the aged floors near the seats of the counsellors. He notices a few of the council slabs appear loose and giving way.

"What is it?" asks Anna peculiarly, as an intriguing smile looms across the face of Wraithe. Suddenly, he pulls out his blade. "What are you doing?!" exclaims Anna oddly. Wraithe lifts his sword above his head, and with all his might; drives the edge of his sword forcefully into the council's floors. Suddenly, there is a great rumble beneath their feet, as sounds can be heard crashing and crumbling below. The floors circled about the counsellor's chairs begins to cave in, falling about in a downward spiral amidst the center of the council. Anna and the others watch on in astonishment.

"They built the council atop it," mentions Wraithe grandly in discovery. "With all their years of searching! None thought, to look beneath," he adds, as the ancient stairway appears circling beneath the three council's seats. "Welcome to the chamber of Aldrig!" he exclaims, leading them all below. Immediately, Anna and the others follow after him.

"Guard! Torches now!" orders Lady Elaine, before joining along the abysmal stairway. "No one is to pass here!" she instructs firmly. Etched into the circular column of the stairway holds the petrified wooden remains of the chamber's torches. Each take up a piece of wood, sharing from the flames of Lady Elaine and continue their descent into the mysterious shadows below. Finally, they arrive at the chamber's floor, a hot and humid clearing, surrounded by thick walls of stone. Lighting along the walls, Anna feels her way through the dried-up vinery, her fingertips running along the rigid barrier.

"So, what is this place?" opens Siff in question.

"The ancient chamber of Aldrig, it's where Mitrefys, the fate of nature, sealed away the white lotus, behind a great curtain of stone, to be guarded only by the most noble of knights, it was to protect against her kin, who sought out its gift," tells Wraithe fully, also feeling his way along the dusty walls. Anna then feels a sudden sensation among her hands. Looking to her palms, the lotus symbol luminates.

"What magic is this?!" gasps Lady Elaine, grasping onto Lord Asher.

"I feel something!" exclaims Anna fascinating at her palms. Immediately, Wraithe, Terra and Siff draw nigh to her. A peculiar sound hisses among their ears. "What is that?" murmurs Anna curiously. She then quickly digs within her satchel, pulling out the omni. She shakes at the staff, sprouting it to its full length, as a sizzling spark lights at its center. Carefully, she holds at each end of the staff. When suddenly, it splits, with a loud clink. The staff separates into two. A pulsating pull draws Anna to the walls of the chamber. Her luminating palms sizzling painfully, as she forcefully hurls the ends of the staff into the wall.

"AGHHHH!!" she grunts, as her staff presses further into the wall, followed by a shuddering rumble, as the etched encryptions of the curtain of stone begins to glow. With a final great push, Anna turns the ends of her staff, churning the circular encryption of the chamber's door. The omni appears to have operated as an ancient key, unlocking the very doors of Aldrig. Suddenly, The curtain of stone draws away, revealing a chambered oasis of hidden white lotus. Instantly, the withered vines along the chamber's walls sprouts back to life, with flowers appearing in full bloom. The chamber of Aldrig has been found, and vibrant with life.

"All those years!" whispers Lord Asher, circling in astonishment. "All those years and it was just below our very feet?!" he jumps in amazement.

"The knights had the council built atop the chamber for fortification and also deceit. The enemy would not look somewhere so obvious as the council itself; its location was perfect," tells Wraithe looking about them. Meanwhile, Anna proceeds along the path amidst the clear pristine pools of Aldrig. Four large pools, plentiful with floating pads of white lotus surround about them. Suddenly,

Siff stumbles upon something peculiar. He glimpses a trail, lining along the borders of the chamber, surrounding the pools of lotus. Kneeling to investigate, he holds his torch closer to view. Meanwhile, A piece of ember, drops onto the trail. Instantly, it sparks alive a trail of flame, giving light about the whole chamber.

"Praise be to the fates; look at all this!" proclaims Lord Asher joyously in disbelief, as the vibrant greenery of the inner walls bursts to life. "This is truly an act of the mother fate herself!" he goes on to add.

"The mother is no more," utters Wraithe bluntly in reply. "Her gift embodies within someone else," he tells further. The counsellors all look to the revenant in confusion.

"What be this of which you speak?!" utters Lord Asher upon hearing this. Wraithe then looks to Anna, notioning their attention towards her. Lord Asher then does a double-take between Wraithe and Anna.

"The girl?!" questions Asher in disbelief. "The mother fate entrusted immortality into the hands of you?" he points gauntly in saying.

"Absurd!" exclaims Lord Rollins, equally in denial. Anna then steps forward, revealing the lotus hue embedded within her palms.

"She entrusted it to me, that I may do whatever I can to keep it from falling into the hands of our enemy. WestSkye must not fall! Its people must prepare for the lycans arrival, otherwise, Maurdis will gain unlimited power, and we be no more!" tells Anna gravely to the elders. Silently, they search among themselves.

"Well then!" utters Lord Asher from the silence. "WestSkye will take up arms!" he vows solemnly in reply. "We must prepare the city immediately!" Anna then looks to Wraithe with a smile, as Siff and Terra stand proudly at his side. Their journey had officially become a success! WestSkye would stand against the threat of Maurdis and would finally prepare for war!

Chapter 8
The Order of the Pact

Beyond the walls of WestSkye, and the forests of Nostalgia, past the hills of east, A lone male journeys. His feet sore of his wandering; weak of strength and spirit broken with sorrow. His journey for truth compels him into the remnants of the great oasis of Equilibrius. Having made a great journey, Sept returns to the garden; where his father, Maurdis, patiently awaits.

Plagued by his distorted past, he enters the garden, through the remains of its fallen passage. An emptiness welcomes him; a lifeless wind carrying through the decimated valley. The ashes of its destruction remember his steps, as he trudges through the forest's remains. His father, Maurdis, nor the pact come out to meet him, as he continues to the one place his father would remain; the foot of the 'Divine Tree.' The journey to its location is clear, a seemingly never-ending rug of ash, leading ahead to its grounds.

As he approaches, Sept notices a structure in place of the former tree. It is a throne, carved of stone, with tall torches rowed along its path, where his father sits unmoved of his return. Sept arrives at his father's seat, where stands gathered, the pact. The men look on quietly in disdain, awaiting word from their lord.

"So, you've arrived?!" exclaims Maurdis unceremoniously, as Sept approaches the throne. Looking at his left, Sept glimpses Tidas standing in wait at his father's side. Tidas grins in contempt watching as his rival appears before them, meanwhile, Sept turns away, returning his attention towards Maurdis. "I sent you on a beginner's errand, and you failed… as expected," utters Maurdis in dismay. "I could've sent omega, to handle such a task," he compares bleakly in mentioning.

Sept boldly faces to him, "Father, give me another chance! I will avenge us! Our lord! I can retrieve the lotus!"

"I GAVE YOU A CHANCE!" roars Maurdis furiously, standing from the throne. "But I was wrong, you lack resolve; you are weak, and not worthy to be one of us! Not worthy of my blood!" he rages on. "You have failed! Now! Your fate will be decided by the pact!" condemns Maurdis harshly in decision. A shadow casts over Sept, as a rage boils within him.

"I SERVED! I GAVE YOU EVERYTHING!" Sept retorts angrily, looking to his father from beneath the throne, "AND WHAT OF EVERYTHING I'VE DONE! IS IT NOT ENOUGH!"

"The words of a fool! Your failure has betrayed the order of the pact!" condemns Maurdis further. Sept suddenly goes silent, as a striking thought comes to mind.

"And what of mother?!" he lifts his head in question. Maurdis stands bewildered by this.

"Sceptra?! Your mother? Ha," he scoffs in disgust. "You be both of the same!" adds Maurdis coldly in reply. The welling eyes of Sept widen with disbelief.

"By the fates, what did you do?!" cries Sept in question. Maurdis returns with a sinister smirk, stepping down from his throne.

"Your mother's fate was written by her own hand the moment she betrayed us!" he whispers madly in return. It is these words that sends Sept into a fit of rage.

"YOU BASTARD!!!" roars Sept, charging towards him in attack. Suddenly, he is caught; having been snatched by the throat at the hands of Maurdis, lifting him from his feet.

"Foolish child! Thought yourself a worthy challenge for me?! You are NOTHING!" scoffs Maurdis, casting Sept aside. "You know the order of the pact!" exclaims his father turning to his subjects, as Sept struggles to his knees.

"Challenge or exile!" uproar the men in chant.

Maurdis grins, turning to his son. "That's right! Challenge or exile!" he repeats to him with disdain. "You have lost your place, as my son, and my successor!" adds Maurdis, as Sept slowly musters to his feet. "You will now have to fight for your place in the pact!"

"Now!" exclaims Maurdis momentously, turning to his men. "Have we any to claim the rite of challenge?!" he utters openly to the gathered. Suddenly, Sept's wound awakens with a sharp searing pain, as he quickly grasps at his shoulder.

"I claim the rite of challenge!" answers Tidas boldly stepping forth. He grins connivingly as Sept wallows in pain. A familiar scent hints at his nose; immediately, he senses Sept's injury, seeing the saturated stain at his right shoulder. He has chosen the perfect chance.

"There is no quarrel with this request?!" asks Maurdis outwardly to the gathered. "None of you?" he looks to them once more in saying, as the men utter not a word. Finally, he returns to Sept and Tidas, singled out among them. "So, let the challenge," grins Maurdis smugly, looking into the eyes of Sept. "BEGIN!!" he sanctions with a wave of his hand.

Tidas then steps forth to Sept in saying. "I've long awaited this!" he tells encircling about him. Meanwhile, Sept's sight follows Tidas' every step, as he readies for his attack. "It's because of you! The pact is weak! But I, will bring about perfection!" rants Sept wildly in contempt.

"Whatever victory you think you'll have, all ends today!" retorts Sept breathily in reply, as both men ready their swords. Tidas impatiently rushes towards Sept, swinging wildly for his throat. Meanwhile, Sept groggily manages to duck, weaving from the edge of Tidas' blade. With a clever swing, Tidas anticipates the dodge of Sept, and as he rises, strikes him with a swing of his fist, rendering Sept mildly off balance.

"Is that all!" laughs Tidas in enjoyment, as Sept wipes away the stain of his soiled lip. Collecting himself, he advances to Tidas, swinging for his rival's head; he misses, and as he turns, he is met by another hefty fist from Tidas. This time, Tidas follows up with a finishing swing, to which Sept manages to weave away. Weak and exhausted, Sept has very little strength to defend himself, as Tidas attacks once more. This time, Sept joins in swing, as both swords clash in meeting. Tidas moves in, attempting to drive his sword into Sept, however, he slips away. As Tidas' sword glides by, it cuts at Sept's side and the two enter a violent grapple. Sept then grips onto the forearms of Tidas and delivers a crashing headbutt. For a moment this dizzies Tidas, who then responds by pressing his thumb into the open wound of Sept's shoulder.

"Arghhhhh!!" screams Sept in agony, as he draws Tidas into him, and rolls to his back, hoisting his enemy over him to the ground. Tidas quickly musters to his feet, picking up his sword and diving towards Sept, who scarcely manages to avoid the blade's edge. However, upon drawing back his blade, he again manages to cut Sept, this time, along his right thigh.

"Arghhhh!!" cries Sept painfully, grabbing at the wound. Tidas swiftly advances in attack, yet Sept again, weaves away, countering with a hefty uppercut, stunning Tidas, placing him off balance. Tidas grins in amusement, as he charges towards him. Sept anticipates, patiently rushing forth; however, he feints below and with a sneaky kick at Tidas' foot, trips him to the ground. Frustrated, Tidas strikes towards the ground in a fit of rage, growing weary of their battle.

Rising to his feet, Tidas dusts himself of dirt. "ENOUGH OF THIS!!" he snarls in saying, looking to the sky as the moon takes over the horizon. Tidas then steps forward, forming into a fearsome, gray lycan. Sept looks on, his shoulder writhing in pain; he can no longer prolong their battle; he realizes he will have to put Tidas down, once and for all. Sept transforms; appearing as a lean, dark-coated lycan. Tidas, the more fearsome of the two, appears taller and much larger in physical build. Teeth bared, gnashing in contempt, the two beasts clash! Meanwhile, from the throne, Maurdis looks on in enjoyment.

Sept pins Tidas to the ground, when suddenly, Tidas reaches around, crunching down upon the injured shoulder of Sept, following with a powerful kick, tossing the lycan off of him. Sept whimpers, limping to his feet, turning to face Tidas. A sweep of the forest's ash is hurled into his sight. Stumbling back, pawing the dust from his eyes; Tidas rushes upon him, biting down upon his left shank, causing Sept to yelp in pain, as Tidas hurls him across the way.

Beaten, exhausted and in considerable pain, Sept drops into his human state, as Tidas creeps upon him, preparing to finally put an end to their hostile rivalry.

Sensing his impending victory, Tidas returns to his human state. Slowly, he approaches Sept, who struggles to his knees. Tidas retrieves his sword, standing over Sept, grinning as he relishes his moment.

"I don't understand how the pact stomached such disappointment as yourself! You are nothing! You will always be nothing, compared to me!" whispers Tidas coldly in saying, as he lifts his blade to deliver the final strike. When suddenly, Maurdis rises from the 'throne.'

"ENOUGH!" Maurdis halts abruptly, stepping down between them. He brushes Tidas aside, standing before his son. Meanwhile, Sept struggles to his knees. "I'm disappointed in you my son," utters Maurdis cruelly. "It'd been better if you had not returned! Dispose of him," he instructs coldly, patting at Tidas' shoulder. Maurdis then turns away, leaving Sept behind, groveling in pain at the mercy of Tidas. Quickly, Tidas calls over two nearby men, who approach, lifting Sept from the ground. Dragging Sept by his arms, they begin pulling him across the way. In final insult, Tidas grabs at Sept's jaw, facing him towards the men.

"See how the pact looks down on you in shame!" he whispers into the disoriented gaze of Sept. "I hope you can swim!" he chuckles evilly in smiling. "You will need it," he tells, releasing his grip upon Sept's face. Tidas turns away, pausing, and with a swift spin, Sept meets the blunt handle of Tidas' sword, rendering him unconscious. "Throw him in the river!" orders Tidas mercilessly to the men, as he proceeds to the throne, where Maurdis sits in waiting.

Looking over his gathered subjects as Tidas attends before him, Maurdis stands in speaking. "MY BROTHERS!" he addresses. "We have been dealt unjustly by fate! Mankind thinks us weak! They doubt the pact's power… banished our lord! And deemed our order a curse!" rants Maurdis wildly in saying. "We are hated for our indifference, when it is our salvation! I ask you this day? Shall you tolerate this insolence anymore?" he roars aloud in question.

"No!!" proclaim the men in uproar.

"Our freedom lies none other than in the western haven! WE shall tear through their walls! Rip through the very fabric of their souls! Avenge our lord!! And take our IMMORTALITY!!" proclaims Maurdis in conquest. The men uproar, clamoring in applause, as their voices and deep howls echoes into the night.

Chapter 9
A Narrow Fate

Beyond the void of Equilibrius; edge of Nostalgia, and the great river's pass, the counsellors of WestSkye, presume orders in preparation for Maurdis and his legion of lycans.

"All women and children will safety themselves within the council! Guards positioned at every entry!" orders Lord Asher dutifully to the men, as he, alongside Wraithe and fellow counsellors continue in strategy. "I want all able hands to protect against entry of the council! If Maurdis seizes it; then may the fates be with us all!" he mutters gravely. Suddenly, Wraithe steps forth, as Anna and the others listen on.

"If I may?" Wraithe humbly joins in. "There is little to be done once Maurdis and his legion are to enter the city. By that time, it would simply be survival. Use some leverage and place as many men atop the city walls, and roofs of the main path! An enemy from below, cannot fend against an enemy he can't see!" suggests Wraithe to the inexperienced seniors.

Lord Rollins moves by them, "The knight is right, the city has much tall households along its main path, we can use them for an edge in battle!" he looks to Wraithe in agreement.

"I also stand with the idea; a life not within reach is a life saved!" answers Lady Elaine, nodding in approval.

"Then it is settled! The people must be pulled from their homes and evacuated to the taverns along the eastern wall. That escape route, would ensure safe secret passage, should WestSkye be invaded!" ends Lord Asher in decision. "I stand with the knight!" turns Asher to them in agreement. He then looks to Wraithe, who has disappeared. "Ummm, knight where did you go?!" he calls to Wraithe in question. Suddenly, he is seen strolling off in the nearby distance, leaving behind the perplexed group.

"For a drink, good sir! Seeing that your canteen is along the city's main path, I figured it won't be open during our preparations!" answers Wraithe in telling, turning to them as he departs.

"Ah," utters Asher reluctantly in reply, looking among the men, who chuckle among themselves.

"I leave you all to carry on! Don't mind me!" voices Wraithe, continuing in his way. Anna and Siff then look to Terra, who notions for them to follow after him. The youngsters enter the bustling canteen where droves of townspeople and travelers alike line each table. Both arguments and laughter rage throughout the crowded space, as they creep along the merry crowd, who look puzzled, as the younger Anna and Siff follow towards the bar's counter. Bottles of alcohol line along the shelves behind the wooden counter, as individuals are seen grabbing up the large mugs and slamming silver pieces noisily along the countertop.

"There he is!" tells Terra turning to them, as she points to the end of the bar counter. Following Terra's notion, Anna catches glimpse of Wraithe handing a few pieces of silver to the bartender. Quickly, the three sidestep their way through, until finally arriving at his side.

"Ah, there you all are! Nice of you all to join me!" he utters reluctantly, looking to them in saying. "Join me in seating!" he tells, patting at one of the few wooden stools at his side. Quickly, the three sweep up the seats, when suddenly, the bartender approaches. "A beer!" orders Wraithe bluntly to him, with a nodding smirk. The male goes off swiftly in retrieving the order. Again, Wraithe returns to the three. "We need to be quick," he warns. "Maurdis may appear at the city gates sooner than we think! And the two of you have no skill whatsoever, our odds do not look promising," he goes on to tell. Meanwhile, the bartender approaches; in hand, a tall iron mug which he places in front of Wraithe. Anna and Siff fascinate in the foamy beverage, its content running slowly down its sides. They watch as Wraithe grips the mug, tilting it to his mouth and gulping the beer filled mug within seconds. He rests it aside, slamming a few extra pieces of silver onto the counter.

"We must be quick? What is it?" looks Anna to him curiously in question.

"I said five days..." Wraithe pitches up, dusting his sleeves, "But they might come sooner!" he tells, quickly turning to leave. The three abandon the wooden stools, keeping a foot behind him, as they continue in questioning.

"Why do you think it may be earlier?" Anna goes on to ask.

Wraithe pauses, turning to her, wary of her questionings. "The blood moon!" he utters in whispering, continuing towards the canteen's exit. Shoving open the shutter doors, they reenter into the city's main path. "It is a time that passes once every twenty years. Where the lycans can pass on their curse to whomever unfortunate soul falls victim to their bite! It is also a time where they are most powerful! Maurdis was wise in choosing his strike!" utters Wraithe gravely.

"What will we do?!" voices Siff looking to each of them.

Anna silently ponders to herself, facing Wraithe boldly in saying. "I mustn't run, the council has chosen to stand and fight! As we speak, they prepare the city for threat of the lycan's attack, Mitrefys gifted me this; the lotus is a part of me, and I, a part of it! I cannot allow it to fall into the hands of him! I want to stand and fight!"

This statement crosses Terra and Siff by surprise, as they both look to Wraithe for his response. Wraithe turns away, closing his eyes in thought, breathing slowly, as he returns to her with his answer. "This what you ask of me, the fate you have chosen; should Maurdis kill you and take the lotus, he will be unstoppable," mutters Wraithe severely.

"I know, but no more running, if he wants the lotus, he'll have to come to us!" utters Anna stoutly in reply.

Wraithe smirks reluctantly, as a brief thought of 'Arthur' comes to mind. "So be it," he answers. "I will train you; both of you!" he also looks down to Siff. "But not here... and definitely not now!" he goes on to say.

"W-Wait what? w-why not now? When is the next blood moon?" stutters Anna confused at his reply.

"The next blood moon is within four days, so we'll be training until the second Muardis arrives!" adds Wraithe calmly, strolling along the brick lain path, passing by the tall houses and rickety chariots. "I overheard a few of the gaurds speaking of a courtyard, just beyond the rear of the council, it'll serve us well for your first lessons!"

"I'm ready!" utters Anna anxiously in saying. "Siff?" she turns to him beside her, who also nods in agreement.

"Good! We shall see," comments Wraithe in reply. Again, the four arrive at the council's doors. This time, they are met by a guard, who immediately bids them to enter. Once more, they proceed by the noisy bids of traders, bustling plethora of market stalls and traffics of livestock within the council's great hall.

"Good sir, we are wary there may be a courtyard beyond the rear doors of the great council, would you be so kind?" murmurs Wraithe lowly to the guard, as he escorts them along the crowd.

"Of course, right this way!" notions the guard, directing them left, and along a stone stairway, leading to the council's upper chambers. The four follow along the stairway's curve, circling them to its peak, where lies a dreary corridor. "Down here," tells the guard, reaching one of the torches hung nearby, as they move along the shadowy corridor. They pass rows of wooden doors along each side; however, it is surprisingly quiet. At its end lies a double door, approaching it, the guard fumbles his keys into its lock and with a great shove, opens to a beautiful lush green courtyard, alive with trees, and undisturbed view of WestSkye below. Anna and Siff rush over to the balcony's walls, looking down among the frolicking children and passing horses. They also glimpse the smoke, presumably from the city's bakeries and blacksmiths. It is a spacious area, enough for their training to be officially carried out. Just as the sun slowly lowers beyond the horizon, and the moon peaks its head, Wraithe calls over the pair.

"Anna, step forth!" commands Wraithe vaguely, as he watches from along the patio, facing towards the lush courtyard. Puzzled, Anna takes a step ahead of Siff, looking to Wraithe for instruction. "Good!" he utters, moving his sights to the right. "Terra, do step forth!" he orders further. Terra quickly follows the revenant's instruction. Anna feels a sudden skip in her heartbeat, as she gears her mind into focus. The two females stand exactly center of the courtyard, both awaiting word of Wraithe.

"Face one another!" adds Wraithe in instruction. Swiftly, the two spin into eye contact. "Two-minute combat until yield! Begin!" he commands jarringly. Terra immediately yucks her sword from behind, having drawn it from her satchel strapped across her shoulder and bosom. Meanwhile, Anna nervously fumbles the omni, pointing unsurely, as she readies for an attack. Terra charges towards her, swinging viciously for Anna's head. Anna's only instinct; to also attack; as she hurls the omni in striking, causing the two blades to meet with a thunderous clash. Terra then kicks at Anna, knocking the inexperienced female off-balance. Wasting not even the slightest second, Terra makes another great swing towards Anna, who ducks, as the blade's strafing breeze whistles overhead. Anna rises with a block, struggling against Terra's push.

"Defend yourself! Advance!" coaxes Wraithe fiercely to Anna, watching on. Meanwhile, Siff's heart also races in anticipation. "Do not allow her to keep taking your ground!" adds Wraithe in saying. Shoving Terra off, Anna makes a hesitant strike towards her, yet Terra glides effortlessly beneath her sword. Anticipating Anna's next move, she hurls her blade with all her might, and the two females' blades meet again in another thunderous clash.

Anna slowly grows weary of their battle, meanwhile, Terra eyes her with a grin. "Always expect the unexpected!" she mutters smugly. Suddenly, she stomps at Anna's foot, putting her slightly off balance, as she hops in pain. With a swift strike of her elbow to Anna's face; she is stunned. Terra then shoves her off, putting space between them, as she poses confidently. Meanwhile, Anna's momentum causes her to trip, falling to her back. Quickly retrieving her fallen sword, Anna turns, coming face to face with Terra's blade, rendering her into submission.

"Enough! Terra wins," informs Wraithe, gesturing the battle's victory over to Terra. Defeated, Anna's head drops in a disgruntled shrug. Meanwhile, Terra catches wind of Anna's frustration, and proceeds near her. Anna then feels a shadow looming over her and looks up, seeing Terra's hand extended to her in sportsmanship. She reluctantly grasps it and is assisted to her feet. Suddenly, a sharp pain tingles behind her.

"Oww!" groans Anna, painfully grasping at her lower back.

"What's wrong?" chuckles Terra, lightly patting her shoulder.

"Well, you got me," nods Anna painfully in humor.

Again, Terra pats at her shoulder. "Chin up!" she replies. "You did great, lasted the full two minutes! You won't learn everything in a day," she adds encouragingly. Wraithe is then seen approaching the pair, as Siff watches idly, from the sidelines.

"You got sloppy," he scolds harshly in mentioning, as if Anna's spirits weren't dampened enough. "You allowed yourself to be beaten once you gave up your ground! But…" he tells with a brief pause, as Anna lifts her head in hearing. "You lasted the full two minutes, against a formidable opponent. You did better than expected," adds Wraithe in saying, impressed at her resilience. This causes a small blossom of confidence to fluster within her.

"We will work on your speed and precision, but above all your defense," tells Wraithe straightly. "As for the boy…" he adds, turning his attention towards Siff. "I have something special for him! Follow me!" he leads. Drawing them closer to the edge of the courtyard, near the very walls that overlook the stony brick paths of the city, Wraithe points ahead. "Over there!" he ushers, vaguely showing across the way.

"What is it?" utters Anna questionably, as the sights of what Wraithe speaks goes unnoticed.

"You must be able to sense the threat," answers Wraithe in teaching. "Among the trees, do you see it?" he voices further. Seconds later, Siff glimpses a target, etched into the trunk of a tree.

"I see it!" exclaims Siff, as he jumps in pointing.

"Good!" answers Wraithe shortly. "Now you use your bow!" he tells pacing by Siff, who looks up puzzled in expression. "You will take aim and strike at the eye of the target," Wraithe goes on to explain. "Your friend had her share of training, now we shall see yours!" he goes on to say. Siff nods quietly, as Terra nears him, handing over a bow with arrow in her other a hand. He accepts and proceeds to Wraithe's side, lifting it up in aim.

Wraithe leans closer to his ear in whispering. "Calm your senses," he instructs, noting the nervousness within Siff's breathing. "Slow your breaths and draw your weapon," he continues calmly. Collecting his nerves, Siff draws back the arrow in aim of the cutout target. "Measure the wind! use it to your advantage!" continues Wraithe in instruction. Siff closes his eyes, feeling as the cool winds whisp by his face. Opening his eyes in exhale, he fires slightly in the direction of the breeze, timing its break. Suddenly, a light gust of wind blows by, as the arrow is within flight. Their eyes follow along the arrows direction until finally it strikes the tree.

Excited, Siff rushes over to check out his shot. As he approaches the target, he is quickly disappointed. The arrow has landed slightly left of the bullseye. Wraithe, however, remains undeniably impressed. "That was a difficult shot! Into the wind, and still you almost made the mark," he mentions impressively. "You have a steady hand," he adds further in encouragement, calling to Anna, and Terra to view the arrow's mark.

"You did that! That's amazing!" exclaims Anna proudly to Siff. Terra also smiles equally impressed. Wraithe then slowly walks by.

"Be forewarned… talent does not trump skill, we now have three days," he stresses urgently to the three.

"I thought you said there would be four?" voices Anna in question.

"That would be the night of the actual blood moon, by then, training wouldn't matter, only death! Three days! We have much more work to do!" he adds bluntly, turning to them in haste.

"Well, I'm ready!" replies Anna eagerly in determination. Siff also stands at her side, nodding in agreeance.

"Me too!" he voices, readying his bow.

"Good," nods Wraithe. "Let us begin!" he commences emphatically. With that, Anna and Siff's preparation for the fight against Maurdis and the lycans, has officially begun. They are led once more to the center of the courtyard, beneath the full moon. Wraithe and Anna draws away, jousting their blades in practice, meanwhile, Terra lifts Siff's arm in aim, as he steadies his shot.

"Watch your step! Swing and pivot!" Wraithe instructs as the two spar along the center of the courtyard. "Underneath!" he tells, jousting forth as Anna dives below his sword.

Meanwhile, Siff fires his shot; yet again, the arrow falls short of the target's eye. "A little short," shrugs Terra lightly in saying. "Here, watch this!" she utters, lifting her bow to her sights. With a calm breath, she measures the breeze, tilting her aim slightly and releases. The arrow's whistle leaves them behind; within seconds striking dead center of the bullseye. this leaves Siff speechless, as he turns to her in gaze. "You'll get there!" comments Terra with a chuckle. "Come on, we have lots to do!" she adds, returning to their practice. The four would then continue tirelessly through the night, until the next morning arrives.

The dawn approaches quickly, meeting the four well into their training, drenched of the sweat of continued sparring and exercises. "Quickly step!" instructs Wraithe, as his and Anna's sparring intensifies. Following his instruction, Anna moves forward, diving toward him with her blade. "Good! Now defend yourself! anticipate the enemy!" he tells impressed at her advance. Finally, he presses towards her in return, with fierce strikes of his sword. Anna slips and weaves away, making a low sweep towards his foot. Wraithe quickly withdraws his feet with a feint spin. Meanwhile, Anna continues with a confident rush towards him, advancing with continuous jousts of her sword.

"Good, good, step forth!" Wraithe encourages among their clashing of swords. "Duck and weave," he adds, making a sudden joust towards her with his sword's tip.

Meanwhile.

"Hold it steady!" instructs Terra to Siff, both taking aim towards the target. "Mind your breathing, but most of all, trust your shot!" she advises calmly. With that, the two release. Once more, Siff scurries towards the target. He approaches, glimpsing Terra's arrow having landed dead center. Finally, he quickly strolls over to his target, this time, his arrow lies just beyond the eye's center.

Again, Siff shrugs in disappointment. "I missed!" he tells frustratingly, kicking at the dust. Meanwhile, Terra approaches from behind.

"Hmm, not bad, let's try again," she encourages, returning across the courtyard. "Come on!" she calls to Siff, who reluctantly follows behind.

The four continue to train throughout the full day, taking little break, as the dusk finds them among the courtyard, sharpening their new skills for the impending threat.

The next day approaches quickly, finding the counsellors busy about the city streets, giving orders to each guard in WestSkye. Lord Asher is leader among them, instructing both his fellow counsellors and guards alike. "The great river's stream flows through the center of our great city, our eastern and western walls are far too exposed, and vulnerable, we've made the decision that the city's natural water supply be cut off!" informs Lord Asher regrettably, striking an uproar of murmuring among the men.

"And what of our families?!" voices one from the crowd indistinctly.

"Yeah, if the city's water is cutoff, we'll die of thirst, there wouldn't be need to prepare for an attack then!" adds another.

"QUIET! There must be order!" exclaims Lord Asher, capturing the silence of the complaining group. "If we allow the river to continue its route through the city, the lycans may use it for easy passage to infiltrate us. It is within our better judgement, we bid the citizens to collect as much water storage as they can. Then, and only then, we fortify the walls of the great river to better defend against an attack along the city's sides!"

"It is done!" agrees Lord Rollins, stepping forth in decision against the commotion. "Notify every household! Water must be collected before dusk; else it will be their sorrow!" he ends, turning away from the disgruntled crowd. With that, the soldiers reluctantly make their way throughout the city's paths, knocking upon every door, telling every ear of the council's decision. Its urgency immediately placing the people on edge, as they rush to gathering among the city's wells and streams in collection of water.

After word has been spread throughout the city, the guards begin lining pillars of sand along the great river's entry and exit of WestSkye. They begin feeding the bags of sand into its six-foot stream, until the very last bucket is filled from the remaining pool. It is almost evening, when finally, the last sandbag is hurled atop the huge pile, shutting out the waters of the river's stream. the waterway finally becomes nothing more than a lengthy wet ditch, as the remaining waters of its current flows out of the city, thereafter, walled off by the pillows of sand.

Meanwhile, Dusk has begun to fall, as Anna and the others having taken a break from their intense training, casually stroll about the restless paths of WestSkye. "The city hasn't slept in three days," mentions Anna, as guards are seen toting bales of swords and archery along the paths. Further along, carriages follow in line, carrying what seems as huge woven balls in direction of the city's main gates.

"What are those?" looks Anna to Terra in question.

"They're for the catapult; coated with oil, they're set afire; a form of long-range defense, it'll be needed in this fight," answers Terra firmly, as they continue on. Meanwhile, Siff who lags slightly behind, takes a hard swallow, as the anticipation and preparation of the lycan's arrival looms.

The dawn arises, upon another day, again meeting the pair in training. This time, however, it is Anna and Siff engaged in close combat sparring, as Wraithe and Terra look on from the steps of the courtyard's edge. Anna and Siff confidently trade strikes towards each other with their swords, stepping into jousts and spinning attacks. Seeing their progress, Wraithe mutters lowly to Terra, standing at his side. "Now," he utters bluntly. Terra immediately skips down the steps, entering the courtyard, with a stern fixed focus, as she approaches the sparring pair.

Distracted by their sparring, Anna advances. "Mind your step," she tells Siff, who stumbles in blocking her strikes. "Good, now follow through!" she encourages as the pair thrash blades. Looking down, Anna glimpses a shadow, leaping towards them. As she peers up, her eyes widen. "Lookout!" she exclaims to Siff, shoving him out of the way, when Terra rushes in with a downward strike of her sword. Getting to her feet, she stands ready between the surprised pair.

"Ready yourselves!" informs Wraithe stoutly to Anna and Siff. "Terra!" he orders with a nod. Meanwhile, Anna clenches tightly at her sword, as Terra rushes in to engage.

"Siff!" calls Anna. "Keep your distance... keep her on her toes!" she orders, hurling a fierce strike in defense against Terra. The two women hash out their blades, meanwhile, Siff remains distant, as he takes aim against Terra, and fires. As she and Anna struggle in a push of swords, Terra glimpses Siff targeting her along her blade's gleaming reflection. She thrusts off Anna, tumbling her to the ground, as she dives into a roll, with the arrows searing breeze whistling by.

Anna recovers, and remains relentless in her advance, rushing into Terra with fierce strikes of her sword, placing her slightly off balance. Meanwhile, Siff continues in firing arrows, as each do their part in keeping the experienced warrior to her toes.

"Good!" utters Wraithe impressed at the pair's efforts. "As a unit," he goes on to instruct. Finally, Siff releases his last arrow; this time, managing to cut at Terra's boot. In that second, Terra is surprised and distracted, making a sudden stumble. Anna however, capitalizes, and with a swift kick, knocks Terra to the ground. Terra quickly rolls, gathering to her feet; however, she is met by another powerful left swing from Anna. She quickly blocks, shoving away Anna's blade, sending her into a spin. Using this momentum, Anna's sword transforms into a broad circular shield, spinning into a block of Terra's next attack. She thrusts Terra off with her shield and twirls about, splitting the shield into dual blades. Anna fiercely rushes towards Terra, attacking with random swings of the swords. Terra counters, parrying one of the blades, attempting to strike Anna. Anticipating the attack, Anna returns her weapons into the firm shield, yet again thwarting Terra's strike. With a swift duck, Anna sweeps at her foot, falling her to the ground with a thud. Terra quickly sits up, coming to a pause, as her eyes rise to meet Anna's blade, poised towards her face.

"Yield!" demands Anna sternly, standing victoriously above her. Terra's expression grows to an impressed smile, as she rests her forearm upon her knee.

"Okay, I yield," utters Terra reluctantly in smiling, casually accepting her defeat. Anna's face brightens to a smile, leaping for joy, as she extends her hand to Terra, helping her to her feet. Once to her feet, Terra pats at Anna's shoulder in sportsmanship.

"Good job!" she tells proudly, turning to Wraithe, who remains composed in grin. Siff is seen rushing towards them, elated of their small victory.

"We did it!" he exclaims jumping in excitement.

"We did," replies Anna with a smile. "But we're far from through," she adds, looking over to Wraithe, who continues watching from the courtyard's edge. Terra resumes at his side, as Anna and Siff finally make their way towards them.

"Very good…" congratulates Wraithe bluntly to the pair. "However, we have much to do, we will resume combat!" Instantly, Anna and Siff look to each other in disbelief, as Terra chuckles to herself, passing them by.

"Well, you heard him… let's go!" she adds humorously. "And this time, I WON'T be going easy," Terra scoffs in laughter.

Anna and Siff reluctantly follow out into the courtyard, where they meet Terra grinning in wait. Siff readies his bow, when suddenly, Wraithe intervenes. "No arrows, this time!" he exclaims from the courtyard's edge. "The enemy we face is fierce, and sooner or later, you will face them, and there'll be no distance enough to protect you, so, without further ado, swords only!" Immediately, Siff rests his bow and arrow bag aside with a shrug, pulling out his blade tucked between his belt and tunic. Siff then readies his stance, firmly positioned beside Anna.

"Begin!" gives Wraithe in order. Immediately, Terra rushes towards them. With a heightened strategy, the pair take turns in blitz towards her. Terra skillfully slips and dodges between their attacks, removing her feet and abdomen from Siff's low strikes, meanwhile also diving below the hefty winds of Anna's blade. "Continue! As a unit!" encourages Wraithe strongly.

Anna and Siff continue their rotation of attack, taking turns between fierce and swift strikes. Terra quickly counters, targeting the weaker Siff. Sweeping at his foot, she falls him to the ground. Instantly, Anna follows through, with continuous blinding strikes towards Terra, allowing Siff enough chance to his feet.

"Hurry Siff!" yells Anna, struggling to fend against Terra. With a twirl of her sword behind her back, and a beautiful spin, Terra blocks Siff's surprise attack with a smirk. Meanwhile, Anna joins them with a fierce strike, as the three swords tangle amongst themselves. As each withdraw their swords, Terra juggles between the pair, both attacking and defending against their rush. All the while, the sun finally begins showing signs of descent.

Finally, Wraithe steps in, looking to the looming red sky. "Enough!" he exclaims. "We have covered the basics of battle, for now, we must rest, the enemy is soon to approach, we shall continue in the morning," tells Wraithe bluntly, as he abruptly turns away, leaving the courtyard and the three amidst their duel. Reluctant of his sudden change of plans, the three quickly collect their items, and follow swiftly behind, as Wraithe shoves open the chamber's doors, entering the gloomy corridor.

"The doors to your left and right be the washrooms, I've instructed the guards to have provided water for you all to cleanse. You will also find protective attire, you will need them, for now, rest up! I will meet you all in the morning," tells Wraithe, as he departs down the corridor. Meanwhile, Anna and Siff stare puzzled amongst each other, both slowly turning to Terra.

"I don't know," shrugs Terra, watching as he descends the stairs of the hallway's end. "He probably is taking time to gather his thoughts on a strategy against the lycans, let's do what he says, we'll need all the rest we can get," tells Terra, pushing open the creaky wooden door. Little mice and few roaches can be seen scurrying across the floors, as the feint light from the torch casts into the humid dark room.

With that, the four relieve themselves of their weaponry, and sweat-soaked attire, cleaning themselves within the washrooms of the hall. Anna washes with the cloth, tilting the wooden bale over her head, as its waters splash down, rinsing her of the day's filth. Walking across the stony floors, she retrieves a dry cloth. As she pats dry, her mind wanders heavily. Would they actually be able to withstand the might of the lycan's army? Would the great city of WestSkye fall? Would Maurdis finally retrieve the white lotus? Her mind would race uncontrollably for the next few moments.

Suddenly.

"Anna! Anna!" utters a voice, shuddering her into reality. It is Terra, standing at the door of the washroom, amidst the hallway. "What's wrong? Any drier and you'll be a raisin, come on!" she calls to her. Anna reluctantly tosses aside the cloth, grabbing at her robes, having been placed along the washroom's post by the guards. Anna joins, as the three retreat into the makeshift rooms along the gloomy hallway. She enters the bedroom, and to her surprise, meets Siff fast asleep. Their comforts are spreads of layered mats, sprawled along the stone floor, neatly laid alongside each other. Anna kneels along her spread, covering herself between the itchy quilted sheets.

"Great job today, you fought well!" mentions Terra, slightly startling Anna, who inches beneath the quilts. She flips her sights to a drowsy-eyed Terra, facing her, as they lie along the floor.

"Thanks, but it took two of us to even put up a fight against you, we won't be a match for Maurdis," mutters Anna in a discouraging sigh. Terra ponders her words, as she looks to Anna.

"We can't afford to think like that, there are children in this city, the fate of sky leans on the victory of this battle, if Maurdis gains the lotus, he as well as all those that follow him will be unstoppable. You're the lotus; Mitrefys chose you! Not us! YOU! You are the symbol of hope; for all of us!" ends Terra confidently in saying. Anna is struck with silence, searching inwardly at herself. "Get some rest, okay? It's almost midnight," mentions Terra, rolling over to sleep. Anna however, remains wide awake, plagued by fears, and thoughts, shrouding her conscience. Doubt would cycle her mind for hours, until in a blanket of fatigue, she is pulled into a deep sleep.

Hours go by, finding Anna tossing and turning in her sleep, as the winds clap the wooden shutters along the window. "No No, Father don't leave! No, No!" she twists and murmurs within her sleep, her eyes finally opening to the ceiling. She sits up from her mat of slumber, rubbing her hands to her dreary face in sigh. As she looks up, she notices a cast of light, lighting the wall ahead of her. Anna quickly spins about, facing the door, leading into the chamber's hallway. A shadow can be seen quickly brushing past the door's crack. Curious, she tosses aside her quilt, scampering to her feet, creeping quietly towards the room's door. Slowly pulling back the room's door, Anna pokes her head into the hallway, glimpsing the cloaked figure, proceeding to its exit, where outside lies the courtyard. Striking her as odd, she turns to see both Siff and Terra still fast asleep. Anna then squeezes through the doorway, keeping silent of its creaking. Pulling slowly the door shut behind her, she makes her way along the hallway, following after the cloaked shadow. As 'they' arrive at the corridor's end, the shadow stops. With torch in hand, 'they' turn about, as the panicked Anna scampers to the side, perching up against the corner of a doorpost along the hallway. The cloaked figure casts the torch's light down the hallway, their sights searching along the corridor. Her breath held, Anna perches to her toes against the door, sucking in her gut. Appearing satisfied, the stranger returns to the courtyard's door. Twisting its lock, they open the doors to exit, shutting it closed behind them. Anna exhales a breath of relief, as she finally steps back into the hallway.

"Where are you going?" whispers Anna to herself in question, as she approaches the courtyard's doors. She slowly pushes open the doors, peeping her head out into the courtyard's balcony, however, it is empty! And there is no sign of the cloaked stranger! Again, Anna looks left and right, as she steps out into the moonlight. Taking a few more steps away from the door, she is suddenly snatched from behind, in a hold about her neck, with blade poised to her face. She hasn't the time to escape or move.

"You should be in bed," utters a familiar male voice in her ear.

"I had a feeling it was you; who else would be up this late?" murmurs Anna breathily in reply.

"Oh yeah? Well, what if it hadn't?!" snarls Wraithe in question, releasing his hold. "You would've been dead," he comments further, as Anna rubs her hand upon her throat. Wraithe turns away, and steps down into the courtyard, overlooking the city of WestSkye.

"Why do you linger out here?" asks Anna calmly to him, as he leans along the posts of the balcony's edge. Wraithe however, appears to ignore her presence, and remains silent. Finally, Anna makes her way down the steps, uneasily approaching behind him. Joining near his side, they overlook the city.

"You truly should rest; you'll need every bit of strength for what's to come," scoffs Wraithe reluctantly to her in reply. Hearing this, Anna quietly looks down in thought, as questions boil over within her mind; from the arrival of the lycans; to their fearsome leader, Maurdis! Her thoughts race continuously.

Finally, she turns to Wraithe in question. "This Maurdis…" begins Anna in saying, walking towards Wraithe. "Why does he hate my father? Why does he hate you?" minces Anna at her words, seeing as he draws in a deep breath.

"We were one. All of us. But betrayal befell us; on both sides, it is then, you learn, some sins can never be forgiven!" murmurs Wraithe darkly in reply. "Our oath, our Order, was what we lived for, sword and sword; blood and blood, we were bound to it, our knighthood," he pauses, looking towards the night's sky. "In the order, we had what was called a 'blood debt.' I had previously spoken to you all of a knight being unable to raise their sword against another; but it would be shame to believe that were true. If a wrongdoing be deemed severe in its action, the order would remove its restrictions and the knight's dispute would be settled at their will. I and your father understood this; Maurdis had reason to have sought us out. The fate, Fenrifrys, the lycan's ruler, poisoned his soul. Maurdis… lost his way… his family… mine," breaths Wraithe heavily, "All slain by his hand."

Anna breathes silently in empathy of his loss. She fumbles words to continue their conversation, and for a few moments, there is a silence.

"So, I was right?" Anna replies, continuing their gazing over the city. Silently, Wraithe looks to her, as she meets him also in stare. "This is personal for you… me… all of us," she adds conclusively.

Wraithe slowly returns his sights towards the city. "Everything's personal," he utters clenching his fists tightly in emotion. Although sharing few words, Anna hears his silent pain, and sets her sights towards the stars.

"Well…" answers Anna. "Let's not let our loved one's deaths be for nothing," she tells earnestly in reply. Wraithe sighs, quietly looking towards the luminescent, full moon, lost in thought. He doesn't speak, yet, silently nods his head in agreement.

"You're right, get some rest," he tells bluntly, turning to leave the courtyard. "The blood moon is almost here, Maurdis and his men are not far," he adds in mention, as he breezes by. Meanwhile, Anna lingers, watching as he returns through the chamber's doors. She breathes out, as she gently rolls herself along the courtyard's lawn, facing the night's sky, freeing herself of her thoughts.

Meanwhile…

Far away, beyond the forests of the west, and Nostalgia, among the ashen gardens of Equilibrius, bubbles erupt from the river's surface, as the rays of the peeping sun's light, shone across the water's glistening surface.

"My son… wake up!" utters a calm, comforting female voice. "Sept wake up!" it repeats. "Wake up!" it continues to shout, when suddenly, he emerges from the surface with a loud gasp for air. Coughing and choking up mouthfuls of water, he slowly paddles towards the shoreline, managing to pull himself along the riverbank. There, he collapses to his back, passing out from sheer exhaustion, beneath the bright, morning sun.

A couple hours pass, and finally the young man awakes with a loud gasp. Sitting up, he looks around him, shuddering in shock. Alone, he weakly gets to his feet, stumbling near the edge of the forest, leaning onto anything offering support, as he continues his way through the barren garden.

"Father!" calls Sept out into the emptiness, pushing himself forward, from leant along a large boulder. "FATHER!!" he cries out again, as the fading smoke surrounds him, choking his voice. He looks around at his marred, hollow surroundings, as not a thing stirs from among the silence. "Father! Answer me, you coward!" he yells furiously, as the wounds of his father's betrayal settles in. It is amidst the forest he finds himself scarred, lost, and enraged, as nothing but ashes and death surround him.

"Y-you murderer," he murmurs tearfully, collapsing to his knees, at the foot of the petrified 'divine tree.' There he sits, uncomfortably in stare, questioning himself. Could he have served all his life, and for nothing? It is this very thought that plagues him, as he battles in and out of consciousness. Across the way, he notices what appears to be a few of the men's coats hung upon a nearby log. Sept quickly scrambles over to pick them up, as his clothes are torn up and ragged from his journey. He picks up the thickest dark coat, sprawling its hood over his head as he checks its pockets in preparation to leave the empty garden. As he limps by where once stood the divine tree, he glares at his father's makeshift throne.

Sept pauses, seeing a small patch of grass, where once lied the lifeless body of the fate, Mitrefys, and returns to his father's throne. "I may not serve you, but I will never serve Fenrifrys or my father again! I will avenge you mother, I swear you," murmurs Sept in vow, as he departs the garden by passageway of the fallen cave. He abandons the 'Order of the Pact, leaving behind all he has ever known, thus forging a new journey. He hastily heads off in the direction of west, in pursuit of his father.

Meanwhile.

Distances away, within the walls of WestSkye, the sun finally rolls over the courtyard, its rays penetrating her soft face; suddenly, Anna awakes, sprawled along its lawn. She sits up, rubbing her eyes as she shields from its blinding rays. Immediately, she hears a voice sounding as it approaches.

"Anna! Anna get up! Let's go!" it continues to call. Finally, Anna turns to realize it is Terra running towards her, she appears distraught.

"Hey…!" Terra calls, standing in front of her.

"Hey," stretches Anna in yawn, "What's wrong?"

"Get up... you should see this!" tells Terra vaguely in reply, spinning in the direction she came, quickly leaving Anna behind. Drowsily getting to her feet, Anna follows, as Terra leads down the chamber's hallway. "Grab your stuff, quickly!" she tells, shoving open their room's door. Anna paces inside, tossing off her gowns and fitting on her tunic and trousers. She fumbles her way to the door, stomping and fixing on her boots, behind the hasty Terra. The pair scamper down the chamber's stairs, entering through the council hall. To Anna's surprise, it is empty.

"Where is Siff? And Wraithe?" utters Anna curiously, as the two make their way towards the main doors.

"Outside!" informs Terra from slightly ahead. Arriving at the door, she gives a great shove, as they enter the welcoming rays of the sun, coming to the rear of a corralled crowd, gathered along the council's front doors. This time however, the people do not clamor to get inside, rather, they are quiet, with silent mumblings amongst themselves. "Come on!" calls Terra, leading through the crowd, towards the forefront of its commotion. Anna is instantly reminded of what occurred in Nordeskye, as she looks down in horror at the sight.

Three bodies lie lacerated along the ground, a young child, huddled between her two parents. Siff, finally seeing Anna for the morning, rushes to their side. "It's the lycans," he tells standing near. "Wraithe says we have less than a day!" he stresses worriedly.

Immediately, Anna pans around for signs of Wraithe. "Where is he?" she turns to Siff in question.

"Council meeting..." answers Siff straightly.

"That can't be, we were just there!" utters Terra in reply, looking to Anna in disbelief.

"He left, with the three counsellors, I swear! They're there! In meeting!" voices Siff assuredly. Upon saying this, the three turn in direction of the council doors, skipping up its steps, and reentering behind the large, wooden doors.

"He must be among the council's main seats!" suggests Terra, as they hastily jog by the empty stalls and tents along its markets. The open floor of the main council is within sight, and the three can hear the indistinct voices sounding in the distance.

As they appear from about the corner, and into the council's sunlight, Wraithe is seen standing center of the council floor, appearing to be conversing with its elders. Hearing the footsteps approaching from behind, he turns to see the three jogging near to his side. He then returns to the council, dismissing himself respectfully and proceeds to meet them.

"They're considering giving Maurdis the flower in exchange for the city to be spared," Wraithe whispers in detail. Immediately, Anna eyes widen at this resolve, as she looks to him in disbelief.

"What? No! they can't!" she refutes quietly, rushing by him. Quickly, Wraithe snatches at her forearm.

"You must mind your tongue! This city is in fear, they are subject to many of decision, even you!" murmurs Wraithe sternly to her.

"They must fight, Maurdis will not show mercy if he gains the flower, he will destroy not just this city but all of sky!" argues Anna fiercely in reply.

"I know that more than anyone, and as you saw, I've spent the last couple of hours trying to convince them of the same! They're scared! They all are! Worst of all, they know the lotus also abides in you, even you, may be used as a bargain for them! leave this to me! You three, must leave here at once!" instructs Wraithe swiftly, nodding to Terra, as he releases her forearm.

Terra then walks up from behind, placing her hand upon Anna's shoulder. "Come on Anna," she encourages, notioning her to join them in leaving. Anna however, remains unmoved, rushing by Wraithe, before the council's seats.

"This matter is beyond you, the council has made its decision, we will negotiate terms with the enemy!" refutes lady Elaine sternly to her, as Anna approaches. "Guards!" she orders. "Seize her!"

Immediately, two of the nearby guards hold at Anna's side, stopping her before the council. "Listen to me!" cries Anna in pleading. "This Maurdis, spares no one… he will take what he wants, and destroy everything, you cannot negotiate with the enemy!" cries Anna desperately, struggling against her restraints. "He will never stop at one! We can save our future and many others, if we stand and fight! You think once Maurdis gains the lotus, he will uphold his word?! He will destroy us, and all of Skye, there will be nothing left!"

"What you propose is that we commit our men to slaughter! The blood moon approaches, and we have not the slightest fathoming of how powerful the enemy might be!" exclaims Lord Rollins in reproach. "Enough of this! Remove her!" he orders finally.

"Take me!" exclaims Anna bluntly, puzzling the council and everyone.

"What did you say?!" utters Rollins peculiarly in question, lending his ear.

"I said take me!" repeats Anna boldly, shaking from the perplexed guards. "Mitrefys herself bestowed upon me the lotus, I also carry its gifts, have Maurdis take me instead," she adds further. This action disturbs Siff who lunges forth, grasping her forearm.

"Anna what? Do you hear yourself, Anna, NO!" Siff refutes sternly. "I can't lose you!"

"Siff, stand aside!" commands Anna in reply, gently shoving him aside; she then turns her attention forward to the council. "You may offer me up to Maurdis in exchange for your peace; but I ask you, If he betrays you, and know you in yourselves he will, what hope have you then?!" steps Anna forwardly in question. This silences the council's elders, each knowing amongst themselves the lycan lord is not to be trusted.

"Convincing is she not?!" mentions Terra reluctantly, standing along Wraithe's side.

"Enough of this!" voices Lord Rollins impatiently. "Guards, remove her from the council!" Immediately, Siff rushes in to defend her, when he is rudely shoved aside by one of the guards. Suddenly, the guard finds himself to the floor in a deafening thud, as Terra strikes from behind, having swept him to the floor. Wraithe also dives in, as the remaining guards quickly encircle them. The three stand firm about Anna, as the guards uneasily inch closer.

"Wait!" halts Lord Asher, flailing them to cease their advance. "She is right," he adds in agreement, appalling his fellow counselors. "A liar is a thief, and a thief a murderer! Maurdis' word is not to be trusted, WestSkye must not allow its fears to cloud its judgment!" proclaims Asher boldly in reply.

"Lord Asher!" exclaims lady Elaine in utter disbelief of this sudden conviction. "You would sentence our great city to its death?!" she baffles in question.

"Open your eyes Elaine, we would only secure our demise in such decision, we must stand against our enemy," Asher continues in answering. Lady Elaine turns her rage towards Anna, standing below the council's seats. "You've poisoned the minds of our people; convinced them that death be our only choice, how could you?!"

"I understand that you're terrified, but this pales in comparison to what will happen if we simply give up, you must stand and fight. Let our descendants know we choose to die on our feet, than slaughtered amongst our knees," voices Anna heartedly. "WestSkye shall not fall!" she raises in saying, as the guards suddenly clamor in agreement.

"Convincing isn't she not?" scoffs Terra lightly.

"Well, let us end it, nothing would ease my pain enough than to rest this blade," tells Wraithe anxiously in reply.

"Amen," nods Terra in agreement. Under the leading order of Lord Asher, the city continues its preparations for war, as the looming threat of the lycans nears ever so closer!

Chapter 10
The Brother's Blood

Meanwhile.

Within the forests just outside the walls of WestSkye, Maurdis and his legion creep upon the wayward hills overlooking the gorgeous city tucked within the valley. He looks down in conquest, upon the seemingly unsuspecting city.

"We should attack now, my lord, while they have little chance of defense!" voices Tidas anxiously, appearing at his side. Maurdis grins, chuckling to himself.

"They already know we're coming," answers Maurdis calmly in reply. "An attack in broad day would be foolish, would it not? Especially when our abilities would be at its peak in but a few short hours. "Patience is a key virtue… even for us! We will attack; but under shelter of the blood moon," tells Maurdis, walking by the men, who follow in waiting until dusk falls.

All the while, within the great city, preparations are just about ready, as Wraithe and the others join in the readying of battle.

"Sir Wraithe?!" calls a common guard pacing over to where they stand. "All preparations have been made sir… now we are just in waiting!"

Wraithe nods silently. "Good!" he utters, "Have the archers taken position along the walls?" he adds in question, leading off down the path, with Anna and the others a step behind

"Yes Sir… but they are a few sir," adds the nervous guard, stumbling alongside them. "M-Many of th-them be not experienced sir!" he stammers in saying.

"Well, no better time to learn than the present!" voices Wraithe reluctantly in reply, before spinning to Terra and Siff. "Terra," he calls, as she obediently steps forward. "You, and the boy will assist along the wall, the lycans must be kept from entering the city, for as long as possible!" he instructs firmly, "For if they get through… then may the fate's help us all!" tells Wraithe gravely, as he returns forward. "For now… go, they need you!"

Siff looks at Anna, who face reads of worry. He gives an uneasy, tearful smile and the two rush into a final embrace, as each recognize the possibility of this being their final goodbye.

"You stay safe…" sniffles Anna tearfully in instruction, glaring into the eyes of her young friend. "You damn well better come back to me!" she warns lightly, drawing him in once more.

"I will," chuckles Siff in reply. "You'd better do the same!"

Hugging tightly, the two let go, as Siff steps back into the arm of Terra, which she places about his shoulder with a playful, mischievous grin to Anna in farewell.

"You stay alive! I only can watch your friend here for so long!" she jokes in saying, looking down at Siff, shaking him closer to her bosom. Anna nods with a smile, swiftly leaving to follow after Wraithe, who proceeds off in the distance.

She quickly paces up to his side. "You didn't tell her goodbye?" looks Anna to him curiously.

"Terra is a skilled and experienced warrior; she will be fine!" he answers bluntly in reply. "Now isn't the time for pleasantries, she has received her duties, we must now make sure we carry out ours, this way!" he informs, leading along the main path.

"So, what shall we do?" continues Anna in question.

"We must protect the council, and its chamber beneath it! Muardis knows not that you are the lotus, we must keep it that way, but he mustn't reach the hidden chamber! Our task is to protect from the ground." tells Wraithe fully in reply.

"No more running," breathes Anna inwardly, mustering her courage.

Meanwhile, Terra and Siff attend the front wall, kneeling in wait, as daylight fades to dusk. The hearts of the men race in anticipation; their eyes watching as the sun disappears behind the hills of the west. Worried murmurs and prayers sound amongst them, as they count the seconds of their enemy's arrival. A few minutes pass, and anxiety continues to build, meanwhile, Siff grows impatient with worry and looks over to Terra.

"Where are they?" he asks anxiously, glaring to the horizon. Terra however, remains quiet, her sights fixated near the hills of the west. "It's almost nightfall, and I can't see a thing," complains Siff, seated in waiting.

Just beyond sight, atop the hills, with eyes peering through the forest's edge, Maurdis and his legion wait in ambush. Suddenly, Tidas steps forth, approaching at Maurdis' side, as he looks to his leader awaiting command. Maurdis grins smugly, looking down into the valley. "Inside those city's walls, hides our immortality, find it!" he instructs in conquest.

"My lord… it is done!" affirms Tidas, immediately turning to the men. "My Brothers!!" he utters openly. "They are fearful! Our destiny lies within those very walls! FOR YOUR ORDER! SEIZE YOUR GLORY!!" he proclaims, as the men uproar in sounding. With that, they stampede from the forest, descending into the valley towards the city.

Meanwhile, Terra closes her eyes listening carefully.

Seeing this, Siff calls to her. "Hey! What is it?!" he asks. Terra however, continues to listen carefully, suddenly hearing the minute stampeding of feet, tremoring within the distance. Quickly, opening her eyes, she rushes by the men.

"Ready yourselves! she exclaims in warning, signaling the horns to blow. A bellowing horn sounds from each corner of the wall, alerting of the lycans arrival.

"We can't see anything!" complains the guards indistinctly, peering out across the valley. The darkness has provided the perfect cover needed for the lycan's attack. Terra quickly rushes near one of the walls mounted catapults.

"Oil!" she orders hastily to the nearby men. Quickly, she is handed a scoop of oil, to which she coats the loaded woven ball. "Flame!" she orders once more. Terra is handed a torch and ignites the large ball. She turns, slashing at the rope's tension, with her sword, catapulting the fiery shot into the night's sky.

As it hurls over the valley, it lights the landscape, revealing a legion of men headed for the city. "They're in the valley!!" exclaims Terra in discovery. Moments later, a second horn signal is blown.

Within the city, Wraithe hears this, turning to Anna in realization. "They're here!" he tells bluntly.

Meanwhile, atop the wall, Terra continues her orders. "ARCHERS!" she signals, calling them to the forefront. They ready their arrows against the bowstrings, preparing a hailstorm of defense. The nearby guards also begin coating the large woven balls with oil, igniting them with torches, and slicing the ropes tension in release. As the fiery projectiles make impact, they ignite the valley's forefront, blazing the night sky a fiery dark red.

Atop the wall, all bear witness to the legion's transformation! An innumerable army of lycans weave their way through the blazing valley, entering range of the city's archers.

"NOW!" orders Terra fiercely. "RAIN FIRE!!" Immediately, every archer atop the wall releases their shot firing off into the valley. The Lycans are then struck by a hailstorm of arrows, decimating their numbers, leaving many dead and many others gravely wounded.

Hearing his pact's cries enrages Maurdis, who then looks to his right. "Tidas!" he growls furiously, looking on at the slaughter.

"My Lord!" answers Tidas, taking place at his side.

"Go!" orders Maurdis straightly. Immediately, Tidas is joined by another wave of lycans, quickly descending into the valley.

"Shit! There's more of them!" mutters Terra in saying, speedily turning to the men.

"What? What is it?!!" asks Siff worriedly, seeing her expression.

"I should've known it couldn't have been this easy!" scoffs Terra frustratedly in saying. "We need more arrows!" she orders hastily to the guards nearby. Meanwhile, Tidas' wave gains, as Terra hastens to the men, until finally, they receive their much-needed supply. The men swiftly take aim; when in an instant, the lycans disperse into three; two groups headed to opposite sides of the city, left and right, meanwhile, the other keeps straightaway. This perplexes the archers, who are rendered unsure of their next defense. Meanwhile, Terra follows along the wall, realizing their scheme.

"NO...NO...NO...NO...NO, they're trying to surround us!!" she exclaims to the men. "QUICKLY, RAIN FIRE!!" she rushes to command. The archers focus aim to wherever the lycans lead, dwindling the splitting numbers as many as possible. However, it is not enough, as many of the lycans have made their way towards the northern and southern sides of the wall.

"No, No, No!" mutters Terra frustratingly, following the evading horde along the wall. Their defence has become somewhat compromised, as the archers disperse, hurling strikes towards all lycans within sight.

Terra continues giving orders, when a soldier rushes towards her. "Ma'am! Ma'am" he calls. "T-Th-They appear to have fully surrounded the city!" he shudders gravely in telling. "The western walls entrance may be reinforced, but the others be vulnerable to a breach! We have fortified as best we can, but I fear they can only hold off for so long!" he adds further.

"Fates, help us!" mutters one of the nearby soldiers fearfully.

"The fates can't help us in this fight! This one we do ourselves!" retorts Terra strongly in reply. She hastens by the line of men. "You... you and you! Come with me!" she selects quickly. "Siff... you too!" she adds. "You may be the youngest, but you're the best shot I've seen in a long time, I need you!" tells Terra, placing a trusting hand upon his shoulder.

Siff looks into her eyes with solemn nod. "I have your back!" he tells confidently.

"And I have yours!" answers Terra assuredly in reply. She quickly turns, rushing past the men, with Siff at her side, as they gather up a few arrows. Siff also snatches a random blade rested atop a nearby barrel, stuffing it comfortably within his waistband.

"We must confirm of the enemy's possible breach of the wall, and provide any stand necessary, should there be any turn for the worst!" briefs Terra to the nervous group. "The fates be with us all!" she prays openly, leading them down the stairs of the wall into the city's main path.

One of the guards, clearing his throat speaks up from behind. "Ma'am, the great river's stream, runs directly through the center of the city, by entry of the northern wall! It should be the very first possible entry to be checked!"

"There's not enough time," Terra answers hastily. "The city has been fully surrounded, the lycans may have very well gotten through! We must pair up and check each possible entryway, returning here as soon as the points have been checked!"

The men measure each other, as each loosely wear the look of fear upon their faces. "May the fates protect you all," tells Terra, as the group disperses. The four pairs make their way through the city's paths, to where the city's edge and its wall meet.

"We make sure no entry has been made… and return, the lycans must not reach the council!" utters Terra to Siff, as they travel to the southern wall.

Meanwhile, "Clear!" confirms one of the guards, investigating along the eastern wall, it is a lesser gate, at the rear of WestSkye, continuing along the flow of the valley. Having been reinforced with huge barrels of oil, and pillows of sand, its structure remains sturdy, seeming undisturbed. Quickly, the pair make their way in return to the city's main path.

All the while, Terra and Siff, follow along the city's edge, in search of signs of breach. Not too long after, they arrive at the great river's stream pass. It is a brick lain pathway, effortlessly flowing from its entry of the northern wall to its exit through the southern wall, where investigates Terra and Siff. Only puddles remain in its path, its exit also enforced with wattle and stone, layered upon with sand pillows. "No threat seen," mutters Terra in telling, kneeling to investigate.

"So far so good," adds Siff in relief.

"Let's return to the group!" she tells hastily, as the pair begin making their way back to the city's front gates. Meanwhile, near the northern wall, and entryway of the great river's stream, the group's last pair creep upon the fortified entry.

"Take a look!" whispers one to the other.

"Why me?" the second replies.

"Fine, we must be heading back quickly, I'll go and get it over with," shrugs the first in annoyance. When suddenly, the rustling and fall of a few nearby baskets garner the pair's attention. Immediately, both men spin about, flashing the lanterns along the shadows nearby.

"You heard something?!" trembles the second in saying. "I-I-I k-know you heard that too? That was something close," he mentions, flashing the lantern over the fallen basket of fruits. "No way that fell just by itself!"

Suddenly, a stray dog bolts between the pair, startling the first, who standing near the trench's edge, stumbles backwards, splashing into the shallow brick stream below.

"Ha Ha! It was but a stray!" chuckles the second in discovery, shining his lantern's light, into the trench upon his comrade. "We can head back now," he exclaims happily.

While in the trench, slowly getting to his knees, as he sits soaked along the waters. "W-We have to move quickly!!" the first answers hastily in reply, erasing the smile from his comrade's face, "They're in the city!" he tells further.

Finally, the second realizes the stream has somehow begun to flow, as his friend sits among the waters. The return of the stream's trail can only mean one thing. The wall has been breached! Immediately, his knees begin to tremble. "Adamus, quickly! Give me your hand!" he calls to the first, diving towards its edge, as he lends his hand. Suddenly, they hear a series of running footsteps, sounding from ahead, blanketed behind the ghostly shadows.

"W-What's that?!" panicks the second, turning about. Meanwhile Adamus takes a few steps forward, shakily holding his lantern ahead. Finally, they glimpse the gaped hole within the pillar of sandbags, as the stream steadily flows down the sandpile.

His eyes widen in fear, as he spins back to the other in saying "Let's G…!" When suddenly, without a breath's notice, he is lept upon by a fearsome black figure. "AGHHHHH!!" he screams helpessly in horror. Meanwhile, startled by the sudden attack, the second guard soils himself, as he frantically starts down the path. A resounding howl is heard nearby, churning a deep fear within his gut.

"No No No!!" he pants fearfully fleeing in return to the group. All the while, the snarling pants of his pursuers follow his every step within the darkness behind him. Recognizing the main path ahead, he frantically stumbles about the sharp corner. In the distance, he glimpses Terra and the others, who await gathered along the main path. "Hey!! Hey!!" he cries out desperately to them from the distance, immediately, the group turns towards his direction, alerted by the voice.

"What is your name guard? And where be your second?" asks Terra concerningly, as he frantically stops to catch his breath, he takes another look behind him, slumping to his knees in fatigue, as the group looks about the empty path.

"My name is David, Ma'am, th-they… th-the lycans they got Adamus!!" he pants gravely in telling, with tears felling his eyes.

Suddenly, a pair of footsteps sound from behind them, as Terra and the others spin to see who approaches; it is Anna and Wraithe.

"The lycans have breached the city," tells Anna as they approach. "As to where they may be, we have yet to find out!" she goes on to add.

Meanwhile, Terra looks past them up ahead. "Well, look no further," she mentions, drawing out her sword. Immediately, Anna and the others turn about, seeing a line of fearsome wolves standing off in the distance. Suddenly, a male steps forth from among them.

"Ready yourselves!" urges Wraithe drawing his sword.

Commotion is also heard sounding from atop the wall, as Terra turns her attention to the indistinct shouts of the men. Seconds later, a loud crash is heard, sounding behind them. The group spins, appalled to see the city's main gates collapsed, as the walls having been barged open by a storm of men. The intruders cast aside the large tree used to ram open the sturdy gates. They enter the main path, as each drop to their knees, shaping into fearsome lycans. As the dust settles, a tall man, draped in a black fur coat appears, as the lycans clear his path. Fanning the dust from her sight, Anna and the cloacked male make eye contact, as he wears a smug sinister grin. it is Maurdis, he has arrived!

The waiting growls of the surrounding lycans, anxiously anticipate their leader's order. Maurdis confidently struts to the forefront. "YOU KNOW WHY I'm here!" proclaims Maurdis boldly. "The flower…OR PERISH!!" he snarls. "We can smell each and every one of your fear; as blood in water! Provide it and half of WestSkye will be spared!" Immediately, the city's men nervously murmur amongst themselves.

"You lie! Maurdis!" voices Wraithe strongly in reply. "You? Spare them? These people stand justly against you!"

Meanwhile, Maurdis grins in humor. "I ask you?! Great men of the western city, which of you wishes to be spared?!! Take hold the words of this fool, drawing your worthless souls behind him in losing battle? Or make known the flowers whereabouts, so that your household be spared?!!" asks Maurdis openly towards them. There is a silence among the main path, as each of WestSkye's men searches within themselves. "Choose you to live… or, suffer be your fate?" he utters once more, as the snarls of the lycans increase. Seconds later, one of the guards bolts from Terra's group.

"I'm sorry! I'm sorry!" he cries out shamefully, fleeing into Maurdis' bargain.

"NO!!! You fool!!!" roars Wraithe in reply.

"Fates! I have failed you!" whimpers the guard, as he nears the lycan ruler. "I wish for me and my household to be spared!" he pleads desperately. "The lotus, it lies beneath the council, a circle of descent! This be true; I swear it!!" pants the guard in detail. Maurdis grins in enjoyment, as Wraithe's expression fills of rage.

"Good," answers Maurdis in reply, as he looks to Wraithe. "You see brother, there is no loyalty!" he tells, quickly drawing his sword and thrusting it into the unsuspecting guard, killing him instantly. "The council! Find it!!!" proclaims Maurdis turning to depart in search of the city's council, "Rid us of them!" he sanctions Tidas in instruction, as he brushes by.

Terra swiftly looks to the roofs above. "ARCHERS!!" she voices in command. Suddenly, men gathered upon the roof of every household lining the main street appear, each with bows and spears drawn in attack. They immediately rain fire upon the lycans; Maurdis and a band of his subjects flee the attack and begin search for the council.

Quickly, Wraithe looks to the three. "I will pursue Maurdis, you three and the men must hold them here, he cannot retrieve the flower!" tells Wraithe hastily in instruction, he then quickly fights his way through the jaws of the attacking lycans in pursuit behind Maurdis and his men. Anna leads a fearless war cry, as her, Terra, Siff and the others continue the fight against the lycans along the main path.

Leading the lycan's attack, Tidas orders a few of them to gather torches, and lanterns hung along the path and use them to set ablaze the buildings where the city's men are positioned. Each door is kicked open, as torches are swung inside, burning everything within, swiftly forcing the archers to abandon the rooftops. The fires catch wildly and pretty soon all the buildings along the path are set aflame. As Tidas rips through Westskye's guards, he notices the familiar faces of Terra and Anna, and begins making his way towards them, as their battle ensues.

"Anna!" calls Terra, fending off the jaws of an attacking lycan, meanwhile, Anna is hurled to the ground, as the gnashing teeth of one of the beasts, is held away by leverage of her staff. Suddenly, an arrow is shot through the eyes of the lycan, as it collapses dead at her side. Anna startles into sitting upright, turning to glimpse Siff lowering his bow, as he breathes in relief.

Tidas sees this and is infuriated, charging his way towards Siff, meanwhile, Terra calls to her once more. "Anna! The real fight is not here! Take Siff and protect the chamber!!!" voices Terra amidst the battle Terra barely finishes her warning, when suddenly, Siff is snatched from behind; lifted at his neck by Tidas. "NOOO!!!" screams Anna in horror, rushing to Siff's aid.

Tidas grins smugly at the squealing and struggling Siff. "Your death will mean nothing!" he leans, whispering into the boy's ear. Anna screams, as her staff wields into a two-edged sword, hurling for the head of Tidas. Quickly, he tosses Siff aside, as he ducks beneath her wild swing. "Hahaha!" he chuckles hysterically, as Anna misses wildly, rolling to the ground in momentum. "You have no experience of battle whatsoever!" he turns to her scoffing arrogantly. Suddenly, Terra leaps into the midst, slashing her sword, towards him in attack, as Tidas weaves just beyond reach of her blade, when with a feint spin, Terra slashes at his leather tunic, cutting across Tidas' chest.

"She may not; but I do!" she replies readily in challenge, Tidas looks down at his soiled tunic in grin, as he quickly rips away his upper clothing.

"Not bad!" he utters reluctantly, as he circles about them, meanwhile, Anna shields Siff behind her. "In the end, it is futile… immortality WILL BE OURS, THE FATES WILL IT SO!!" he snarls wildly. Dropping to his knees, Tidas transforms, appearing as a large lycan before them.

"You're nothing but a pawn… and your leader will never take the lotus, you'll die an arrogant fool!!" refutes Terra fearlessly in reply. Enraged, the lycan charges towards her, Terra blocks feinting off his attack with a shove of her sword, as Anna leaps atop Tidas' back, as the lycan thrashes and attempts to bite and toss Anna from its back. Finally, he returns to his human form, reaching over his shoulder and hurling Anna off of him. Quickly, Terra darts towards him, jousting her sword at his abdomen. Tidas swiftly steps aside, catching her blade with his hand, as his blood runs along her blade. Terra attempts to withdraw her sword from his grip, and struggles, having to throw a hefty, left punch at his face. She pauses appalled, as his head merely turns from her explosive strike; turning with a smirk, Tidas wipes the blood of his lip with his sleeve.

"Is that it?!" chuckles Tidas hysterically, delivering a powerful, front kick, knocking Terra across the way. "How disappointing!" he flails in gloat. Walking up to Terra as she rolls along the ground, he kicks at her ribs, causing her to curl in pain. "Whatever made you think you could stand against me?!" he laughs in enjoyment, again kicking at her side. Finally, he presses his foot on her throat, when suddenly, an arrow is fired into his shoulder.

"Argggghhhhh!!!" he roars out in pain. Enraged, he turns to Siff, who being petrified at his angered gaze, lowers his bow. "I've had enough of you!!" he snarls, removing himself from Terra and charging towards the frozen boy. Anna leaps to the rescue, running her sword into the male's back. Hollering out in pain, he spins to her, only to meet a flipping kick from Terra. His face begins to shift as he begins his transformation.

"Quickly!" urges Terra, "Before he transforms!!" she goes on to command. Siff follows up with a strike of his bow, and Anna her staff, followed by a swipe of Terra's blade, as the trio blitz in attack. Finally, with a twirl of her staff, and Terra joining in spin, the two females plunge their blades through the chest of Tidas. He gasps suddenly, looking down at the two silver swords entered through his body.

"Tell me, whatever made you think you could stand against us!" mutters Terra ironically in reply, as he collapses to the ground with a thud.

"Quickly, we must aid Wraithe, he will need help against Maurdis!" exclaims Terra hastily.

Meanwhile, Maurdis and the lycans make their way through the city. Wraithe follows along the shadows, creeping behind their every step, as they hunt for the lotus. Suddenly, Maurdis stops as he approaches the city's open marketplace. "You will never desist, will you? Old friend?" he pauses abruptly to say.

Finally, Wraithe steps out of the shadows, appearing before them. "I will stop at nothing to keep the lotus from the hands of you, even until the end of time itself!" rebuts Wraithe boldly in telling.

Maurdis chuckles to himself smugly. "Unfortunately, your time draws nigh, Old friend," he turns away in saying, as four of his subjects lunge forward, shaping into ferocious lycans. Instantly, they charge towards Wraithe. Meanwhile, Maurdis hastens for the council, glimpsing its tall pillars, and large wooden door's entrance. Tucked away inside, counsellors Rollins, Asher, and Elaine, ready the men to stand guard behind the council's doors.

"Do you think they invaded the city?!" pants lady Elaine anxiously to Rollins in question. Lord Asher interrupts, confidently placing his hand upon Elaine's shoulder.

"We should have nothing to fear, they are heavily fortified, and with firm defense, the lycans may very well be slain before even making it into the valley!" Asher assures in reply. When suddenly, there is a loud thud, as the council's tall wooden front doors, shake, frightening the gathered inside.

"What is that?!!" jumps Elaine fearfully, clinging tightly onto the forearm of Asher.

A voice is heard yelling from just beyond the door. "WestSkye! We have come for the lotus, give it or perish!!" roars Maurdis ultimately in demand. This scampers the fearful counselors, who look to Asher in command. He turns to them, looking to Rollins and Elaine in final decision.

"Listen to me!" he opens in telling. "You have to gather the people of WestSkye from hiding and lead them in escape! Me and the men must hold them here! WestSkye has a chance if you escape now!" he goes on to tell, as Rollins and Elaine look to him in utter disbelief.

"You cannot be serious?!!" voices Elaine incredulously in return.

"Asher, why must you stay behind?! We must all escape!" urges Rollins in reply. "If we leave now, we can all survive, there's no escape if we linger here much longer!" Suddenly, there is another great thud along the council's door. This startles everyone in the room, as the doors ready to give way, the men stand unsurely on guard, searching the courage within themselves.

"Please," utters Asher earnestly to them, as he looks towards the shaken entrance. "I can draw them away if you make leave now!"

Lord Rollins silently steps forth, and grips at the forearm of Asher, firmly shaking his arm, as the two men stare into each other's eyes. Finally, Rollins releases the arm of Asher, his eyes shedding a tear, as he turns away, pulling along a distraught, speechless Elaine and their group of soldiers making headway in escape. The eyes of Asher well of tears, as he prepares himself, turning to face the council's front doors. Another loud thud is heard, thrashing open its front doors, its slams hurling the dust of the floor. A male figure appears before him, cloaked in a dark maned robe. His skin is of tan, as his streaks of gray coil through his dark hair. A pack of wolves follows after him, upon entering into the council.

"This is him!" trembles Asher to himself in thought.

"Destiny has arrived!" he exclaims momentously, admiring about the huge structure. "More importantly, I have!" he goes on to add.

Lord Asher stands alone, amidst the council floor, his palms sweaty and shaking uncontrollably. He grips at his tremoring hand, taking a hard swallow, as he steps forth towards them. "You be Maurdis?!" voices Asher in question.

"I be the one to retrieve the lotus under name of the pact, and our fallen lord, I am Maurdis grand alpha of the pact!" he proclaims proudly in reply. Asher firmly makes stand, drawing his sword, as he prepares to defend against the lotus' capture. Maurdis grins at this, as his pack paces forth, encircling about the petrified counselor. They anxiously await the order of their lord, growling about the feet of Asher. Maurdis grows impatient, lunging towards the counselor. "Where is it?!" he roars in demand, grabbing at the face of Asher. "You'd better speak quickly!" he warns, when suddenly, the low growling and gnashing of teeth, forces two figures from the shadows. It is lord Rollins and Elaine, having been captured hostage by the lycans. Lord Asher breathes heavily, shocked to see his fellow counselors captured.

"Noooo!!" he muffles desperately in screaming, as the pack encircle the frightened pair.

"Now! I won't ask again!" he snarls maliciously, as the lycans tighten their circle about them, their teeth bared, readily to attack. Asher looks to the horror-written faces of his fellow counselors and opens his mouth to answer.

"B-Beneath t-the council's chamber!" he muffles in saying. Maurdis then releases his grip about Asher's mouth, dropping him to the floor. "It is beneath the council, within the chambers!" he utters in repeating, struggling to catch his breath.

"Good," grins Maurdis devilishly.

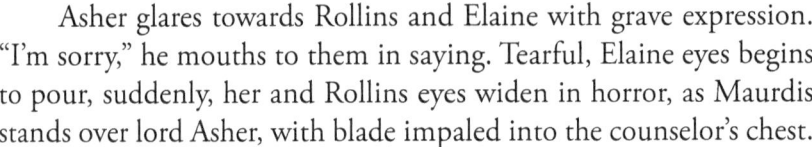

Asher glares towards Rollins and Elaine with grave expression. "I'm sorry," he mouths to them in saying. Tearful, Elaine eyes begins to pour, suddenly, her and Rollins eyes widen in horror, as Maurdis stands over lord Asher, with blade impaled into the counselor's chest.

"Pitiful..." mutters Maurdis in disgust, as he pulls his sword from the lifeless body of lord Asher.

"Nooo!!" cries Elaine gripping tightly upon the arm of Rollins, as she turns muffling her tears upon his shoulders. Maurdis smiles in enjoyment, as the reddened eyes of Elaine stare him down in contempt. "You are a monster!" she curses tearfully in saying.

Maurdis steps closer, hovered near the pair's face. "You sit upon your seat in the judgement of others, as if your hands be tidy; you've spent your whole life in the act of judgment, now here's yours; you will show me to the flower, and then, you will die!" snarls Maurdis in telling. "Now! Show me to the chambers!" Immediately, Maurdis pack nip and bite towards the counselors' feet, driving them forward. Lord Rollins and Elaine lead them into the council's main hall, where the three judgment seats sit center of the hall, beneath the gloomy night sky, peering through the pillars of its open roof.

For a moment, Maurdis admires the majestic details engraved into the tall columns supporting its large structure, the artful beams that make up its open roof, and priceless treasures, lining between each pair of the tall pillars. "Grandiose is it not!" utters Maurdis reluctantly in saying, looking about the hall. "Limitless power placed in the hands of mere man, who has oppressed the very 'powers' created to control them, the fates have made a grave mistake!"

Suddenly, a clunking thud is heard, sounding before them. Alerted, the lycans begin to growl, looking towards the council's seats. There, within the silhouette of darkness, sits a dark figure, as the clunking thud resounds. As all heads turn, to what lies ahead.

"The brother's blood"

"Powers?!" scoffs a male voice in humor, sitting comfortably among one of the chairs. "You mean curses... one should not speak of such abominations in such manner," Wraithe tells satirically in reply.

Maurdis, however, laughs in recognition of the familiar voice. "It appears you're ready to perish brother," tells Maurdis, standing at the forefront of the judgment seats. Finally, the light of the ghostly moon, reveals Wraithe seated comfortably, upon the counselor's chair, his feet stretched across its podium.

Meanwhile, Maurdis, enraged at his frivolous response, looks to his subjects. "Kill him," he orders stoutly, as the lycans make charge towards Wraithe. Quickly drawing out his sword, he leaps from atop the seats, landing as he drives his sword through the skull of one of the beasts. Wraithe advances forth, dodging and slashing through the pack, and with a final downward strike, slays the last of them. Getting to his feet, he and Maurdis lock their gaze. Until finally, Wraithe looks to the shocked counselors, who stand appalled.

"Leave! Now!" orders Wraithe hastily to the pair. "I will deal with this!" with a shivering nod, Rollins pulls at Elaine, and the two quickly begin to flee, leaving behind Wraithe and Maurdis amidst the council.

"Be not mistaken, I will find them brother, however, I won't delay your death any further!" snarls Maurdis in telling, grinning eagerly towards Wraithe.

"Your ambitions are that of a fool, they drive you only to carnage, and ultimately, your death!" condemns Wraithe stoutly in disgust.

Meanwhile, Maurdis grins drawing his blade. "Come brother!" he tells momentously, "Let us embrace!"

All the while, Anna, Siff, and Terra have begun making their way towards the city council. Terra leads the trio, as they turn the corner of the main path. "Wraithe should've cut them off by now, or even worse, they may have actually made it to the council!" warns Terra in saying. "We must hurry!" she hastens.

Meanwhile, Maurdis, and Wraithe waver back and forth in combat. "You've grown slower brother…" scoffs Maurdis reluctantly in saying. "Not even half the warrior you once was!" he adds in laughter, as the pair struggle in a push of blades.

"How you've fallen, you once sought to protect, now, only destruction be your ally!" retorts Wraithe in disappointment, "You are not half the man, you once were! Vaiya, would be ashamed!" adds Wraithe in disdain.

This infuriates Muardis, who tosses Wraithe away with a shove of his blade. "I gave up those hopes, a long time ago!" roars Maurdis coldly, seeking to strike at Wraithe. He manages to strike left, stunning the revenant, following with a wild swing for his head. Gathering himself quickly, Wraithe ducks beneath Maurdis' sword, throwing a swift kick to Maurdis' shin, dropping the tyrant to his knee. Wraithe follows through, with a heavy right fist, dizzying Maurdis.

"It doesn't matter if I'm old or crippled... you're no match for me!" tells Wraithe, rising up and lifting his sword above his head to finish Maurdis. When suddenly, Maurdis infuriated by having been bested by his enemy in combat, lifts his head, catching the blade of Wraithe. Meanwhile, the moon reaches its peak among the night sky, as its galleon boasts a glowing dark red. The blood moon has arrived! Wraithe struggles to withdraw his sword from Maurdis' grasp, as the lycan stands to his feet, his piercing yellow eyes staring into Wraithe's.

Maurdis pulls greatly against Wraithe and drives his forearm into the broad side of Wraithe's blade, shattering it. Taking its broken edge, he drives it towards Wraithe's abdomen. The revenant seizes Maurdis' arm and struggles to prevent the blade from penetrating his body, it is a battle of wills. However, Maurdis feels a sudden surge of strength, as he quickly overpowers Wraithe, with the moon looming just above them. He shoves the blade's edge into the abdomen of Wraithe, while also driving the revenant backwards.

Wraithe struggles to keep Maurdis at bay, to prevent the blade from entering deeper. Meanwhile, the lycan grins reveling in his struggle, as he removes his hand from the blade, quickly lifting Wraithe overhead and tossing him across the council's floor. As he lands heavily, Wraithe clutches painfully at his wound, staggering away from Maurdis, as he struggles to get to his feet. As he spins to face him, Wraithe is welcomed by a powerful kick from Maurdis, tumbling him back to the floor.

"Your death is inevitable!" scoffs Maurdis in enjoyment, slowly stalking the revenant. Meanwhile, Wraithe continues to drag himself away. "I've waited ages for this moment!" tells Maurdis momentously, grinning smugly in amusement towards Wraithe.

"You betrayed the order, allowed yourself to be succumbed to the darkness, your honor will forever be soiled!" voices Wraithe in disdain, continuing to creep away.

"There's no honor between wolves, and men…" laughs Maurdis coldly in reply. "On your feet brother… let us end this!" he exclaims, picking up his sword lying nearby, and tossing it to Wraithe. Suddenly, Maurdis begins to quiver, dropping to his hands. Finally, he lifts his head, rising into a fierce large black wolf. The most fearsome Wraithe has ever seen!

His canines bared, and ears erect as the tuft patch of fur upon his back raises upright, he readily awaits Wraithe, to continue their battle. Injured, Wraithe slowly gets to his feet, he is exhausted, he firmly holds his sword, readying himself for an attack.

"Yes brother," breathes Wraithe in reply, "It is time to end this! Once and for all!"

The two make a charge for one another, with Maurdis leaping towards Wraithe. As Maurdis dives towards him, the revenant slides across the council's floor, gracefully leaning below his attack. Wraithe quickly spins about and makes a charge for the lycan. He thrusts his sword into the lycan's shank, as Maurdis yelps with a great howl, jolting and riling about. A blunt kick hurls Wraithe to the floor, when suddenly, an intense, excruciating pain is felt, as Maurdis bites down onto the forearm of Wraithe. A loud crunch is heard as the right forearm of the revenant is broken.

"AGHHHHH!!!!" hollers Wraithe painfully, punching in an attempt to get Maurdis off of his arm, suddenly, he is violently swung and hurled across the way. Landing to his back, the reality of him having been bitten settles in, and during the blood moon! Immediately, he glances for his sword, glimpsing it nearby, and scampers towards it. Maurdis transfigures back to his human state, slowly stalking Wraithe, who drags himself across the council's floor.

"Now, you will understand how it feels to have fought for something all your life, and to have it been for nothing, tonight, you die as one of us!" Maurdis chuckles sinisterly. Wraithe's hand runs cross a bit a sand along the floor, as he quickly grasps, and hurls it towards the face of Maurdis, blinding him. Quickly, he leaps forward in reach of his sword, and severs his right forearm.

"AAGHHHHHH!! DAMN YOU!!" cries Wraithe in agony, gripping at the wound, he then tears as his sleeve, and begins tying it about the wound, tightening it. "GRRRRR!!!" he mouths painfully, pulling at the tourniquet with his teeth. Suddenly, Maurdis pounces upon him. Wraithe makes a swing with his blade trying to fend off the lycan lord, however, Maurdis catches the sword, and the pair enter a struggle as Maurdis begins to direct the blade back to Wraithe. Maurdis grins devilishly, as he continues to force the sword towards Wraithe's chest. With all his strength, Wraithe holds against the might of Maurdis.

"<u>A narrow fate</u>"

"This is the end for you brother!" laughs Maurdis evilly. Suddenly, an arrow pierces Maurdis' left shoulder, the sudden strike infuriates the lycan, who swiftly spins to glimpse his attacker. Maurdis sees the three standing across the way of the council; Wraithe glimpses Terra preparing another arrow, as Anna and Siff stand at her side, they have come to his aid. Quickly, seeing he is distracted, Wraithe pulls the sword from Maurdis' grasp. Surprised, Maurdis returns his attention to Wraithe, when he is met by the strike of his blade, slashing at his right eye.

"GYAAHHHHHHHH!!" screams Maurdis painfully, grasping at his face, as he coils to the floor. Wraithe swiftly gets to his feet, and limps away in escape. Enraged, Maurdis roars out in fury, as he alters into his fierce lycan counterpart.

"Run! Run now!" orders Terra hastily, nodding them to flee. Maurdis charges towards Terra, as she quickly fires another arrow. The lycan ducks as the projectile strafes through the fur of its back, continuing towards her. Terra readies another arrow, when Maurdis leaps towards her; hastily rolling out of the way, she releases her shot. To her astonishment, it is caught midair, in the mouth of Maurdis, who crunches the arrow, tossing it aside with a vicious snarl. Terra quickly reaches for another, and suddenly realizes, she has run out. Swiftly, she turns to flee, with the lycan starting after her. Meanwhile, Anna and Siff creep their way over to Wraithe, who lays injured, immediately, they help him to his feet, as Anna leans him upon her shoulder in support.

"Hurry to the chambers, we'll burn it, Maurdis must never get the lotus!" instructs Wraithe to the pair. All the while, Terra flees into the council's market, with Maurdis swiftly behind. She dives into one of the stalls, as Maurdis thrashes his way through. Tearing through the tents and toppling the tables and items, Terra scampers through the stalls, until tripping over a group of baskets. Maurdis pulls and tugs against the restraints of the torn tent's coverings laced about his neck. Until its coverings and wood come crashing down upon them.

Terra feels a sharp numbing pain suddenly pierce through her thigh. "AGHHHHH!!" she screams out painfully, as the nails of the heavy wood drives into her flesh. She struggles desperately, to push the heavy wood off of her legs. Meanwhile, Maurdis, the lycan appears, growling as he creeps slowly towards her, seeing this, Terra struggles frantically, pushing with all her might to remove the large wood, to no avail. She searches about nearby for her blade, a weapon or anything that could be used to defend herself, however, time has run out. Finally, she comes face to face with the great lycan, as he breathes down her neck.

Maurdis steps onto the wood, draped over the legs of Terra, pressuring the puncturing nails deeper in her thigh. "Aghhhhhhh!! Son of a….!" mouths Terra gritting her teeth in screaming. She stares fearlessly into the piercing-yellow eyes of Maurdis. "Kill me if you want, but you will never get the lotus!" Instantly, the lycan's eyes widen, as if in realization; its attention spins back towards the main council, swiftly making its return to Wraithe and the others, leaving behind a helpless Terra.

The lycan arrives at the main council, and to its surprise, there is no sign of Wraithe. It searches about the council floors, glimpsing a trail; the soils of what could only be Wraithe's blood, droplets that would lead his pursuit, with a whiff of its scent, it is all too clear, and quickly, the lycan starts after them. Meanwhile, beneath the council, Anna's staff once again begins to shiver, sparking and sizzling at its center. Leaning Wraithe nearby, she takes both ends of her staff, as it splits in two. She thrust its ends into the engravements of the chambers wall, and with a great twist, unlocks the chamber of Aldrig. Siff runs over to Wraithe, supporting him, as they proceed to enter the chamber.

"Wait!" utters Siff, turning towards the shadowy stairway, as he listens quietly. Wide-eyed Siff looks to them in hastening. "He's coming!!!" he utters, hearing the snarls of Maurdis, clamoring his way down the stairway.

"Quickly, he is almost here!!" hurries Wraithe. "The order laced the chamber with oil patterns throughout, the knights grew paranoid of Aldrig's discovery, so they ran trails throughout, so that the chamber may be destroyed before falling into the wrong hands! Find the trails and light them all!" instructs Wraithe quickly, meanwhile, the chamber's walls slowly begin to conceal themselves, as the earthly stone walls shifts, drawing to a close.

"He's almost here, hurry Anna!" exclaims Siff hearing the snarls and growls of Maurdis, he closes in on the chamber. Anna looks along the walls of the chamber, brushing away the thick vines that blanket throughout.

"I found it!" she exclaims, quickly placing the torches flame along the trail, as the fires immediately, flush throughout the walls, burning away at Aldrig's interior. As the chamber is set aflame, the lotus' that sit afloat its pools of water, begins to wither, as the connecting life is rendered to ash. The chamber's walls nearly shuts, when with a great leap, the lycan bounds into the chamber, behind the sealed walls. As the stones and rubble tremors and shifts shut. Locking Maurdis and the three within the great burning chamber.

His eyes reflecting the sight of the garden, looking around at it all having been set aflame; Maurdis stands to his two feet, with mouth gaped in utter silence. He watches helplessly as the flames engulf his hopes of immortality. Reaching into the shallow pool, he picks out a lotus, withering to ash before his very eyes, as a cold shudder, travels down his spine. Maurdis drops to his knees in disbelief, as he holds the dying flower within his palm, mystically evaporating to ash.

"W-What h-have you done?!" stammers Maurdis deliriously, as the lotus' remaining dust silks seamlessly through his fingers, and the silent shudders of anger, ushers throughout his body. His head sinks in despair, as his reflection looks to him from the water's surface. "You have no idea… what you have taken from me," his voice trembles lowly in saying. "Denied me my very destiny, THAT IS WHAT YOU HAVE STOLEN ME!!" roars Maurdis furiously, erupting into the fierce black lycan once more.

"Ready yourselves!!" warns Wraithe imperatively, mustering to his feet.

"Right!" answers Anna, readying her staff, as does Siff, drawing out his blade tucked within his pouch, hidden behind his back. Wraithe leads the charge with Anna, and Siff a step behind.

"Anna!" signals Wraithe, as Maurdis lunges towards him. "Now!" he exclaims, diving to his knees, allowing Anna, pacing behind, to catapult herself from Wraithe atop the lycan's back, as the revenant rolls to safety. Anna, twisting herself above the jaws of Maurdis, manages to grab onto his back. Her staff, now two-edged sword, she prepares to drive between the shoulders of the large lycan. When suddenly, Maurdis riles up, hurling Anna to the floor.

"Anna!!" screams Siff charging to her aid. The lycan turns its focus to Siff, who stops, petrified as he glares into the piercing, yellow eyes of Maurdis. Spinning about in fear, Siff flees, with Maurdis behind. Soon, Siff is cornered, seeing there is no escape, the chamber walls having been closed shut. His panicked breaths slowly turns to face the growling stare of Maurdis, who lunges towards him. Suddenly, Wraithe rallies himself into the body of Maurdis, tackling the lycan aside.

"Run boy! The both of you!" exclaims Wraithe, cautioning Siff to flee. Suddenly, he is clutched at his throat and his body lifted from the floor.

"This is the last breath you shall ever take!" snarls Maurdis, as the fires rage within his eyes. Suddenly, something catches his attention, as Wraithe struggles within his grasp, wheezing for air, he tosses Wraithe into the pool, as he steps into the water's shallow. It is a single lotus, the last of Aldrig's chamber, the fires hunt at the flower, burning away at its lush vinery. Maurdis floats in wake of the lotus, miraged in the glory of completing his conquest.

"Finally, you are mine, and my destiny shall be fulfilled!" he utters anxiously, his hand extended in reach. Suddenly, there is a drag at his left foot, as he turns to glimpse Wraithe straddled about his leg.

"Anna!!" shouts Wraithe in command, when Maurdis, upon hearing her war cry, turns to see Anna charging into him with sword drawn, piercing his abdomen. Curling to his knees, the lycan lord watches as the flames finally engulf the last of the white lotus, its single petal floats onto the shallow's surface, immediately, breaking into ash, with remnants dispersing across the waters. In that instant, there is a great shift within the chamber, as the stones, and rocks of its ceiling begins to decay, falling to the ground. Meanwhile, motionless, Maurdis wallows within the shallows, as years of conquest have come to an end, his head lay lowered in wake of his failure. His shoulders twitch, shuddering in his realization. Enraged, he delivers a blunt strike at Wraithe, freeing himself of the revenant's grip, as he steps to his feet. He locks his hand onto Anna's forearm, and with the other, pulls the blade from his abdomen. Meanwhile, Wraithe locks his arm about Maurdis' neck, tightening his choking grip. Maurdis then pulls at Anna's sword, again thrusting it into his abdomen, and also into the stomach of Wraithe, who then drops into the shallow. With a deafening strike of his forearm to her face, Maurdis topples Anna to the ground, finally drawing her blade from his flesh. He stands over Anna, preparing to joust his final strike. For Anna, escape is futile, as her dizzied gaze renders her unable to swiftly evade. Her eyes begin lowering, as Maurdis thrusts the blade forward. There is a silence, as the blade's edge faces her, and her eyes look upon the back of Siff, as the Omni's blade has been driven through his chest! Immediately, the eyes of Anna widen in utter disbelief, as Maurdis tosses aside the body of Siff from the blade.

"NOOO!!!" echoes the scream of Anna throughout the crumbling walls of the chamber. She swiftly lunges towards the omni, rolling it out of the hand of Maurdis', with a quick spin, she slashes at the tyrant's leg. Finally, Maurdis shapes himself once more, into the fierce, black lycan, yet wasting little time, Anna catapults upon his back. Immediately, she drives her blade into the lycan's shoulder, as it yelps and thrashes in attempt to dismount her. Suddenly, a stone breaking away of the chamber's ceiling, falls upon the head of Maurdis, stunning the great lycan. With a sounding war cry, Anna draws the omni from Maurdis, her blade splitting into two, she drives both swords into his hide, silencing him with a whimpering yelp. Maurdis drops to his knees, panting his final breaths, as Anna then stands before him, glaring soullessly into his eyes. It is in that moment, Maurdis realizes the strike having been made to her face, has been fully healed!

With a smug grin, he wheezes in cough. "Soooo… It's you?!" he mutters in discovery. Meanwhile, Anna silently creeps towards him, placing her hand upon his shoulder, and poising her blade to his chest.

"For my father, and for Siff!" exclaims Anna, driving her sword into the lycan ruler's chest. Maurdis then takes his final gasp, falling face flat into the chamber's shallow. Swiftly, Anna scampers over to the body of Siff, who lies motionless within the shallows.

"Siff! Siff!!" she cries desperately, shaking at his shoulders for him to reply, as there is another great quake felt within the chamber.

Suddenly, a startling hand grabs at her arm. It is Wraithe, having rushed over. "Quickly!" he exclaims. "We must hurry, the chamber is about to collapse!" he hastens her to follow. The pair picks up the body of Siff, and begin their escape, as the chamber's walls finally give way. The pair make their way up the wayward stairs, as every passing stone tremors about them. Finally, the entire council's floor gives way, crashing down upon the lower chamber and stairway. Meanwhile, above the collapsing floors of the council, Terra stands leant against one of the pillars, her eyes widened in disbelief of the unrecognizable council's floors.

"Anna!!" she calls out above the debris. "Wraithe!!!" she shouts. "Siff!!! Where are you??!!!" her eyes frantically wander over the sea of stone. Her breaths panicked, as she cries out once more. "Answer me!!!" she lingers in gaze. The pain of her leg returns, as she slides down the pillar, to her knees in weeping.

Moments later, the toppling of stones can be heard, as there is a shift beneath the rubble, immediately, Terra turns to the bed of rocks. A shield appears from the rubble, revealing the three, having sheltered themselves beneath the omni's shield. Anna quickly casts the body of Siff atop the rock bed's surface, as Terra slowly makes her way over.

"Siff?!" sobs Anna desperately. "Siff please! Wake up!" she cries, shaking at her friend's body. Meanwhile, Wraithe musters up from behind, standing beside Anna, as both he and Terra standby silently. The tears of Anna trickles upon the dust covered face of Siff, as his body remains motionless.

Terra grunts holding at her side, as she leans to place her hand along Anna's shoulder. "I'm sorry…" she whispers softly in reply. Anna lowers her head onto the chest of Siff's body, as she sobs uncontrollably. Suddenly, a feint glimmer of thought comes to mind, as Anna reaches for her staff. Wielding as a sword, Anna cuts at her palm. Her blood runs, as she squeezes her fist over the abdomen of Siff. The droplets of her blood, seep through to his wound, as she then opens her palm to reveal her hand fully healed. Meanwhile, Wraithe and Terra standby, puzzled as to what she is attempting. Anna waits for a few moments, remaining at his side. Slowly, her head lowers in dismay, realizing his body remains motionless. Seeing this, Wraithe and Terra also continue to lower their heads in silence.

Suddenly, Anna feels the rise and falls of Siff's chest, as the young boy coughs back to life, sitting up from the rubble. He is immediately met by a smothering hug from Anna, whose face is worn of tears. Meanwhile, Terra smiles, as Siff glances towards them.

"Great, you're back, I like you better alive!" jokes Terra reluctantly in saying. "So…?" gestures Terra to her leg and side. "Any help with these?" she chuckles further, as Anna and Siff turn to her in smile.

Wraithe wears a subtle grin, as the trio banter back and forth, yet, for a few seconds he returns his gaze towards the collapsed chamber about them.

Seeing this, Terra pats at his arm. "Hey, it is done now," she whispers calmly. "He is gone." Wraithe then looks to her with silent nod, as the four make their way towards the council's front doors.

In an instant, the council's doors are flooded, as the city's remaining guards flock to the council, as the noise of its collapse garners the city's attention. Anna and the four are met by counselors Rollins and Elaine, who both steps forward from the looming crowd. Rollins then leads in hopeful question, stepping forth to meet them. "I-Is it over?" he utters nervously in question.

looking through the distraught gaze of the elderly counselor, Anna steps forth in reply. "It is done, Maurdis is no more." Rollins nearly loses his breath in relief, as he excitedly bows his head to the four, and quickly turns to face the crowd.

"People of WestSkye!! The lycan's reign of terror, IS NO MORE!!" he roars in acclaim, flailing to the gathered crowd of the council. "Let all of Skye know the name of Anna Valor, Saviour of the west!" voices Rollins further in acclaim. The audience clamor and uproar in celebration, as guards begin relieving themselves of their weaponry, casting their swords along the city's path, as they also join in cheering. Skye has finally ridden itself of Maurdis' treachery!

Wraithe leans closer to Anna, proudly placing his hand upon her shoulder. "I knew you had it in you," he smirks in telling. "… Arthur would be proud." These very words hit deeply at Anna, who slightly sheds a tear, as her sights set upon the sky.

"It is done father, I've avenged you, Skye is finally safe…" she whispers solemnly in promise, as she returns to the cheerful, celebrating crowd, who proceed to clear a welcoming path for the four, as the name 'Anna' is suddenly chanted all throughout the city's main path.

Meanwhile, beyond the chanting voices of the city's crowd, and shaken walls of WestSkye, a cloaked straggler looks on, from atop the valley. They watch as smoke of the burning city continues to fill the air, the aftermath of the tremendous battle, and the many slain, whose bodies horde outside the city's walls. Removing the cloak's hood from their head, it is Sept, who looks on silently. His fist clenches in rage, as his motion remains still. Finally, he shrouds his hood over his head, taking final glance towards the city, as he turns away retreating to solitude within the forest.

Back within the walls of WestSkye, Rollins and Elaine meet with Anna and the others, to the counselor's astonishment, they meet the four readily packing their belongings onto their horses.

"My? In an awful hurry, are we?!" he chuckles in bewilderment. "Must you be in such hurry?" Rollins goes on to ask.

Finally, Anna turns to him in speaking. "We must, I bear the lotus, fate itself is bound to find me, WestSkye will never truly be safe if I stay here, I must leave!" tells Anna earnestly in reply.

"B-But if you leave, it would be unrest, there will always be those that seek after, here within the city we can offer you protection!" utters Rollins in suggestion

"She won't need it," adds Terra stoutly in reply, as she trots near atop her horse. "She has us! She has all the protection she needs," utters Terra with a smiling glance to Anna, Rollins sees this, and steps back with a grin.

Looking to the four sincerely in gratitude, he bows in saying. "You have saved us from peril, our city, and many more after us, are now safe… the people of Nordskye, and in respect of your father would be proud!" he adds earnestly with grateful nod, as does Elaine.

"You're very much welcomed to visit at any point of your journey, WestSkye's repairs will surely bring about an even greater city!" joins Elaine joyously in saying. "Until we meet again!!" she waives.

"Until we meet again!" utters Anna in farewell, preparing to join behind Terra atop her horse, when suddenly, a series of whinnying is heard approaching nearby, as two guards' appear, in hand, the reins of a pair of horses.

"We saw it fit to bestow two of our finest steeds to serve you on your way," comments Rollins in kind gesture, as he offers the horses to Anna and Siff, who excitedly receive their own horses.

"Woww, easy boy!" utters Siff, gently patting alongside the beast's neck. Quickly, Anna and Siff mount atop the fine steeds, bowing in thanks to the counselors, as they finally make off behind Wraithe and Terra, proceeding beyond the main gates of WestSkye.

As the four make headway towards unknown, what be that of the vast forest ahead of them, Anna turns in final glance of the city of WestSkye. "Will we ever return?" she looks to Wraithe curiously in question.

"That I can't say, it would be if the fates deem it so!" answers Wraithe stoutly, tutting at his horse to pick up pace. "For now, we train!" he adds bluntly.

"Train?!" turns Siff puzzled in reply. "For what?"

"For what's to come," utters Wraithe bluntly in telling, keeping focused ahead, as the four finally enter beyond the curtain of forest, disappearing into the great, mysterious land that is Skye.

MEANWHILE…

Five days after the departure of Anna and the others, and their return to Nordskye, lord Rollins carries out dutifully within the city. The council has begun its restoration, as citizens receive rations and food within the council's market, now a refuge for WestSkye's homeless. Stepping just outside the council's doors, Rollins is suddenly rushed upon by a panicked guard.

"My lord?!" exclaims the soldier, as he approaches and bows respectfully. "If I may?"

"But of course, go right ahead," permits Rollins kindly in smiling.

"My Lord, restorations of the council's collapse have revealed something rather disturbing Sire!" answers the guard gravely in reply.

This pulls at Rollins' undivided attention, as he draws the guard a way off in further conversation.

"You may freely speak," tells Rollins preparing to listen intently.

"We have stumbled upon what we believe to be the remnants of the great chamber, it be fully destroyed sire!" exclaims the guard panicked in detail.

"Yes, Yes, I know this, go on," Rollins replies anxiously, as he continues to listen.

The panicked guard tells further. "We have stumbled upon a body, Sire! We believe it to be the body of Maurdis!" he goes on to add.

Immediately, the eyes of Rollins widen. "Ha, well, we must retrieve it! And we will reduce the corpse to ash!" scoffs Rollins in chuckle, as he turns away. However, the guard continues behind the counselor in telling.

"That be it Sire, he be alive!" exclaims the guard further in disbelief, putting the aged counselor at pause. Struggling to swallow, as a sinking nervousness fills his gut, Rollins turns to face the guard, who stands by, awaiting the speechless counselor's orders.

To be continued...

www.ingramcontent.com/pod-product-compliance
Lightning Source LLC
LaVergne TN
LVHW021711060526
838200LV00050B/2615
* 9 7 8 1 6 8 4 8 6 1 5 7 6 *